PEN[...]

BIHA[...]

Amit Lodha is an Indian Police [...] [...] holding the rank of inspector general of police. Over the course of his career, he has been part of a number of successful operations, including the arrest of gangsters and rescue of kidnap victims. He has been awarded the prestigious President's Police Medal for Meritorious Service, the Police Medal for Gallantry and the Internal Security Medal for his work.

Amit enjoys playing tennis and squash, and is an ardent fan of Kishore Kumar. He regularly writes for the *Times of India* blog. He can be reached on Facebook and Twitter (@Ipsamitlodha7).

ADVANCE PRAISE FOR THE BOOK

'India has had very few tales of valour and heroism that are both real and inspirational. *Bihar Diaries* is one such tale about a top cop who takes his work seriously and the cause of national service even more so. The book is anecdotal to the point of being refreshing and leaves the reader with insights that only someone at the front lines can capture. Amit's style of writing and the way he weaves the storyline reminds one of those fine thriller writers who can leave you at the edge of your bed whilst you savour their tales.'—Suhel Seth

'It's more than just a thrilling cop story as it's real and contextual. Best read at one go as it's unputdownable.'—Ronnie Screwvala

AMIT LODHA

Foreword by Twinkle Khanna

BIHAR DIARIES

THE TRUE STORY OF HOW BIHAR'S MOST DANGEROUS CRIMINAL WAS CAUGHT

BLUE
SALT

PENGUIN BOOKS

An imprint of Penguin Random House

PENGUIN BOOKS

USA | Canada | UK | Ireland | Australia
New Zealand | India | South Africa | China

Penguin Books is part of the Penguin Random House group of companies
whose addresses can be found at global.penguinrandomhouse.com

Published by Penguin Random House India Pvt. Ltd.
4th Floor, Capital Tower 1, MG Road,
Gurugram 122 002, Haryana, India

First published in Penguin Books by Penguin Random House India and
Blue Salt Media 2018

ISBN 9780143444350

Typeset in Adobe Garamond Pro by Manipal Digital Systems, Manipal
Printed at Replika Press Pvt. Ltd, India

www.penguin.co.in

*To all the unsung heroes of our police and paramilitary forces,
the bharatkeveer.
Let us make ourselves worthy of their sacrifices.*

Contents

Ranks in the Indian Police   xi
Foreword   xiii
Introduction   xvii

1. The Jailbreak   1
2. 'What Is the Score, Uncle?'   13
3. The 'Shunting'   29
4. The Fall   35
5. The Massacres   42
6. *'Kursi Sab Sikha Deti Hai'*   48
7. Copulating Lizards   55
8. Back to Work   59
9. The Making of a Butcher   69
10. *'Loha Hi Lohe Ko Kaat Sakta Hai'*   79
11. *'Aap Suspend Ho Gaye Hain'*   84
12. 'You Are Eunuchs!'   90
13. The Cable TV Connection   93
14. 'Krazy Kiya Re'   100
15. *'Dekhte Hain'*   109

16.	The Traitor	112
17.	Nature's Call	116
18.	Bhujia	122
19.	*'Bol Bam'*	126
20.	*'Bagal Mein Hai, Huzoor'*	133
21.	The Headbutt	147
22.	Beauty Kumari	150
23.	*'Aloo Le Lo'*	153
24.	*'Suttal Hai'*	158
25.	'My Husband Is the "Famous" Criminal of Bihar'	166
26.	*'Sahib Gusal Mein Hai'*	171
27.	The Interrogation	175
28.	'My Son Will Become a Police Officer'	181
29.	'Shekhpura Police Zindabad!'	185
30.	*'Mard Hai to Aaja!'*	189
31.	*'Jai Chamundi Maa'*	193
32.	*'Phone Kyon Nahin Baj Raha Hai?'*	196
33.	The 'Encounter'	200
34.	*'Network Nahin Aa Raha Hai'*	202
35.	'How Do I Turn Off the Gas?'	209
36.	'You Have Won a Nokia Mobile Phone'	215
37.	*'Ringa Ringa Rojej'*	223
38.	*'Jagah Mil Gayi'*	232
39.	*'Aa Gaya Hoon Chhatt Par'*	238
40.	*'Sir, Pakad Liya'*	242
41.	'Put On Your Uniform'	249

42.	'Saregama'	256
43.	The Attack on Avi	264
44.	An Attack on the MLA	269
45.	'Woh Hi Laddu Hain'	272

| Epilogue | 275 |
| Acknowledgements | 279 |

Ranks in the Indian Police

Director general (DG)

Additional director general (ADG)

Inspector general (IG)

Deputy inspector general (DIG)

Superintendent of police (SP)

Assistant superintendent of police (ASP)

Deputy superintendent of police (DSP)

Inspector

Sub-inspector (SI)

Assistant sub-inspector (ASI)

Senior constable/havaldar

Constable

Foreword

What makes a tale truly gripping? It is a quandary that every storyteller has grappled with from time immemorial. Kurt Vonnegut, in fact, went on to graph the world's most celebrated stories in order to understand this conundrum. One of the most popular themes, he stipulated, was 'Man in Hole', wherein the protagonist gets into trouble, then out of it and is thus better for the experience. *Bihar Diaries*, Amit Lodha's engrossing thriller, is an impeccable example of this particular genre with the graph zigzagging magnificently all over the paper.

The author is an IPS officer and has been the recipient of various awards and commendations, including the Police Medal for Gallantry and the Internal Security Medal. He also happens to be a family friend, and I must add, an engaging conversationalist with innumerable intriguing anecdotes.

Amit pursued a career in the civil services, but he has always been a writer at heart, from being the editor of his school magazine to writing for IIT publications and, recently, the *Times of India* blog.

'Why didn't you write about your days in university? Then you would have also been a bestselling writer like Chetan Bhagat,' I recall saying to him, knowing that they were both batchmates in IIT Delhi in the early nineties.

While Sameer Gehlaut, another batchmate, founded Indiabulls and Chetan penned *Five Point Someone*, Amit felt that his calling was to protect his fellow citizens and he joined the police force.

This journey eventually led him to moving to a dank guest house in Patna in the midst of massacres and mayhem. In the book, he calls it a very distressing experience. And he spent a large portion of his time disheartened and bemoaning the vagaries of fate. But luck, like Seneca said, is a matter of preparation meeting opportunity, and it was his time in Shekhpura that turned out to be a stroke of fortune, both in his chosen career and his vocation as it led him to this intricately detailed book.

When you read the story, you will find that it is vivid and atmospheric because the author has lived each moment, unlike the rest of us who have to often rely on second-hand research and our imaginations while writing from the safety of our armchairs.

This story following the 'Man in Hole' model is as much about the author finding himself at the bottom of a chasm and climbing out, as it is about catching criminals. What I also found very interesting in the book was the role his wife played in hoisting him out of various situations with her astute advice. Well, though most will not admit it, alongside every successful man there is often a woman lending him parts of her multi-tasking brain.

Amit Lodha's absorbing account is soon going to be adapted into a motion picture, truly a triumph for any debut writer. The book does bring to mind another popular movie about a police officer based in Bihar. It starred a rather familiar gentleman and was called *Rowdy Rathore*. I would suggest that someone get hold of that tall actor and get him to do this *chor*–police tale from the same region. Let's call the movie 'Lucky Lodha', and I have a feeling that we may just have another blockbuster on our hands.

Mumbai   Twinkle Khanna
June 2018

Introduction

I am fortunate to be an officer of the Indian Police Service for I find the work of a policeman the most challenging yet immensely satisfying. It is one of those rare jobs where you can see your hard work bear fruit instantly. The feeling when you help unite a mother with her kidnapped child is indescribable. Most people associate glamour with a policeman's job, but in reality, there is a lot of blood, sweat and some tears too. Losing a colleague or having your family in danger is a professional hazard we face almost every day.

As a policeman, I am expected to be someone people look up to. However, I am not perfect. I have my weaknesses and human fallibilities. I do my best to repay the trust that so many people have in me. I am not a hero who kicks open doors and beats the hell out of goons, but I stand by my principles and ethics. I do what is just and right.

In my long career, I have had a number of thrilling encounters, almost all them etched firmly in my memory. I have been very lucky to have worked in Bihar. I received a lot of love from the people of the state and my seniors during my tenure there. It was here that I came into my own.

This book deals with one particular mission, an absolutely determined chase of one of the most dreaded dons of

Bihar—Samant Pratap. Unfortunately, as the book is about to go for printing, Horlicks Samrat, his accomplice, has come out on bail. In view of the clear and present danger to my family and others involved in this mission, the names and characteristics of quite a few individuals, particularly the criminals, have been changed.

During 2006, Bihar was on the cusp of revival. The establishment believed in *sushaasan*, or good governance, and the results are for everyone to see. I was transferred to Shekhpura, a posting I was not exactly looking forward to. It was quite a backward district then where time seemed to stand still. For quite long. I was going through a minor professional crisis and was in no mood to serve in a mofussil town when my friends were doing exceptionally well in life.

Samant Pratap, ably supported by Horlicks, ruled Shekhpura and the adjoining areas with an iron fist. His writ ran large; he was the 'Gabbar Singh' of Shekhpura. For him, a murder was just an addition to his resume, which included killing a former MP, a block development officer (BDO) and a few policemen. After experiencing the pain that Samant had brought upon so many innocent people, I got over my trivial issues and became a man possessed with a sole aim—to bring Samant and his gang to justice. I was lucky to have colleagues who supported me in this dangerous, high-stakes case and helped pursue these brigands relentlessly. And, of course, my wife stood beside me like a rock through this roller-coaster ride—even under grave threat to the children and herself from Samant.

I have been as truthful as possible in narrating this story. No mission, however challenging and dangerous it is, can be without its share of funny anecdotes. There is a liberal dose of humour in this otherwise absolutely serious story about catching dreaded criminals. The book also has a lot of references to movies and sports because I enjoy both of them. I have also recounted some of my experiences from my IIT days that show my metamorphosis from a shy, meek teenager to an overconfident cop.

I would like to remind readers that this book is a work of non-fiction. The views and opinions expressed in the book are only mine and do not reflect or represent the views and opinions held by the Government of India. It is based on actual events that took place in my life and drawn from a variety of sources, including published material. It reflects my present recollection of experiences over time as truthfully as memory permits and can be verified by research. All persons within the book are actual individuals, and the names and characteristics of some individuals have been changed to respect their privacy. The objective of this book is not to hurt any sentiments or be biased in favour of or against any particular person, society, gender, creed, nation or religion.

Through this book, I aim to show readers how much hard work, patience and strength of character is required to pursue a criminal like Samant Pratap, who not only had a large posse of men to do his bidding but also well-wishers in high places. It is also with pride that I am able to talk of the work I do as an IPS officer, which brings me so much satisfaction and makes me believe that I can make a positive impact on the society I serve.

1

The Jailbreak

Nawada, 23 December 2001

A Tata 407 slowly moved towards Nawada Jail. Raushan looked at his mobile phone. It was 9.38 a.m. He had to cover another three kilometres in the next twenty minutes. He was a little ahead of schedule. He motioned for the driver to take it easy and looked back.

'*Sab bandookein dekh lena* (Check all your weapons),' he commanded the motley group of men sitting behind him in the Tata 407. All the men could have easily passed off as labourers.

Raushan picked up his AK-47 and inspected it. Shorter and lighter than traditional rifles, the Kalashnikov automatic is very easy to use because of its few moving parts. This also makes it quite durable and reliable. It can fire approximately 100 rounds per minute in bursts. The 7.62 mm cartridges do not fragment after striking the target, but remain intact even after making contact with bones. They can cause significant damage to tissues. That is why the AK-47 is favoured by most terrorists.

However, even such sophisticated guns sometimes develop technical snags during firing. There was no room for any error today. The bullets *had* to hit the targets in one go.

~

A jail is supposed to be the most secure place in a district. It is usually also the most horrifying. Nawada Jail was no different. It was a veritable purgatory where all the scoundrels of the district were lodged. The compound was overcrowded; the almost 1100 inmates far outnumbered the jail's capacity. The cells were dingy, squalid and had very poor ventilation. The kitchen was right next to the common toilets. A nauseating smell would emanate from the often overflowing toilet waste. It seemed as if some depraved architect did not want the inmates to even eat without escaping that terrible stench. Yet, life went on. One can only marvel at the great adaptability of the human body and mind in such situations.

Contrary to popular belief, the district police do not usually guard the jail. There is a separate jail guard for that purpose. The people who make up this jail guard are the poor cousins of the district police in terms of training and equipment.

In 2001, the Nawada Jail administration was terribly understaffed. There were just four or five unarmed administrative staff—including the warder, jamadar and bada jamadar—and about four or five jail guards. The jail superintendent would inspect the jail every day after 11 a.m. At that time, the jailer and assistant jailer would make sure the prisoners under trial appeared in court. Some of the jail staff also allowed inmates to meet their relatives—at a price, of course. Some prisoners who were in the good books of the jail administration were often given the task of 'monitoring' the visits or *mulaaqat*s. It was a win-win situation for everyone. The money was distributed almost equally among the conniving jail staff. The prisoners who acted as 'monitors' also got some money sometimes. And there was no one to check them.

~

Twenty-third December 2001 was another cold and depressing morning in Nawada Jail. A lone jail guard was sitting on top of the observation tower, which was about 30 feet high. With deft movements of his palms, he prepared his *khaini*, the local tobacco, and packed it around the gums, exposing his dirty yellow teeth. There was nothing better to do.

In the courtyard below, a warder was moving towards the jailer's chamber. His daily responsibility of lining up all the inmates for a headcount was quite monotonous, but had its benefits. He could make a decent collection every day from all the visitors and the prisoners for various favours. These ranged from allowing pornographic magazines inside to letting home-cooked food be delivered to an inmate. Different rates were fixed for different things. The rates were always quite high, but negotiable if the prisoner belonged to the same community as the conniving jail staff. The jail staff somehow always managed to fulfil all the eclectic demands of the inmates. Some '*bahubalis*', or strongmen, even had desert coolers in their cells. The VIPs were obviously the most privileged lot. With just one medical report, they could be in hospital, enjoying all manner of luxuries for months on end in their air-conditioned wards.

~

Samant Pratap stretched his arms and yawned. He heard rumbling sounds from the nearby hills. Illegal mining was a routine activity in those hills, literally a stone's throw away from the jail premises. He surveyed the jail compound, the huge courtyard and the crumbling ramparts. He liked the place. After all, the jail administration treated him like a king. He believed he had earned it.

All the inmates roamed around the compound, mingling freely with each other. The next headcount would be at 2 p.m. Samant's eyes sought out his best buddy, Horlicks Samrat. Horlicks was a small, frail man, a first-time resident of the Nawada Jail. But à la Satya of the eponymous, iconic movie, he had greatly impressed Samant Pratap.

'You are destined for bigger things, my brother,' Samant had proclaimed in many conversations. The two criminals had got extremely close to each other during the time spent together being locked up. Even Samant's aides in jail realized that he couldn't stop raving about Horlicks Samrat. It seemed that Horlicks too could lay down his life for Samant without batting an eyelid. Horlicks became very loyal to him as no one else had treated him with so much respect in his life.

It was obvious to those who knew Samant that once out of jail, Horlicks would join the gang as one of his top aides—a straight promotion to the rank of CEO for a fresh MBA graduate.

~

As the jail warder went through the parcels, he yelled out, 'Horlicks Samrat, your tiffin has come from home. It seems your wife has made some delicious hilsa. Enjoy,' handing over a tiffin box. Horlicks looked at the clock. It was ten minutes to 10 a.m. His wife had been punctual. Timing was very important for their plan.

As a concerned wife, Shanti Devi did not let her husband eat the almost inedible prison food. She would prepare the choicest of Bihari delicacies every day and deliver them for her husband and his friend, the legendary Samant Pratap. Horlicks was not surprised by Shanti's fascination for Samant. She always liked powerful people, be it the SP of a district or a local don.

'*Aapke dost Samant ko achcha laga* (Did your friend Samant like the food)?' she used to ask Horlicks whenever she got a chance to meet him.

The delivery required some money and a sweet smile for the jail guard. That was it. The guards used to inspect the tiffin in the beginning, but after a few months, it became too routine for them to pay any attention to it. 'What was the harm in letting a wife deliver some home-cooked food for her husband?' they thought. On their lucky days, the guards also got their share of some litti chokha and puri bhaaji.

Horlicks opened the large tiffin box to inspect his lunch. The top container had a number of besan laddus. He looked at Samant and nodded.

Samant took the container from Horlicks and walked over to the jail staff.

'*Arre, sipaahiyon, aap log khaiye* (Guards, please have these). These are my favourite laddus. *Ghar ka banaa hai* (It's home-cooked)!' exclaimed an excited Samant.

The prison guards and the staff had been enjoying many treats from Samant and Horlicks over the last few days. After all, who could refuse those delicacies?

'*Dhanyawad, Samant Bhai* (Thank you, Samant Bhai),' said the warders while grabbing a handful of laddus each.

'*Aur lijiye na* (Take some more),' Samant Pratap said as he went around distributing the laddus.

The other prisoners salivated at the sight of the laddus, but kept a safe distance from Samant. He was no ordinary criminal.

He was the butcher of Nawada and in jail for the murder of at least thirty people.

After ensuring that none of the four jail staff in the courtyard had missed the laddus, Samant looked at Horlicks. Horlicks immediately opened the second container of the tiffin.

The aroma of fish curry wafted through the air, mingling with the stench coming from the toilets. Yet, it was inviting enough to make quite a few prisoners turn their heads in Horlicks's direction. However, Horlicks was least bothered about his favourite dish right now. His eyes were searching for something far more appetizing. He opened the next container.

He found the desi revolver wrapped between the crisp rotis. Samant had specifically asked for an indigenous version of a .38 revolver. It would be quite easy to use, even for a first-timer like Horlicks. Its original, the Smith & Wesson .38, is often carried by women in their purses for self-defence in the USA. The tiffin had been an excellent means to smuggle letters, and now, the gun, thought Horlicks. The revolver would come in handy if things did not go according to the plan.

Suddenly, the jail warder felt a sharp pain in his temple. He felt as if his head would explode. He knelt down, clutching his head in both hands.

Another jamadar was in an even worse condition. He had vomited blood and was clearly in excruciating pain. One by one, all the jail staff fell down, in no position to hold themselves upright.

The inmates could not fathom what was going on. But one thing was clear—the laddus had some ingredient far more harmful than sugar. Samant smiled. He was sure Shanti Devi had laced the laddus with the right amount of rat poison.

~

The truck took the bypass towards Nawada Jail.

There were a number of signboards just outside the town. They all had the same message on them—'Smile, for you are in Nawada'—painted in garish green.

Raushan looked at the dreary landscape and smiled. 'We're about to reach our destination in a few minutes. Get ready.'

The sentry at the jail gate waved and stopped the truck.

'What is it? Who all are in the Tata 407?' shouted the guard. Another guard was busy reading *Manohar Kahaniyan*, a bestseller that printed sleazy crime stories. One of their colleagues had gone to buy some vegetables.

Both of them were totally oblivious to the events unfolding inside the jail compound at that very instant. The inner wall and inner gate ensured that the two guards were isolated from the happenings inside.

'Sir, we have come to repair the toilets of the prison. I am the contractor,' said Raushan with folded hands.

'Wait here. I'll check the truck,' the guard said in a firm voice.

'*Aane do*. Let them come. The toilets are really in bad shape. *Bahut bura haal hai*. They need immediate repair,' shouted the assistant jailer, his boss. Hurriedly, the guard came back and opened the gate.

'Okay, all of you get down and go inside,' he gestured to Raushan and his men once he had opened the prison gates. The assistant jailer curled his lips and gave a sly smile. He was retiring next month. His desire of owning a two-bedroom flat in the posh Gardani Bagh area of Patna would finally come true. The local neta had been very helpful in arranging the deal.

Raushan just looked at him and nodded slightly.

The 'labourers' picked up their 'implements'.

'*Maaro, bhoon daalo* (Kill them, gun them down),' commanded Raushan at the top of his voice. The gangsters jumped down and opened fire at the two jail guards. Both of them fell down instantly. With great speed, Raushan and his men entered the jail premises.

On hearing the gunshots, the jailer rushed to the courtyard with his two guards. He was in for the shock of his life. Four of his staff were lying on the ground in unbearable agony, their mouths spewing bloody vomit all around.

The jailer looked towards the gate. Raushan and his men marched in like the marauding Genghis Khan and his soldiers. The jailer and the poorly trained sentries simply froze when they saw the gangsters. Their English vintage .303s were no match for the bullet-spewing AK-47s anyway. A burst of fire from Raushan had the jailer writhing on the floor. The two guards ran helter-skelter to save their lives. One of them somehow managed to crawl to the office and sound the alarm, but unfortunately, it did not work. It was not surprising since hardly anyone checked those 'routine' things. Luckily, the gunshots were heard by the labourers working in the nearby mine, who alerted the police.

Raushan smiled at his seemingly easy success. The response of the jail staff had been just as Raushan expected. Samant had briefed him well about the strength of the guards and their daily movements. He had been planning this daring operation for the past two months. Nothing, not even the minutest detail, missed his eye. There were just eight to ten staff in the jail at any given time, and only half of them were armed. The jail staff were not allowed to carry arms inside the premises for security reasons. In theory, a group of prisoners could overpower and snatch the weapons from the guards. Even the SP and other policemen had to deposit their weapons in the jail superintendent's office before entering the jail premises. Thus, the unarmed jail staff in the courtyard were in no position to retaliate. But that day, in any case, they were all sprawled on the ground, clutching their heads and groaning in pain. The handful of armed sentries at the gate had been taken care of. Raushan and his men had memorized the sketch Samant had drawn. They knew exactly where to go in the compound. All the letters delivered by Shanti Devi were coming to good use today.

Suddenly, Raushan saw Mukesh Kumar, one of his men, grimacing in pain. A bullet had pierced his arm. Raushan whipped his head around, frantically searching for the source of the bullet.

He looked up and saw the guard in the watchtower, crouching and taking aim. The guard now had a chance to prove he was good at not just making khaini. Raushan cursed. The guard was at a vantage position because of the height of the tower, which cleared his line of sight for firing. Samant could not move towards the jail gates without risking getting shot at.

Raushan took cover behind a *chabootra*, a raised platform, and gestured to Samant to catch his attention. He pointed his index finger towards the guard on the watchtower. Samant and Horlicks looked up. There was no way of shooting the guard from where they were standing; he was well-protected. Suddenly, Horlicks sprang into action. He took out the revolver from the tiffin and started crawling towards the watchtower. Once he reached the base, he slowly pushed the door of the staircase leading to the top. The *sarkari* latch came off instantly and the door opened. He climbed up the stairs in a jiffy.

The guard heard the soft click of the revolver but did not have any time to react. His head exploded like a watermelon. The trigger action was quite smooth, and there was hardly any recoil. Horlicks caressed the gun with his palms, savouring the feeling of having killed someone. This was the first of the many cold-blooded murders Horlicks would commit in the future.

The compound was in absolute pandemonium. Samant and his men, with their superior weaponry, had won the battle easily. And they were definitely more motivated. The incapacitated warders had somehow managed to get up and run for their lives, ducking in different corners and waiting for the police reinforcements to come quickly.

Raushan shouted at Samant, 'Come quickly! The district police will be here any minute.'

Suddenly, Samant turned around.

'Bhaiyya! Where are you going?'

Samant looked menacingly at Raushan. He snatched the desi revolver from Horlicks and ran towards the toilets. The assistant jailer was hiding in one of the cubicles. Samant found the hiding spot and kicked open the door. The man's eyes were wide open in horror and shock. He realized that there were no free lunches in life.

'*Yeh le apna Patna ka dera* (Here's the final instalment for your Patna apartment)!' said Samant as he pumped all the bullets into him. Then he ran back, and both he and Horlicks jumped on to the Tata 407 and sped away.

'Haha! *Mazaa aa gaya* (That was fun). Horlicks Bhai, you are a naturally gifted sharpshooter. *Kali Mata ki kripa hai* (Goddess Kali has blessed you). You showed a lot of *jigar*, guts and talent, in killing that sentry. Welcome to the company!' said Samant.

Both of them smiled and hugged each other like long-lost brothers.

~

Nine hardcore criminals escaped in the ensuing melee. It was one of the most daring jailbreaks in the history of Bihar, probably second only to the Jehanabad jailbreak on 13 November 2005.

About 340 prisoners had escaped then, after 200 Naxalites had attacked the Police Lines and the jail simultaneously.

The dreaded serial killer Charles Sobhraj had escaped from Tihar in an almost identical fashion in 1986. He had left behind him two Tamil Nadu special police sentries outside the prison, and six jail officials lying inside the compound in a drugged state. Apparently, Charles made the jail staff believe that he was celebrating his birthday and had them eat various delicacies like burfi and petha, all laced with sedatives. Both escapes had eerie similarities.

The Nawada police, under the able leadership of SP Dayal Pratap, quickly got on to the case and after follow-up police action, three of the escapees were killed. But it was little solace. Samant Pratap was free now, and even more dangerous. He had a lot of unfinished business.

~

While all this was happening, I was busy with my office work in Nalanda, the district under my command, barely 50 kilometres from Nawada. Tariq, my telephone operator, rushed to the lawns, panting heavily.

'Sahib, there has been a jailbreak in Nawada. Samant Pratap and some of his associates have escaped from the jail after killing the jailer and injuring at least three or four guards!'

I knew about Samant Pratap. He was the mastermind of one of Bihar's cruellest massacres, at Apsadh village in Nawada, which had taken place on 11 June 2000. Around 100 armed men, dressed in black like commandos, had suddenly arrived and started firing indiscriminately on the family of the independent MLA Aruna Devi, wife of Akhilesh Singh, Samant's arch-enemy. They then cut the victims with swords, slit their throats and stabbed them in the stomachs. Even a four-year-old girl was not spared. The conspiracy was so deep-rooted that even a DSP and the brother of a state minister were named as accused in the first information report (FIR). The DGP, K.A. Jacob, had to personally go to Apsadh village to quell the simmering tension.

That was the age of the 'jungle raj', as the media called it, in Bihar. Being the SP of the neighbouring district, even I was often directed by the Police Headquarters (HQ) to 'camp' in Nawada.

Still, I was not exactly worried. I knew well that Nalanda was the last place Samant would seek refuge in. After all, he had been arrested in Nalanda during my predecessor's time. Nevertheless, I directed Tariq to alert all the police stations in my jurisdiction.

Little did I know that one day, both Samant and I would be baying for each other's blood.

After just ten minutes, Tariq was again standing in front of me, accompanied by a lungi-clad man. Two children were clinging to his neck.

'*Kya hai?*' I asked, a trifle surprised.

'*Sahib, meri biwi apne aashiq ke saath bhaag gayi hai* (Sir, my wife has eloped with her lover). Please find her.'

'You should be happy; you have got rid of your wife,' said Tariq, laughing mildly.

I knew that the joke was in bad taste.

'I don't mind her running away. But she should have at least taken the kids with her. You have to get her back!' the man said. 'Or else ask her to take the kids. I can't take care of them. Find her. This is your job,' he continued after a pause.

I remained quiet. It was just another day in my life as the SP of a district.

2

'What Is the Score, Uncle?'

27 July 2004

'Sir, the SBI manager who was kidnapped last week—we rescued him early this morning,' I briefed C.A. Shankar, the Patna IG. Fatigued by lack of sleep on account of working overnight to recover the manager, I didn't expect much from Shankar, an acerbic but straightforward officer. But today he was in an unusually foul mood. Choosing the choicest of expletives in Hindi, the urbane and 'English-type' IG cussed.

'I don't know what the **!& is happening to Bihar! Which manager are you talking about? When was he kidnapped? I have lost count of kidnapped people. I'm out on the roads of Patna in my pyjamas looking for a boy. Just twenty minutes ago, Ayushman, a student of Delhi Public School, was kidnapped. He was forcibly taken in a Maruti van.'

Instinctively, I instructed my telephone operator to alert all police stations on the Patna–Nalanda highway about the incident and went off to sleep. It was hard to be fully focused on a kidnapping in Patna, at least not right now, when I needed some sleep. I consoled myself saying that someone in Patna was in charge of it and looking for the child.

~

Patna had become the crime capital of the country in those days. Extortion, murder and kidnapping were rampant. Hardly a day passed when someone was not kidnapped in some part of Bihar. Lawyers, doctors, contractors, businessmen and school students were the prime targets. Things had become so bad that even a *rickshaw-wallah* was not spared. His own neighbour kidnapped him when the news spread that the rickshaw-wallah had sold a small plot of land for one lakh rupees.

Hundreds of well-to-do people migrated to other states or sent their children to boarding schools outside the state. One DG, known for his outlandish statements, had famously stated, 'Kidnapping is a full-fledged industry in Bihar!'

Kidnapping was a low-risk, high-profit business. The algorithm was quite simple—survey the victim's habits and schedule, wait for an opportune moment to kidnap the unsuspecting target and then make a phone call to the victim's home. The helpless family would invariably pay the ransom amount out of fear as quite a few of the victims had been killed.

There were many professional kidnapping gangs operating in Bihar. In fact, some groups specialized in just providing a safe passage or a safe house to the main gang. Sadly, this was an ideal example of outsourcing in Bihar during those days. The beleaguered police was extremely understaffed and had hardly any resources to tackle an organized crime like kidnapping. Though the police tried its best and was successful in quite a few cases, kidnapping continued unabated. The situation in Bihar at that time was a fitting example of the 'broken window theory'.

Just about an hour after I went to sleep, I was woken up by the incessant ringing of my phone.

'Sir, Bada Babu Nagarnausa wants to speak to you urgently,' said my telephone operator.

'Sir, we have recovered the Maruti van and caught the driver. There's no trace of the boy and other criminals. They probably got down when they saw us checking all the vehicles at the naka,' said an excited Mithilesh, the SHO (station house officer) of the Nagarnausa police station.

The kidnappers had made a blunder. Apparently, on seeing the police barrier, they had got down with a sedated Ayushman. In their wisdom, they somehow assumed that the van would be allowed to cross the naka by the police and they could use it again after it crossed the post. Except, they forgot that Ayushman's school bag was in the van. An alert constable saw the bag and immediately detained the driver.

I promptly called the Patna IG and briefed him about the development. He was quite excited by the lead. I started off for Nagarnausa. It was almost midway between Patna and Nalanda. Throughout my journey, I sincerely hoped to find the young boy in a safe condition. I also wondered how the kidnappers could have reached Nagarnausa, almost 80 kilometres from Patna, without being stopped anywhere. As it often happened during those days, the most basic tenets of common-sense policing were overlooked. If the police had put barricades along all possible exit routes, the van might have been stopped right in the Patna district.

On reaching the police station, I saw a hapless man. His clothes were tattered and he looked harassed, probably exhausted from the interrogation. The man was the driver of the van.

Though kidnapping was quite common in Bihar, the abduction of a young student from one of the most prestigious schools in the state capital was too big an embarrassment to the state machinery. The opposition had got a golden opportunity to call for a Patna bandh. All the schools and colleges had also called for closure till Ayushman was recovered safely.

The entire Patna police force, led by Shivender Bhagat, the DIG of Patna, descended on the Nagarnausa police station. Bhagat Sir, one of the most sincere officers, usually went by the book. But right now, he was desperate. He stared hard at the man and started questioning him.

The man kept shouting, 'Sahib, I'm innocent. I'm just a driver. I don't know anything about the kidnapping.'

Unable to bear the prolonged and fruitless questioning of the man, I requested Shivender Sir to let me have a chat with the driver. Sir himself was exhausted.

'Who are you? What is your role in the kidnapping?' I asked the driver, increasingly believing my gut feeling that he was not a kidnapper per se.

'Sahib, I'm a poor driver. My boss gives cars for hire. Two people came to our office yesterday and told us that they had to take their nephew from Patna to their ancestral village in Nalanda. They specifically asked for a Maruti van. This morning, they asked me to wait in the van at the Boring Road Chauraha. After some time, the men came with a semi-conscious boy, dressed in a school uniform. They told me that their nephew was not well; he was under some kind of a spell. They had taken special permission from the school authorities to take him to Nalanda for a puja to ward off the evil influence on the boy. I was a little suspicious, but then, as a driver, I ferry all kinds of passengers. Also, we often go to *tantriks*, *ojhas* or quacks in rural areas. I didn't bother much and kept driving towards Nalanda. When we were about to reach Nagarnausa, the two men asked me to stop the vehicle on the pretext of meeting a relative. They told me that they would be using my car again in the evening. I drove a little farther before I was detained by the police here.'

I had very little doubt that the man was telling the truth.

'Do you have the numbers of those guys?'

I deliberately did not ask for the names. I knew that even a novice in the world of crime would not reveal his actual name.

'No, sir, who remembers numbers nowadays?' said the driver. He was still shielding his face with his hands.

'*Dar mat, nahin maaroonga* (Don't be afraid, I won't beat you).'

The driver was right. I too did not remember any numbers except those of my home and my boss, the DIG of Patna. Mobile phones had increasingly reduced our ability to memorize numbers. I asked for the mobile phone of the driver. I checked the logs and showed all the numbers to the driver.

'Which one is it?'

The driver pointed at one number on the screen.

'Sir, I received a call from this number in the morning today. The guy asked me to reach Boring Road Chauraha by 6.40 a.m.'

I requested Shivender Sir to let me help with the case, although the kidnapping happened in Patna.

'Sir, I will work in my own way. Let me make use of technology. Meanwhile, police teams can raid the hideouts of all suspects.'

Being an IITian, it was natural for me to use the latest technologies and gadgets to solve cases. Shivender Bhagat had no hesitation in letting me work independently as I had successfully handled quite a few kidnapping cases earlier.

We were racing against time as Ayushman's father had already started arranging for the money. Ayushman was the only child of Nilesh and Madhu Gupta, a reputed couple from Patna. I instinctively knew that the kidnapper would not let the boy live even after getting the ransom.

~

I rushed to my residential office and immediately called the general manager of Reliance Telecom in Kolkata. I had called Ghosh many times in connection with different cases and had developed a personal rapport with him.

'Ghosh Babu, please send me the call details of 94****3654. It's urgent.' By that time, my wife, Tanu, had entered the office and sat down to have her tea with me, her standard ritual every day on my arrival.

She could sense that I was disturbed about work. '*Aapko Ayushman mil jaayega* (You will find Ayushman),' she said, her eyes expressing confidence in me.

Ghosh called me again and told me that the number had not been used at all except for that one call to the van's driver that morning. The call records were blank otherwise. Obviously, the criminal had procured this SIM card specifically for making calls to the victim's family. And of course, the SIM card had been obtained under a fake name. The kidnapper had some basic knowledge about mobiles, but he was probably not as sharp as he thought.

'Ghosh Babu, could you please tell me the IMEI number?'

'In a minute, sir,' replied Ghosh.

IMEI, or International Mobile Equipment Identity, is a unique fifteen-digit serial number given to every mobile phone. A service provider like Reliance or Airtel can run the SIM card number through its database and find the IMEI number being used by that SIM card. Once the IMEI number is known, the details of any other SIM card used on that particular phone can be found out. The reverse is also true. I requested Ghosh to immediately run the IMEI number of the mobile phone of the criminal and see if any other SIM had been used on the phone.

'The person used another SIM on his handset earlier! That SIM card, 94****6381, is of our company too,' said an excited Ghosh in his sweet Bengali accent.

'Can you check if that number is still in use?' I asked, equally excited.

'Yes, of course. I checked it. That number is functional right now.'

It meant the kidnapper had another SIM card that he was using for other conversations.

'Then send me the call details of that number. Just for the last forty-eight hours.'

I wanted to focus on the last few calls only. Obviously, those calls were going to provide the most crucial clues to solve the case.

Ghosh had been of tremendous help. Within a few minutes, the printout of the call details was on my desk. I circled the numbers that appeared a little more frequently in the incoming and outgoing calls list. In fact, a particular number had been contacted a few times just a few hours ago, almost immediately after the van was detained by the police. That number could be the key to our case.

To take a short break, I went into the house to play with my three-year-old son, Aditya. I came back soon and saw one of my finest officers, Sanjay, looking at the printout lying on my table.

'Sir, this number you have circled, it is the number of Shyam, my *spy*!' exclaimed Sanjay. I was surprised by this unexpected information.

'Are you serious?'

'Yes, sir, I talk to Shyam practically every day to gather information about any suspicious activity in my area.'

I could not believe my good luck. I sent Sanjay to immediately fetch the man. After an hour, he came back, but without his informant.

'Sir, I did not find Shyam. I will try again tomorrow morning,' a disappointed Sanjay said. He then saluted and left.

I pondered for some minutes. There was nothing more I could do at that moment about the kidnapping case. I dispensed some office work and decided to catch up on sleep. It had been a long day. I lay down, but my mind refused to switch off. A voice in my head kept saying, 'A young boy has been kidnapped. And you're going off to sleep!'

I tried to pacify myself by thinking I had done the best I could, and would try something else tomorrow, but I couldn't simply switch off and go to sleep. I knew every hour was crucial for the safety of that boy.

I got out of bed, a little irritated, but realizing what needed to be done. I called SI Sanjay.

'*Sanjay, Shyam ko utha ke lao* (Sanjay, get Shyam here). Raid all his hideouts.'

Shyam was our best chance. If the kidnapper had contacted him, there must be a strong reason for that. Sanjay realized that I wanted Shyam at any cost.

I waited anxiously in my residential office and soon heard a jeep rumble outside. Sanjay marched in triumphantly. This time, he had been lucky.

'*Sir, mil gaya,*' said Sanjay. Tariq, my operator, pushed a lanky, thin man towards my table. The fellow was clearly intoxicated.

Shyam was a *nashedi*, a liquor addict, a typical police 'spy' who would provide information about criminal activities to the police for small favours. These informers often commit petty offences, which are sometimes deliberately overlooked by the police, for obvious reasons.

'Whose number is this?' I pointed at the highlighted number in the printout.

'Sir, I don't know—what are you talking about?'

Sanjay shoved him. Shyam fell to the floor. The effect of the liquor diminished considerably with that one push.

'You have talked to this person four times in the last ten hours. The call logs on your mobile screen are clearly showing this. Don't try to play games with us. *Baap hain hum tumhare*,' said Sanjay, pointing at the screen of Shyam's mobile phone.

Realizing that his bluff had been called, Shyam told us that Sukhu Sao had called him. Sukhu was a dreaded kidnapper in Patna, infamous for killing his victims after getting the ransom money.

Sukhu had asked Shyam to arrange a Maruti van for him. The Maruti van was the preferred vehicle of kidnappers those days. The van's sliding doors made it quite convenient to push the helpless victim inside. I am sure this is one endorsement that Maruti did not covet. Shyam was totally unaware that Sukhu had kidnapped a child and the vehicle was to be used for ferrying Ayushman to a hideout.

'Where will you deliver the vehicle to him? Will Sukhu come on his own? Or will you call him? Do you know him well? What does he look like?' I bombarded Shyam with a number of questions.

'Sahib, I met Sukhu when both of us were in Beur Jail, Patna, two years ago. I have talked to him only on the phone a few times since then, but I will still surely recognize him. He's quite tall and burly, and absolutely bald. He told me to come with the van to the booth near the bus stand tomorrow at 8 a.m.'

I checked the clock in my office immediately. It was 1.40 a.m. Sanjay and I went to the proposed rendezvous and surveyed the area.

'Sanjay, keep your men at different vantage points around this area. Take your positions by 7 a.m. Shyam, the moment you are sure that it's Sukhu Sao, just start caressing your hair. Sanjay, this will be a signal for you and your men to catch Sukhu. It won't be very crowded early in the morning, so it will not be difficult for you to arrest him.'

Satisfied with my briefing to Sanjay, I waited anxiously for dawn to break. It was impossible to sleep now. I went home and sat on the rocking chair in my drawing room. I did not enter my bedroom as I did not want to disturb Tanu and Aditya.

At 6.30 a.m., I got a call from Sanjay, who was shouting frantically on the phone.

'*Sir, pakad liya* (Sir, I have caught him).'

It so happened that Sukhu had called Shyam early in the morning and asked him to meet at 6 a.m., two hours before the time fixed earlier. A worried Shyam immediately called Sanjay for instructions. Sanjay, the ever brilliant officer, decided at that instant that Shyam had to meet Sukhu at the stipulated time, otherwise Sukhu would become suspicious. Sanjay left for the bus stand with just two newly recruited constables who were available at the police station at that time. He briefed them on the way. They nodded nervously. Sanjay did not have much time. He frantically tried to call me, but out of sheer bad luck, the call would not connect. He cursed the unreliable mobile phone network. Praying to God, he asked the two constables to take their positions and hoped that everything went according to the plan.

Sanjay waited in a corner with bated breath, every second feeling like an eternity. Shyam paced anxiously in the alley near the booth, his heart beating hard. Then, all of a sudden, a huge six-foot-plus man appeared. It had to be Sukhu. Shyam froze the instant he recognized Sukhu. The expressions on Shyam's face clearly aroused some suspicion in Sukhu's mind and made him turn around quickly. He started moving towards the alley.

'*Sir, pakdo!*' shouted Shyam at the top of his voice. Sanjay ran like a sprinter after Sukhu. He shouted and waved at the two constables, 'What the hell are you two doing? *Boodbak*, you fools, stop him!'

It happens many times in a crisis—the mind goes blank, the body freezes. This is exactly what happened with the two constables. Sanjay just couldn't let Sukhu escape. With all his might, he jumped on Sukhu and knocked him down with his elbow. Sukhu was too strong for Sanjay. He kicked Sanjay in the shin and almost broke free. But the two constables chose that moment to regain their senses and pounced on Sukhu. After restraining Sukhu, Sanjay called me. This time his call connected.

My excitement knew no bounds. I ran out of my house wearing my slippers and hailed my driver and bodyguard. As my beacon-fitted official vehicle could alert any criminal to our arrival, I deliberately decided to travel in a private vehicle.

A Toyota Qualis had been seized just the previous night by the SHO of the Sarmera police station. It belonged to another notorious kidnapper in Nalanda, Chhota Santosh. Santosh was quite short, hence the name, but he was a big pain for the Patna and Nalanda police. The SHO had also seized a horse from Santosh's house. Naturally, it was the Qualis that I chose.

I reached the bus stand in no time. There I saw Sanjay, totally mired in sweat and mud, panting heavily. We put Sukhu in the back of the car, flanked by Ajit, my bodyguard, Shyam and Sanjay. My driver, Chhotu Singh, drove as fast as he could. There was no time to lose at all. I was worried about Ayushman's safety. What if there was someone else with Sukhu Sao? What if the other kidnappers had come to know that we had caught Sukhu?

'Where have you kept the boy?' I slapped Sukhu hard. It hurt my hand, but I didn't show any pain.

We interrogated him in the moving vehicle but he didn't open his mouth. We were losing precious time. 'Sahib, I think he has kept the boy in Saraunja village. He had made a passing reference to Saraunja yesterday while talking to me. I'll take you there,' Shyam finally intervened.

'Let us give it a try,' I said desperately.

I asked Adil Zafar, the DSP of that area, to join us at Saraunja. I also called C.A. Shankar, the IG.

'Sir, I've got the kidnapper. I'm going to get Ayushman.'

The IG was happy to finally hear some good news. He started for Nalanda, along with Shivender Bhagat, the DIG. The IG immediately told Ayushman's parents about the imminent recovery of the boy. Unfortunately, this news was also somehow leaked to the media. Soon, vehicles of the media, particularly news channels, were parked outside my house. Tanu was shocked to see so many OB vans prowling around. The circus-like atmosphere confused our son, Aditya.

We reached Saraunja village after two hours. We checked every house, but did not find anything suspicious. Now we were losing hope. It was getting gloomy outside too.

'Bastard, where have you kept the boy? You will die a horrible death,' snarled Adil.

'Kill me, sir. I'm dead anyway,' a nonchalant Sukhu murmured. He knew that we couldn't do anything to him till we recovered Ayushman.

'*Abe, yahaan kyon lekar aaya* (Why did you get us here, you rascal)?' Ajit was furious. He grabbed Shyam's collar.

'*Sir, galti ho gayi* (Sir, I made a mistake). I thought he spoke about Saraunja yesterday. I am not sure now. Maybe I misheard. I should stop drinking so much *tharra*.'

'*Mat pee itna, bewade* (Don't drink so much, you drunkard)! This intoxication will get you killed some day,' Sanjay said as he stared at him hard.

~

'Amit, any good news?' asked Shivender Sir on the mobile phone.

I took a moment to compose myself before saying, 'Sir, there's no one here. I don't know what to do right now. But I assure you I won't return without Ayushman.'

'That's my boy!'

C.A. Shankar, a chain-smoker, sat in my residential office, enjoying Tanu's hospitality. As he was about to take a sip of his umpteenth cup of tea, Shivender Sir told him of the latest development. The cup almost slipped out of his hands, spilling some tea on his trousers. What if something went wrong now? Ayushman's family was about to reach and media persons were waiting outside like salivating dogs. Yet, somehow, he had a feeling that today was our day, and that everything would end well.

Adil and Sanjay interrogated Sukhu again, but he didn't utter a word about Ayushman's whereabouts. He knew his silence was his passport to safety. If we didn't recover Ayushman, we couldn't take any strong legal action against him. He would be out on bail very soon. I was staring blankly into space; I could not think of any plan.

Then, out of the blue, Ajit handed his mobile to me, saying, 'Sir, the SHO of Deepnagar, Vinod Babu, wants to speak to you urgently.'

'Sir, I have come to know that you have arrested the veteran criminal Sukhu Sao. Ajit told me that you could not find the kidnapped boy in Saraunja. I would strongly suggest that you raid Tripolia village. It's close to Saraunja and has been a traditional hideout of Sukhu and his gang members. I had arrested Sukhu a few years ago from the same village,' Vinod said quickly.

By a stroke of luck, Vinod Yadav had called my residence for an official matter. As soon as he was apprised of the developments in the kidnapping case by Tariq, he had called me. I was glad for

Vinod's knowledge of criminals and his loyalty towards me and the department. This is generally true for many policemen. That is the reason for the success of the police all over the country. When we put on our uniforms, we work as a team.

I had been feeling hopeless a while ago. Vinod's call reinvigorated all of us and we decided to follow his advice. We started walking towards Tripolia—it was about two kilometres away. Our vehicles could not go there as the roads were terrible. My hip joint started hurting all of a sudden. It was clearly an attack of ankylosing spondylitis, an arthritic condition I had had since my training days. I had no option but to ignore it. It started raining heavily. We rolled up our trousers and covered our weapons. I fervently prayed to God and hoped for a miracle.

As we neared the village, we saw a small one-storeyed house on the outskirts. I saw a man on the terrace and the unmistakable shape of a pistol in his hand. I gestured to all my men to take their positions. Before we could even move, a bullet whizzed past Ajit's ear. He was clearly shaken but, the brave man that he was, he immediately fired back. We didn't have any cover to give us protection. Instinctively, we all lay down on the ground and crawled towards the house. My hip and back started hurting like hell. Ajit and Adil somehow managed to pull me away from the volley of fire. Luckily, the man with the gun was not a professional like us. Soon, he had emptied the magazine of his pistol. Too much of an adrenaline rush is bad in such instances. This was a chance good enough for Rajesh, one of Adil's bodyguards. He took a deep breath, held his pistol still and fired at the criminal's chest. One shot was all it took to make the body fall to the ground. Without wasting a moment or caring for our safety, we barged into the house. In the ensuing melee, we forgot about Sukhu. Things had happened in such a rush since the morning that it simply had not occurred to any of us to handcuff him! He tried to pounce on Ajit and take his revolver. But Ajit was an equally tall and strong person. He grappled with Sukhu and had no choice but to fire at him from point-blank range. Sukhu collapsed in a heap instantly. The 9 mm bullet had punctured his lung. Both the criminals would have been alive if they had not attacked us first.

We started searching the house desperately. This time I was sure that Ayushman was somewhere inside the house itself. I went through all the rooms and suddenly saw a door bolted from the outside. I opened it and saw a hapless child, bound and gagged, coiled in a corner. A strange feeling of relief flooded my mind.

Adil and Sanjay ran to Ayushman and set him free. The boy stretched and looked around. Clearly, he was still a little fearful.

All of us remained quiet while we waited for him to recover. Finally, I took a deep breath and said, 'Ayushman, I am Amit Lodha, the SP of Nalanda. The kidnappers are dead. You are safe now.'

'Thank you, uncle.'

'Uncle, what is the score right now?' he asked after a pause.

'What, what do you mean?' I asked incredulously.

'Uncle, the match between India and Sri Lanka!'

I just smiled. This little boy who had been through hell in the last day was asking about the ongoing Asia Cup cricket championship.

'Don't know, *beta*, but you can watch the highlights tonight.'

By the time we came out of the house, the sky had cleared. I shook hands with each of my men and congratulated them. There was tremendous pride in their eyes.

'Sir, good news! I've got the boy. Two of the kidnappers were killed in a clash,' I told the IG, Shankar Sir.

'My boy, I'm so proud of you. Come home soon. Your wife is even more anxious than we are.'

I reached my house at night. We were swarmed by the press. I remained quiet, too overwhelmed and exhausted to speak. C.A. Shankar and Shivender Sir hugged me. It was a wonderful gesture by the two senior officers. Tanu was beaming with pride, standing in the veranda. Finally, I saw Nilesh and Madhu, Ayushman's parents. Tears of joy trickled down their cheeks.

The reporters thrust their mics into Shankar's face and at practically everyone present there. My team and I were still standing with our pants rolled up, sweaty and grimy. One of my slippers' straps had also broken. Ayushman's uniform had been badly soiled too. Finally, they asked a remarkably composed Ayushman about his feelings. Quite an insensitive thing, but the boy answered in style.

'I am happy that I was freed just before the India–Pakistan cricket match. And I want to become an IPS officer like Lodha uncle.'

This headline was splashed on the front page of every newspaper in Bihar the next day. It felt like I was at the height of my professional success. Naturally, the only place for me to go now was downhill.

3

The 'Shunting'

19 September 2005

'Why are you not getting ready? People will be waiting for you,' said Tanu.

'Tanu, nobody comes to these functions on time. I'll go after some time,' I said in an irritated tone.

In the morning, Kripal Singh, one of the most dangerous criminals in Muzaffarpur, had been killed after an exchange of fire. Wanted in scores of extortion and murder cases, his elimination was a huge relief for the traders and businessmen of the town.

My team and I had been invited by the Chamber of Commerce for a dinner. I was not even a bit excited. I had become quite used to these '*samman samarohs*' or felicitation programmes after my numerous 'successes'.

'And why are you not dressed properly? You used to be quite a suave man, or at least that is what you told me about yourself before our marriage. *Khud ki itni taarif karte the* (You would praise yourself so highly)!'

'What is the point of getting dressed when nobody cares? Don't you remember what happened in Hazaribagh?'

'Yes, of course. You made a fool of yourself!' Tanu giggled.

I recalled the incident and could not help laughing too.

A few years ago, in December 1999, just after our training at the National Police Academy (NPA), our batch of five IPS officers belonging to the Bihar cadre had joined the Police Training College (PTC), Hazaribagh, as probationers. PTC Hazaribagh and the NPA Hyderabad were as different as a low-budget movie and the blockbuster *Bahubali*.

The Sardar Vallabhbhai Patel National Police Academy, Hyderabad, is the premier institute for the training of IPS officers before they are sent to their respective cadres. The sprawling campus houses state-of-the-art facilities that include world-class training infrastructure, a shooting range, an Olympic-size swimming pool, a modern gymnasium and a huge library. Of course, hardly any of us ever visited the library.

A regular day would begin with a gruelling run, followed by PT and parade practice. Some of us were made to run extra rounds holding our rifles over our heads. That was the punishment for a poor shave or unkempt hair. Many would opt for the '*katora-cut*' hairstyle to save themselves from any future punishment. After a quick but sumptuous breakfast, we would head for lectures on various subjects, such as forensic science, the Indian Penal Code (IPC), investigations and so on. In the evenings, we had martial arts, horse riding, swimming and team sports. After dinner, it was a mad scramble to finish our assignments for the next day.

Our weekends were reserved for cross-country runs, rock climbing and riot control drills. If you thought these were the only activities we had, hold on. The 'extracurricular' activities included debates, cultural programmes and jungle survival modules. Nowadays, activities like rafting and scuba diving have also been added.

People like me, who were newly engaged, also had to find some time to make phone calls to our fiancées. Those were the days of long-distance calls from phone booths. Almost all of us would wait for 11 p.m. to make calls, when the rates were the lowest. Mobile phone call rates were very high at the time, and of course, social media like WhatsApp and Facebook did not exist. They were beyond our imagination.

Most of us tried to catch a few hours of sleep in the classrooms. The director-deputed marshals in the classrooms would wake us up in case we dozed off, and report us to our seniors. Regular offenders were made to do *shramdaan*, or penal service, too, such as cleaning the campus, planting trees, etc.

We cursed every minute of our existence in the NPA. It was only when we started our careers in the districts did we realize the importance of the solid foundation the NPA had laid. It had made me an officer and a gentleman.

The PTC Hazaribagh was the exact opposite of the NPA.

The building was in a shambles, the infrastructure non-existent. There was no swimming pool, only puddles of filthy rainwater. Instead of horses, we found some stray cattle munching on the vegetation in the campus.

The 'good' part was that it did not have the rigour of the NPA. The training staff itself was poorly trained. Naturally, there were no whistles at 5.40 a.m., no cross-country runs, no checking of our uniform—basically nothing. We were on our own. Fortunately, in the new, changing Bihar, a new ultra-modern Police Academy in Rajgir is nearing completion and should be ready in 2018.

During our days at the PTC Hazaribagh, many people, particularly the youngsters, looked up to us. For them, we were the future 'stars' of the Bihar Police! Some people came up with the idea of hosting an evening for us.

'Sir, as per tradition, a dinner is being organized tonight by a local club to welcome you to the Bihar Police. It will be a good occasion for you to interact with the people,' the portly mess commander of the PTC informed us.

'Friends, we have to make a good first impression. Remember, people observe everything about IPS officers—the way they talk, behave and dress. We should all wear our Jodhpuri *bandhgala*s. And don't forget to put on colourful pocket squares,' said Sahil, our batchmate.

'We should follow all the etiquette we learnt during the formal dinners at NPA. Remember the sequence of using the cutlery, the forks and the knives. And don't forget to raise a toast!' Praveen reminded us.

We all nodded in unison.

That evening, we assembled in the dimly lit corridor of our mess. All of us were looking quite dapper. After lavishly complimenting each other, we reached the club hall.

It was the most grotesque sight ever—the atmosphere was anything but formal. The hall was teeming with people. It was as if we had entered a mela. People were dressed in whatever they felt like. One gentleman was wearing a lungi and shirt. Another was in his shorts and chappals.

A guy nudged Praveen.

'*Arre, thoda machchli lene do* (Hey, let me take some fish),' he said, pushing other people out of his way.

There was a mad rush, particularly at the chicken and fish counters. Everyone's plates were overflowing with rice, topped with dollops of fish and chicken gravy. On the edges of most plates were small mountains of chicken bones. Some men even gargled and washed their hands in their plates. We were absolutely aghast.

The final nail in the coffin was driven in by one particular gentleman.

'*Arre, waiter, zara meetha leke aana* (Hey waiter, get me some sweets),' the man ordered Sahil. The gent's pyjama strings were hanging to his knees and his vest had umpteen holes, as if it had been struck by bullets in a shoot-out.

Sahil violently pulled out his pocket square and stomped out of the dining hall.

All of us looked at each other sheepishly.

'*Bhailogon*, let us leave quietly before anyone else mistakes us for waiters!' said Praveen.

That was the last time I dressed up like that, but Tanu and I have shared many a hearty laugh remembering that incident.

~

That night's felicitation party in Muzaffarpur was similar to the Hazaribagh dinner. There were a series of supremely boring speeches by every Tom, Dick and Harry who wanted to show his importance in the scheme of things in the district. This is typical of any district programme. Most of the time, the people sitting on the dais outnumber the people sitting in the audience.

The speeches would go on ad nauseam. It was as if the speakers competed for the longest and most boring speech. It would have been very difficult to adjudge the winner. A standard speech would start like this—'*Aadarniya* DM Sahib, respected SP Sahib, respected District Judge Sahib, respected DSP Sadar, respected Town DSP' and so on. The speaker would address practically every official in the district. Since Muzaffarpur had a large number of officers, you can imagine my plight. I had to listen to the names of all the officers present for the function. '*Jab se SP Sir is zille mein aaye hain* (Ever since SP Sir has come to the district), crime has been finished. Criminals shudder at just hearing his name!'

I hardly reacted to such flattery any more; I had got used to it. I had the same feeling a superstar has after delivering a number of blockbusters. But little did I know that this feeling was short-lived and soon, I was about to experience what a superstar goes through when he delivers flop after flop.

As another speaker was singing my praises, Ajit sneaked behind the podium and whispered in my ears. '*Sir, aapka transfer ho gaya hai* (Sir, you have been transferred). You have been posted as a commandant in one of the BMP (Bihar Military Police) battalions.'

I left the party without uttering a word. I had been shunted out. In the administrative parlance of Bihar, 'shunted' means anyone who is not posted in the district or someone who has been given an inconsequential charge.

This happens often to government officers, particularly the SP and the district magistrate (DM). They are transferred all of a sudden when they think that everything is under control. Often, they don't even know the reason for their transfer. Not many realize that they are just foot soldiers, pawns in the establishment's game of chess.

4

The Fall

January 2006

I had been living life in the fast lane.

I had made it to the IPS at a relatively young age. Getting the Bihar cadre had turned out to be a blessing, as there was so much a young SP could do. Even my small and routine 'successes' were lauded by the public. The people of Bihar idolize and adulate government officials, especially police officers. Being an IIT graduate had increased my appeal even more, particularly among the youth. I was a regular feature in all the newspapers and TV channels. I was always busy with work that ranged from making security arrangements for the visit of the Prime Minister to conducting parliamentary elections. People would gather around me to watch me at work when I would go for my field visits. The heady cocktail of success, fame and power had made me overconfident. I felt invincible. The trouble was that I had seen too many good things too early on in my career, and I thought that life was going to be one smooth ride.

My fall was equally bad. The sudden posting to the BMP was a huge shock. It felt as if I, like the tennis champion Roger Federer, had been knocked out in the first round of a Grand Slam.

'Sir, I am your reader, Surendra,' said a sweet voice on my mobile phone.

'Surendra, where do I report? Where is the office?' I asked.

'*Huzoor, aaffice kahaan hoga* (Sir, where would the office be)?' he replied.

'Do you have any staff, at least a cook?'

'Huzoor, this battalion has only two people as staff right now—you and I,' replied Surendra nonchalantly.

I did not ask any more questions. My wife, Tanu, didn't bother about any of the accoutrements that come with my service. She happily went about doing all the household chores. More importantly, she wanted to raise the kids in a very normal way. She was my strength and always stood by me. She tried her best to cheer me up, but my frustration knew no bounds.

The battalion under my command had not been sanctioned; it existed only on paper. I was relegated to a post with no office, no phone, no house and no pay. All my fans and well-wishers vanished overnight. The media did not bother; I was no longer a newsmaker. I just could not believe it was happening to me.

I was now totally on my own. Luckily, my most trusted and loyal bodyguard, Ajit, chose to remain with me.

'*Sab theek ho jaayega, sir* (Everything will be all right, sir),' he would constantly motivate me. I thanked God that I had such a loyal man by my side. He had saved my life twice already, once from a mob and once in a Naxal encounter. He used to watch over my family too and was fiercely protective of my children.

From being a poster boy to a persona non grata, my journey was quite traumatic. For one, my ego was bruised and second, the graph of my IIT batchmates was touching stratospheric heights during the same time. Sameer Gehlaut had founded Indiabulls, which is a multi-billion dollar business today, and Chetan Bhagat's *Five Point Someone* had taken the nation by storm.

A few days after I received news of my posting, Sapra, another of my IIT friends, called from the US.

'Amit, thank you so much. I have got admission for the MBA course in Wharton University. It is all because of your recommendation.'

The irony was unbearable—people were getting admission to the world's most prestigious universities on my recommendation and I was not even getting my salary of Rs 18,000. To make some money, I tried my hand at the stock market over the next few months. I started investing—rather, speculating—in the stock market. I lost both my money and my peace of mind, whatever remained of them.

'*Amit, tera sahi kataa hai* (Amit, you're screwed right and proper)! You are a disaster at sex and Sensex! Haha!' Tarun laughed deliriously when he heard of my plight.

When Sameer Gehlaut, a true *chaddi-buddy*, heard about my bad phase, he immediately called me. 'Amit, people are earning in five figures nowadays and your *sarkari naukri* is paying you less than Rs 20,000. Now I have heard that you've burnt your fingers in the stock market too. *Kya faayda aise?* You can join the private sector if you want to. Let me know if you want any help.' Sameer had become hugely successful by sheer hard work, instinct and a lot of gutsy decisions. Like most people growing up in the post-liberalization days of the 90s, he had found my idea of joining a government service quite strange.

I imagined him sitting in a plush cabin in a sleek office, somewhere in a high-rise building, while someone brought him a steaming cup of single-estate coffee as I sat with my one-man staff in Bihar. I stared at the hair protruding out of Surendra's ears and had a strong urge to pull them out.

I knew Sameer was a genuine well-wisher. I thought hard as I disconnected the phone. Everything that could go wrong was going wrong for me during that period. I seriously considered quitting the IPS to join a private sector company. I thank God for not giving me the guts to do so.

~

Unable to get government accommodation, I managed to get two rooms in a small guest house in Patna. Patna was like most of our metropolises. Its basic infrastructure was crumbling because of the burgeoning population. The guest house was in the heart of Patna, the Dak Bungalow Chauraha. The so-called posh locality had a huge garbage dump right in front of my building. It was a favourite place for men of all strata to relieve themselves. Stray dogs and cattle munched on the garbage lying in the open for days. The stench and the abhorrent sight made me really grumpy. For someone who had lived in majestic colonial bungalows, it was as miserable as it could be.

The depressing environment and my disguised unemployment exacerbated my torment.

Tanu had just delivered our daughter, Aishwarya. My frustration made me very impatient and irresponsible as a father. I did not wake up even once to pacify my infant daughter, nor did I try to teach even the ABCs to my four-year-old son, Aditya. The wails of my daughter and the perfectly normal tantrums of my son irritated me to no end.

All I did was listen to the sad and melancholic songs of my favourite singer, the legendary Kishore Kumar. I asked Ajit to get a special compilation from the music shop right across the street. The shopkeeper probably even gave me a discount out of sympathy!

I felt as if I was the most troubled person on this planet, and that everything was an absolute mess. 'How can you become so depressed just because of a posting? These are temporary phases, quite natural in anyone's career,' admonished Tanu. I knew she was right. But I was still finding it difficult to accept my change of fortune.

I had hardly any friends in Patna. My circle was limited to policemen alone. I decided to get out of the house and meet my colleagues. I roamed aimlessly in the gloomy corridors of the Bihar Police HQ and entered the room of any officer who was free at that time. Of course now we have a swanky, state-of-the-art Police HQ. How times have changed!

I preferred to call on officers who were themselves posted to nondescript departments. I used to take solace from the fact that I was not the only one who had been wronged.

Some of the 'shunted' officers were quite cynical. The problem with a senior police officer is that after one has such a heady feeling of power and authority as the SP of a district, it is difficult to come to terms with any other office job, that too, a ceremonial one. It's as if an ageing superstar is forced to play the roles of a character artist in his or her twilight years.

Over endless cups of chai and files kept pending deliberately to create the impression of being busy, I was subjected to their favourite pastime.

'When I was the SP of so-and-so district, I did this and that. People still remember me there. You must have heard. Blah, blah, blah . . .'

Some of us have this delusion that there was and will be no one better than us.

After I had absorbed all the gyan from my equally 'wronged' colleagues, I started knocking on the doors of some 'influential' officers to at least get my salary released.

A decent soul like Shivender Bhagat Sir even took out his wallet and offered me some money. '*Kuchch paise doon tumhe* (Should I give you some money)?'

Taken aback by his benevolence, I politely refused his offer and requested the rightful release of my salary.

The one officer who stood by me and did his best to help me was Kumar Bharat. He somehow arranged a septuagenarian maid, Manju Devi, to work as a nanny for my daughter. She looked even older, like she was touching eighty, but she had managed to work as a staff member by getting a fake age certificate. Getting a fake age certificate was quite common at the time. Whenever I asked a criminal his age, his reply would be, '*Sir, certificate ya asli umar* (Sir, the age in the certificate or my actual age)?'

Manju Devi used to change two buses to reach our house and promptly doze off the moment she entered our guest house, fatigued by the travel. I would fervently pray to God that she should not die in her sleep. At least not in our guest house. I already had enough problems.

~

'Now that we are in Patna, at least get Avi admitted to Noble Academy. It is excellent for nursery students. All your colleagues' children study there,' coaxed Tanu.

I made three rounds of the school but was denied even an appointment with the principal. I felt quite frustrated and angry. Finally, I asked the SHO of Patliputra station, Lalit, to help me with Avi's admission. Noble Academy fell under his jurisdiction.

'Sir, you should have told me earlier. Getting admission to any school is very difficult, but I will get it done for you,' said Lalit.

Eventually, Avi was admitted to the school. That day, I realized the importance of the SHO, the thana in-charge, or Bada Babu, in Bihari parlance. He is the most important cog in the police hierarchy. According to Gangadhar Pandey, one of my trainers, an SHO is an '*ashtabhujadhari*', someone with eight arms. Senior officers expect SHOs to be able to do seemingly impossible tasks with ease.

On the other hand, I had become an *aam aadmi*, a common man, who had to grudgingly collect milk in a utensil from the milkman. My frustration knew no limits.

To make matters worse, I was made the officiating SP of Begusarai around May 2006. My batchmate Rajesh's father-in-law was seriously ill, so I was asked to look after the challenging district in his absence. It felt like I had no power but great responsibility.

I reached Begusarai in an extremely irritable mood. The circuit house was dingy and squalid. The one-man staff would constantly scratch his unmentionables and wipe his paan-stained hands on any curtain within his reach.

'Sahib, what will you have for lunch?' he would ask every time before serving me aloo parwal and lauki. I have a strong suspicion that he had made a month's supply at one go. Anyone eating so much parwal and lauki would go crazy.

I went to the office in the SP's sprawling bungalow every evening to drop off files. I would see the beautiful gardens, the cars parked in the garage and the sentry at the gate. I yearned for the day when I would also become the SP of a district again.

After a week, I called Tanu and the kids to Begusarai to make sure they had a break as well. Suddenly, the Begusarai circuit house became lively. I had still not become a perfect father, but now I enjoyed the shrieks and laughter of my children. Staying away from my family had probably made me realize their importance.

Just a few days later, while walking with Tanu in the Indian Oil Corporation (IOC) campus, Begusarai, I saw Ajit running towards us, saying he had a message for me. As soon as I was back in the residential office, he blurted out, 'Sir, sixteen people have been killed by Samant Pratap in the area bordering Nalanda and Shekhpura!'

5

The Massacres

21 May 2006

Ram Dular had just lit the Kachhua Chhap mosquito coil, hoping that the hundreds of buzzing mosquitoes would spare him that night. It had been a long and tiring day, typical for any farmer in Bihar. His entire clan was sleeping out in the open as it was too humid to sleep inside. There had been no electricity for the last two days. Yet, he was happy—all his closest relatives had assembled for the *grihapravesh*, the housewarming. The ceremony would take place the next morning. He looked at his new house with great pride. He had worked very hard to construct it. He strolled around the courtyard, surveying his labour of love. Suddenly, he stopped in his tracks.

To his utter shock, he saw at least ten armed men staring menacingly at him.

'*Boss, yehi hai* (Boss, this is the one). This swine has been informing the police about our gang's movement,' snarled one voice.

'And he got Lakha Samrat beaten up the other day. What for? Just because Lakha snatched his sister Rekha's dupatta!'

'Five of our brothers were also killed on his information to our enemies, those bastards, Raju and Krishna,' shouted Birju.

A thin, gaunt man came forward, his face covered with a *gamchcha*, a small towel. Ram Dular was petrified when he saw the unmistakable silhouette. It was Samant Pratap. Who didn't recognize those beastly eyes?

'Sahib, what have I done? I would have come personally if huzoor had called,' said Ram Dular.

'*Bahut police se dosti ki hai* (You have become quite friendly with the police). Let me see if those bloody policemen can save you today,' growled Samant.

'Sahib, there must be some confusion. I don't know any policeman. I am simply a poor farmer,' pleaded Ram Dular with folded hands.

Samant dragged Ram Dular by his arm and waved to his henchmen to get his remaining family members.

'Go, get all the family members,' shouted Raushan.

One by one, the family members were rudely awoken from their slumber.

There was a deathly silence, except for the sound of crickets. All eight of them were lined up in the courtyard, too groggy and shocked to speak. They were yet to comprehend what fate had in store for them. It was a scene straight out of the iconic *Sholay*.

'*Dekh le in sab ko aakhri baar* (Look at all of them one last time),' said Samant, holding Ram Dular by his throat.

The ganglord then looked at them and fired with an imaginary gun.

All hell broke loose. Horlicks, now Samant's trusted lieutenant and an ace sharpshooter, fired bullets from his AK-47 at Ram Dular's kith and kin. They started falling like ragged dolls.

Ram Dular was aghast. He started shrieking wildly, trying to break free from Samant's stranglehold. Samant gestured towards

Sukha Singh, who cut Ram Dular's neck with surgical precision. His head was found around ten feet away from the torso when the police arrived the next day.

Happy with the mess his gang had created, Samant sat in his jeep, his leg dangling out to mark his authority.

A man came running furiously towards the jeep.

'Huzoor, we have made a mistake. You came to the wrong Ram Dular's house. The traitor we are looking for has gone to Mannipur village, Shekhpura, to attend a wedding,' shouted a sweating Vakeel Yadav, his informer.

'Boodbak!' shouted an exasperated Horlicks. Raushan slapped him hard.

'Leave him! *Koi baat nahin.* Shekhpura is not far. Let us gatecrash the wedding there. Come on, hop on to the jeep,' said Samant. For him, it was just another day on the job. Killing people made him happy; it satisfied his bestial instincts.

Not one villager in Goachak dared to tell the police what happened that night. Nobody wanted to be the next target of Samant Pratap.

~

The jeep stopped outside the marriage hall. There was a lot of drunken revelry and nobody paid any attention to the gun-slinging men entering the pandal. It was quite common for people to display their machismo by firing in the air. So what if one or two dancers died?

The indifference soon turned to fear when the guests realized in the middle of the wedding that it was Samant Pratap!

The wedding rituals were stopped midway, and beads of sweat started trickling down the pandit's forehead. Samant smiled, grabbing a chicken leg from the plate of one of the *baraatis*.

'Don't worry, I am just looking for Ram Dular. I have some business with him,' announced Samant.

Ram Dular was shaking violently, absolutely terrified. He hid under one of the tables like a child playing hide-and-seek, hoping that somehow or the other, he wouldn't be found.

When no one answered him, Samant dragged the groom by the collar and pointed his finger at the groom's temple.

'I'll blow his head to smithereens if you don't produce Ram Dular by the count of five! No one, I mean, no one, will leave the venue. All you baraatis, stay put!'

The baraatis froze out of fear; they did not dare move a muscle. They knew Samant's penchant for violence. Out of sheer desperation, the groom's father pushed a toddler towards Samant.

'Sahib, this is Ram Dular's grandson. Please don't harm my son. It's his wedding today,' he pleaded, hoping this barter would save his son's life. Samant looked at the toddler, neatly dressed in a pyjama-kurta, looking like a young prince who was about to be butchered by a monster. Samant patted the boy's head and shouted for Ram Dular. His booming voice sent chills down Ram Dular's spine.

Unable to see her son held captive by Samant, the boy's pregnant mother rushed forward and fell at Samant's feet. She pleaded with him to spare her son's life. Now Ram Dular's entire family converged around Samant, praying fervently.

'We'll give you anything you want—we will sell our house, our land. We'll wash your utensils, be your slaves. Please let Golu go. He has done you no harm. He is just a four-year-old child,' wailed Golu's mother.

Ram Dular knew why Samant was looking for him. He had been providing information about Samant not only to the police, but also to Raju and Krishna, Samant's arch-enemies. In fact, when Samant's henchman, Lakha, tried to molest his sister, Rekha, Raju and Krishna had thrashed him black and blue. Not only that, just a few days ago, they had dared to get five of Samant's trusted lieutenants killed in their sleep.

Ram Dular had no choice now. He knew his time was up, yet he hoped that Samant would let some of his family members off. At least his grandson.

He emerged from under the table. 'Sahib, I have broken your trust. Do whatever you want to do with me. Please let my family go,' he pleaded with folded hands, tears trickling down his cheeks.

'*Abe gadha*, we killed another family just because of you. For no fault of theirs. *Bekaar hi mar gaye* (They died in vain).'

Samant thwacked him really hard, bursting his eardrum instantly. He was now bloodthirsty. Within an hour, he had lined up an entire family once more for a massacre. He looked at Ram Dular's family and gestured with his imaginary gun. The always trigger-happy Horlicks opened fire with his AK-47 on Samant's cue, killing Ram Dular's family members instantly. He was about to shoot Golu when Samant stopped him.

Everyone was surprised. Would Samant, the terrible murderer, spare the life of the innocent child? Did Samant really have a heart?

All hope vanished when Samant hoisted the toddler by his ankle. Golu was crying furiously. Samant took out his *desi katta*, a country-made pistol, and pointed it at the boy's head. He looked at Ram Dular with a cruel smile. Ram Dular felt as if his heart had been cut into a thousand pieces. He did not utter a word, but his eyes were pleading. There was a click and a bang.

His face was splattered with blood and tears. He collapsed on the ground.

Horlicks pointed his gun and emptied his bullets into Ram Dular's body. But his life had already left his body.

'Arre, pandit! Why have you stopped the wedding? Come on, it's time to indulge in festivity! Everybody, enjoy! Drink and be merry!' roared Samant, grabbing another chicken piece.

The gang boarded the jeep, leaving behind a wedding and seven funerals.

6

'Kursi Sab Sikha Deti Hai'

Begusarai, 22 May 2006

I got a call from Lakshmi Chandra, a political leader: 'Congratulations, Amitji! You have been posted as SP, Shekhpura.'

I was absolutely devastated. For someone who had been the SP of big and important districts like Nalanda and Muzaffarpur, Shekhpura was the pits. It was like shifting from Miami, Florida, to Mogadishu, Somalia!

Shekhpura is one of the smallest districts in Bihar. In 2006, the Ministry of Panchayati Raj included it in the list of the country's poorest districts.

Some years ago, I had visited Shekhpura to meet my friend and batchmate, Ramnathan, who was posted as SP there.

'Boss, we have to get bread from your district, Nalanda. Even the newspapers come two days late,' Ramnathan had said candidly.

I had felt very bad for Ramnathan on my way back to Nalanda. The road had huge craters, the size you find on the moon. I'm sure the non-stop jolts caused permanent damage to my already precarious back. And now I was to join the same district, that too, in an hour of crisis. I could not believe it— things were just getting worse.

I got a call from the ADG, A.K. Prasad.

'Lodha, the CM wants you to join immediately. We are releasing your salary. We are giving you some Secret Service (SS) funds too,' the ADG said.

I sent my family back to Patna. Tanu had always been remarkably brave, particularly during crises. She wished me luck.

'*Ajit, dhyaan rakhna madam ka* (Ajit, take care of madam),' I told my bodyguard as I bid goodbye to my family.

Outside the Begusarai circuit house waited a rickety, old Ambassador car. Heck, it even had a red beacon and a bold embossing on the plate—'SP SHEKHPURA'. The letters 'SP' somehow rekindled my spirits. At least I was posted as the head of a district.

The joy was short-lived. As I started my journey to Shekhpura, I realized that the road was not meant for driving at all. An erstwhile leader of Bihar had promised to make the roads as smooth as the cheeks of Hema Malini. Unfortunately, the roads became as pockmarked as the cheeks of Om Puri over the years. However, this changed too, albeit after my tenure, and by 2007, Bihar had shown remarkable improvement. Almost all villages and towns are now connected by excellent roads.

The journey got more and more depressing as the evening set in. The atmosphere was quite gloomy and dull, with no lights visible anywhere. It was particularly embarrassing to see women get up from the side of the road and tidy up their saris on seeing the lights of my car because they were forced to relieve themselves along the roads to avoid rodents and snakes.

No wonder our country needs to ensure that the Swachh Bharat Abhiyan is a success. I instructed the driver to switch off the headlights to avoid any further embarrassment to myself and the women.

'*Sahib, bina light ke gaadi bahut slow chalega* (Sahib, the car will go only slowly without the lights),' complained the driver.

'Don't worry, you can drive faster after this stretch,' I replied sternly.

Our car moved forward like a bullock cart, lights or no lights.

I tried to sing Kishore Kumar songs, particularly the all-time classic 'Zindagi Ka Safar'. The driver put on a CD in the car after a few minutes. I took that as a signal for me to shut up. The poor driver could probably not tolerate the murder of music any longer.

I got a few congratulatory calls on the way, telling me that at least I was back in the scheme of the establishment. In any state, the worth of an IPS or Indian Administrative Officer (IAS) officer is measured by the number of districts he or she heads.

'Sir, the government needs officers like you. Only an officer of your calibre can bring law and order back to Shekhpura,' were the statements I heard, typical of the flattery that an officer hears in his or her career, particularly on joining as a district SP. A few officers fall prey to these grandiloquent ideas about themselves. But all good and genuinely successful officers believe in teamwork, delegating power and giving due credit to even the lowest ranked constable. They take bouquets and brickbats stoically, stand by their men in hours of crises and show strength of character in troubled times, à la M.S. Dhoni.

En route, I dwelt on my childhood and IIT memories. I wondered how an absolutely timid and introverted person like me had transformed into a confident and successful policeman, that too in Bihar.

I was a disaster in IIT. Nobody had pressured me to appear for the JEE (Joint Entrance Examination), but I saw all my friends preparing for it. Midway through class XI, I borrowed their books and started studying for the exam, more out of competition with them than any desire to become an engineer. The moment I attended the first class in IIT Delhi, I realized I had come to the wrong place. It was one thing to be good at maths, quite another to find pulleys and lathe machines interesting. I started avoiding going to the classes, flunked mathematics and just about managed to get Cs and Ds. I even wrote a letter to one of my professors begging him not to flunk me. I claimed to be the son of a poor vegetable seller from Rajasthan! I described my imaginary family—a TB patient for a father and an old woman making rotis on the *chulha* for a mother. The professor of thermal energy definitely must have had tears in his eyes as he gave me a D despite the fact that I had attempted just one question out of fifteen.

I tried my hand at everything apart from studies—and failed at all of it. Though I was reasonably talented in all extracurricular activities, I used to chicken out at the crucial moment, be it a match for the selection of the IIT squash team or a quiz competition. I was also an unmitigated disaster with girls. I simply did not know how to converse with women of my age. I used to pay a princely sum of Rs 300 to attend 'socials' with the girls of prestigious colleges like Miranda and Lady Shri Ram. I couldn't utter a word in the presence of anyone wearing skirts. I had two left feet and would start jogging if asked to dance. My thick moustache, heavily oiled hair and ill-fitting baggy pants did not help my cause. Naturally, I could not impress a single girl. I would amble towards a girl and turn towards the buffet table the moment she looked at me. I used to end up eating at least twenty samosas and an equal number of pastries. I could not let my father's hard-earned money be wasted. At that time, I thanked our ancestors for the concept of arranged marriage, otherwise there was no hope for a person like me to get married.

I appeared for job interviews with only Tata Consultancy Services (TCS) and Infosys, as both the companies preferred students with low CGPAs. According to their management, students with poor grades could not turn to greener pastures.

I stammered during the entire interview with TCS. I did not get a call-back from them after the interview. I was rejected by Infosys despite the company's representatives trying their best to take me. I was so disinterested that I didn't even attempt to solve simple questions like calculating the number of diagonals in a cube!

But all this was about to change.

I had always wanted to be a civil servant. This was my true calling. I worked hard and meticulously for the civil services exams. From one of those 'six-point someones' in IIT, I became a member of one of the most prestigious and elite services of the country, the Indian Police Service. I took maths as one of my optional subjects and cracked it. It was the same maths I had failed at IIT. I cursed myself for not making any effort during my college days. My grades would have been much better. I cleared the prelims in the next attempt too, but found the lure of the uniform too strong to take the mains and probably join some other service. The civil services exams take a huge toll, emotionally, mentally and physically. Out of lakhs of young and not-so-young aspirants, only a few hundred are selected. You need to be really lucky to clear the exam and doubly lucky to get a service of your choice. I knew there was no dearth of hardworking and intelligent people in our country. I just thanked my stars and joined the National Police Academy, Hyderabad. My years in IIT had already started making me come out of my shell a little bit, but the days at the NPA accelerated the process. For all my shortcomings, I was always extremely ethical and had a strong sense of right and wrong. This also led to some trouble earlier in my career. With experience and maturity, however, I started looking at the larger picture and learnt not to see everything as black and white.

On getting selected for the IPS, I got the Bihar cadre. All the congratulatory phone calls used to end on a slightly sombre note.

'Wonderful, Amit, we're proud of you. Oh . . . you've got Bihar cadre. Hard luck. Tch, tch,' said the nosey neighbourhood aunty.

Little did they know that I would have the best time of my life in Bihar.

~

I remembered the day I took charge as an ASP in Jamalpur, Munger.

'*Sir, kursi sab sikha deti hai* (Sir, the chair teaches you everything),' said my trainer, SI Harishankar, when I expressed my anxiety. To take charge as a young ASP was an overwhelming experience. I had butterflies in my stomach, and I felt as though everyone was watching my next move. You stand out in a crowd because of your uniform, surrounded by a posse of men. The entire district is your workplace, your office.

Due to sheer hard work, intelligence and some good luck, I had become very successful right at the beginning of my career. I kept getting good postings and made a name for myself. I took every crime as a challenge and confidently solved it. I became a darling of the media and the public. I was drinking the elixir of life, and my stock kept on soaring. The mix of professional success, media coverage and good postings turned my self-assurance into cockiness. My personality transformed. From a meek, gawky student, I became a 'smart, sophisticated and conceited' officer.

However, I was absolutely courteous to the public and my colleagues. Though I did not stop feeling grateful for my successes, I started taking everything for granted. SI Harishankar was right. *Kursi sab sikha deti hai.*

~

On my transfer from Nalanda, almost the entire town descended on the roads to bid me farewell. Life was like a dream. But as is true for everyone, be it a superstar or an ace sportsperson, the good times soon make way for the bad times. You fall when you are at the height of success, when you least expect to fail.

All of a sudden, I was posted as commandant of that non-existent battalion. My world came crashing down. Everyone's attitude changed overnight. Most people started avoiding me as I was no longer 'important'.

'*Tsk, tsk, sir, bahut bura hua aapke saath* (Sir, you have been treated very badly). You have been given quite a bad posting,' mocked a few people sarcastically.

'Everyone loves a fallen hero,' said the devil on my shoulder.

7

Copulating Lizards

23 May 2006

My train of thought was interrupted when we reached Shekhpura. The town, if I may call it that, was the size of a small colony in any other city.

'Sir, this is Dallu Chowk. We are in the heart of the town,' announced my driver, as if he was taking me on a guided tour of Las Vegas.

The streets had an eerie silence, punctuated by the barks of a few stray dogs. Shekhpura looked like a ghost town straight out of the Ramsay Brothers' movies. A few lamps outside the decrepit buildings were constantly flickering, typical of most places in Bihar at the time. Getting an hour of uninterrupted power at proper voltage was as frequent as Pakistan beating India in a Cricket World Cup match. Thankfully, there has now been a sea change in the situation in the state.

'And, sir, this is Famous Tailors—it is really famous for stitching all kinds of suits. Masterji specializes in wedding suits,' added my bodyguard.

'This is Mrigendra Babu's clinic; he is the best doctor in Shekhpura. There are hardly any medical facilities here, not even a Sadar Hospital,' said the driver.

'O lord, please don't let any of us fall ill,' I prayed. I also wondered how we would find vaccinations for our daughter.

We soon reached the circuit house. Worst of all, I saw scores of policemen who looked unshaven, famished, haggard and exhausted, standing on the streets. It often happens during a major law and order problem. A policeman of any rank, be it the DG or a constable, does not know when he will return home. There is no time or place for rest and relief during a crisis. Often, officers and jawans catch some sleep in their jeeps. Food is the least of their priorities. It is difficult for an average civilian to understand what all jawans go through in situations like facing a mob in Srinagar or fighting Naxalites in Bastar.

The DSP of Shekhpura, Yash Sharma, greeted me. There was only one DSP for the entire district. Shekhpura was smaller than a lot of subdivisions in my previous districts.

'Sir, welcome to Shekhpura. Let me give you the details of the situation.'

'There is no need,' I cut him short. I was in no mood for policing. At all.

The senior police officials expected me to hold an emergency meeting with them. After all, Shekhpura had witnessed a massacre, and the SP and DM had been removed. Moreover, my reputation as a successful officer, that too, in the neighbouring district of Nalanda, must have preceded me. But to their utter surprise, I just entered my room and slammed the door shut. My fleeting joy at being posted as an SP had given way to despondency again. Why was I here in this godforsaken place? I did not want to accept that harsh reality.

The circuit house was actually a 'Samudayik Bhavan' or a community centre, originally meant as a meeting hall for the local public. Shekhpura had no sanctioned circuit house since hardly any politician or senior official visited it. Not that the other circuit houses elsewhere in the country were any better.

I surveyed the 'suite' and found quite a few really fat rats climbing up the rods installed around the bed to hold the mosquito net in place. I gingerly pushed open the door of the bathroom, fearing that a rat would jump at me. To my horror, I saw two lizards copulating in the Indian style-loo and a lone frog croaking in one corner. I have faced many dreaded criminals in my life, yet I start shaking the moment I see lizards. If you ever see me standing on a sofa in my house, you can safely assume that there is a lizard on the floor, ten feet away from me.

I ran out of the circuit house, straight to the porch, at a speed that would have shamed Usain Bolt. I commanded two orderlies to get rid of the biodiversity in my room. Bemused, they succeeded in executing the first order given by me as SP, Shekhpura.

'*Huzoor, pakad liya hai,*' said the beaming orderly. The two poor lizards were dangling precariously on the broom. I felt bad for the lizards, for I had disturbed their passionate mating.

With great trepidation, I entered the room again and ordered dinner. I should have guessed I would be treated to the delicacies of aloo parwal and lauki. I am sure the cook of the Begusarai circuit house had sent the leftovers to Shekhpura. After a forced fast, I tried to sleep under the mosquito net, constantly rolling and slapping various parts of my body to kill all the species of insects and mosquitoes whose habitat I had invaded. I think the two lizards and the frog were maintaining an ecological balance in that fragile ecosystem.

The next morning, I woke up to the constant buzzing of mosquitoes. Moments later, I got a call from Kumar Sir, 'Amit, please note down the names of these villages. They are on the radar of Samant Pratap. Please visit these places and ensure that there is adequate patrolling there.'

I was surprised and happy in equal measure. The DIG had also been transferred overnight and Kumar Bharat was to take charge.

Kumar Bharat was one of the finest officers in Bihar. A man of few words, he was a thorough professional and an excellent leader. I learnt a lot from him, not only about technical and legal matters, but also on how to maintain one's dignity in office, when I worked as the ASP, Patna, under his SPship.

He called me again after two hours, inquiring if I had taken any measures. I categorically said no and vented my ire. Sir was remarkably patient and listened till I lamented to my heart's content.

'Amit, I know I am sounding preachy, but this is the oath we took on the Constitution. As IPS officers, it is our duty and moral obligation to the citizens to prevent crime and bring to justice any perpetrators of crime. And apart from that, you are already in the bad books of the establishment. The earlier SP was just shunted out, but you will be suspended in case of another massacre,' he explained in as many words as possible on the phone.

Just afterwards, Tanu called me and asked about my well-being. I ranted about the pathetic condition of the guest house and told her that there was no official house for the SP. As always, she pacified me, 'Don't worry. We will manage. I am happy that all of us will live together. I will reach Shekhpura in a few days.'

8

Back to Work

I knew that Tanu was not really bothered about the pitiable condition of the Shekhpura circuit house. I thought back to our first night in Bihar, on 13 December 1999.

Immediately after our honeymoon in the beautiful city of Udaipur, we had disembarked at the Jhumri Talaiyya railway station, a place famous for all its residents making requests to the All India Radio for playing songs of their choice.

After an hour's drive, we reached the pitch-dark campus of PTC Hazaribagh. I expected a proper reception, just like at the NPA, but was shocked to see just a fat constable emerging out of the darkness. The lantern in his hand created an eerie silhouette, just like that of the caretaker in the movie *Bees Saal Baad*. The portly constable scratched his huge tummy and handed me a Good Knight mosquito coil, a candle and a matchbox. I was totally flummoxed.

'Why are you giving all these things to me?' I asked angrily.

'Sahib, there has been no power supply for the last six hours. How will you see in this darkness? And there are a lot of mosquitoes here. Memsahib will have a lot of trouble if you don't use the coil. Mosquitoes love *gori chamdi* (fair skin),' said the constable, adjusting his lungi.

We somehow managed to reach our room on the first floor. Tanu lit the candle. I opened the tap to wash my hands, only to find all the water falling on my feet. I looked down and saw that there was no pipe. Even the drain was a good five feet away from the basin. I then tried to close the windows of our room, only to discover that they could not be closed from the inside. I went outside the room to check the windows. To my horror, I realized that the window latches were on the outside. That meant anyone who was in the corridor outside our room could open our window! It was absolutely shocking. Our privacy as a newly wedded couple was under threat.

'Why is there no pipe in the washbasin? And why the hell are the latches of the windows on the outside?' I demanded an explanation from the constable.

'Sahib, that *thekedar* (contractor) has not been paid his dues for the last three years by the PWD. So as revenge, he put the windows inside out. And there was no money left to buy the pipes for the washbasin.'

I wondered if Tanu would run away.

'Come on, the "honeymoon suite" is waiting for us,' Tanu giggled when she realized there was no solution to our problems. I was thankful she was not leaving me. Ever.

Tanu has always been the pillar of strength in my life. Being the daughter of a senior IPS officer, she was well aware of the professional challenges I faced and would continue to face all throughout my career. She could make out a lot of what I was going through just by looking into my eyes. Apart from being highly intelligent, she has been a paragon of virtue and ethics. In fact, the first two big arrests of my career which led to my meteoric rise were purely because of lady luck— literally!

~

My first posting was in September 2000 as the ASP of Jamalpur, a small, sleepy town in Munger, once famous for the railway institute, SCRA, an ITC factory and the Yoga School, but now infamous for the production of desi kattas. The British had set up a factory there to manufacture arms for the police and the provincial constabulary. Years later, the factory shut down, leaving scores of gunsmiths unemployed. Knowing no other vocation, they started making guns for the local criminals at a fraction of the cost of the original ones. So skilled were the workers that it was nearly impossible to tell the difference between the original and a country-made gun. And to give it an even more authentic touch, the guns were embossed with 'Made in Italy' or 'Walther PPK'!

Soon, word spread about this remarkable craftsmanship, and hordes of criminals, big and small, started ordering all kinds of guns. The rising crime graph in the states of Bihar and neighbouring Uttar Pradesh further helped expand the business. The gunsmiths were thriving now. Making country-made weapons was now a 'cottage industry' in Bihar. And there was no need for any government subsidy!

As it happens with any young police officer, many people came to see me when I was first posted to the town.

'Sir, Kirtan Mishra is the biggest criminal of Munger. He killed the general manager of ITC just a few months ago. We'd be very happy if you arrest him. The people of Munger are fed up with his extortion. He also killed our cousin last fortnight. Please arrest him. We have great expectations from you,' said an elderly man earnestly.

'Sir, we have come to know recently that he hides in a room next to a tube well near his house. There are two neem trees near that tube well,' said another man.

I wondered why the police could not arrest Kirtan if his hideout was so easily known to those two. I noted down the information reluctantly. If none of my predecessors had caught him, what could a greenhorn like me do?

The next day I raided a few places to seize some illegal arms but did not find anything. I was quite disappointed; I was desperate to make a mark for myself.

'Huzoor, that big house is Kirtan Mishra's,' my driver, Shashi, pointed it out as we were on our way back to the circuit house.

'*Achcha, chalo*, let us check out his house.'

I thought I might as well put my manpower to some use. I also wanted to tell my SP that I had 'raided' Kirtan's house to prove my sincerity.

I entered the house. It was quite tidy and well-maintained.

'Sir, will you have some tea?' asked Kirtan's wife. I was quite amused. I did not know policemen were so welcome in criminals' houses in Bihar. I checked the entire house and, naturally, did not find the criminal. I saw the landline phone and immediately dialled the circuit house number to speak to Tanu.

'Hi, how are you? I'm not in my office, and I think I kept a piece of paper that had an address scribbled on it in your Mills and Boons novel,' I said.

'Don't worry. I will get it and tell you the address,' said Tanu cheerfully.

Within a minute, she read out the address to me. I called Inspector Tiwari, a brilliant officer who was accompanying me.

'Tiwari, can we find this place?' I told him about the tube well and a few other landmarks.

'Sir, this place is quite close by. Let us go,' said Tiwari.

After a few minutes, Tiwari and I found the room next to the tube well and entered it. There was no one and nothing inside except for a bed. I yawned and stretched my arms. Suddenly,

Tiwari aimed his pistol at the bed and shouted. '*Baahar niklo, goli maar denge* (Come out, or I will shoot you)!'

A tall, well-built man with huge arms emerged from under the bed. He was carrying a country-made pistol. I was shocked as well as delighted. Shocked because I just could not imagine that such a huge man could hide under the bed, and delighted because it was going to be my first achievement, the first arrest of my career. I shoved the man hard. Convinced that he wasn't retaliating, I commanded Tiwari, '*Le aaiye isko, Tiwari* (Bring him, Tiwari),' and started walking towards my Gypsy. Just moments later, I saw Shashi jumping jubilantly.

'*Huzoor, kamaal ho gaya* (Sir, a miracle has happened). Kirtan has been arrested,' he said animatedly.

'Where, where is he? Who caught him?' I asked with a hand on my pistol.

'*Sir, woh hi toh hai* (Sir, that is him). The man you just arrested.'

I just could not believe it. Both Tiwari and I had never seen Kirtan earlier in our lives, and here we had arrested the don of Munger without any fuss. We reached the Kotwali thana to a thunderous reception from a huge crowd. Thousands of people came out on the streets to celebrate Kirtan's arrest.

'Sir, you joined as an ASP just three days ago. How did you arrest such a notorious criminal so quickly?' asked all the media persons.

I remained quiet. How could I tell them it was sheer good luck and that my wife had helped indirectly?

Finally, I said, 'It was a secret operation. I can't divulge any more details.' It became my stock answer to countless questions by the press in the future.

A few days later, as I was about to leave for a game of squash, I got a call from an informer.

'Sir, Hari Sinha is about to leave his village. He has just hired a car.'

I was really irritated as I was getting late for my game.

'Do you know which car he will travel in? Or the route he is taking? How will I catch him then?' I shouted into the phone. When I got no answer, I put it down and turned around to see my wife with a stern look on her face.

'I can't believe that a game of squash is more important to you than your police duties!' I tried to reason with her, but to no avail. In any case, I was desperate to arrest Hari Sinha.

I put on my uniform and asked for some additional force to reach the Safiasarai police station. On reaching the station, I kept looking at the flickering flame of the lantern, waiting for some policemen to arrive. But who cares for an ASP? Things become quite different once one becomes an SP. The SP is a *zilla ka malik* in common parlance.

Unable to wait for backup any more, I asked Shashi, my driver, to drive towards Hari Sinha's village. An old Ambassador car passed us. Instinctively, I asked Shashi to stop the next vehicle. Before I could finish my sentence, Shashi blocked the road and stopped a Maruti that was coming from the opposite side. In a leisurely manner, I got down from my Gypsy, only to hear Shashi shouting, '*Sir, neeche jhuk jaiye* (Sir, duck immediately)!'

I saw a man brandishing a country-made carbine from the Maruti. Shashi and my bodyguard, Bhushan, shouted and ordered the passengers to get down from the car. The driver and the gun-toting burly guy raised their hands and came out. The guy with the carbine probably realized that he was outnumbered by the police. In any case, he was an easy target for us as he was sitting inside the car. Our backup team, led by Inspector Tiwari, had also arrived by this time.

'*Sir, aapko bahut yash likha hai* (Sir, you are destined for big successes)!' said a jubilant Tiwari, lifting me up.

We had just arrested Hari Sinha in the most dramatic fashion, with me doing practically nothing except sitting in a Gypsy! I became a super cop overnight for arresting a notorious criminal, wanted in about twenty murder and kidnapping cases, close on the heels of the arrest of Kirtan Mishra. That day I realized that I may have failed at IIT, but I was destined to arrest big criminals and succeed as a policeman.

~

Back in Shekhpura, Tanu's phone call jolted me into action. I started worrying about finding suitable accommodation for my family as there was no official residence for the SP. I summoned the town SHO, Rajesh Charan, a strapping young officer.

'Jai hind, sir, I am the brother of your batchmate Anupam Charan. I had also appeared for the UPSC exam,' he said with a smart salute.

In Bihar, there are quite a few cases of one brother becoming an IPS officer and another a relatively junior officer. You could call it destiny. I could clearly see the scorn in his eyes. I imagined he must have been thinking that he could very well have been my batchmate in the IPS.

I instructed him to find a decent house for my family. Within half an hour, he came back triumphantly, as if he had annexed a small kingdom for me.

'Sir, the junior engineer's house has been lying vacant for years. You can move in right now!'

The electricity supply was quite erratic in Shekhpura and there was not much the junior engineer could do. A few officials of all government departments work like this, in almost all the states of the country. They will make their own houses in the capital city, get their children admitted to good schools, hire tutors for them and settle their families there. An official will try his best to fulfil the aspirations of his family. This is the dream of almost all middle-class people. The officer will travel up and down to his place of posting, maybe once in a few days. But poor policemen like us do not have any choice. We have to actually stay in our place of posting. We can't move to and fro and hope that a criminal will be kind enough to commit an offence only when we are in the district. However, in this instance, I thanked the electricity department and decided to shift into the junior engineer's house.

~

Kumar Sir reached the 'circuit house' and moved into the adjoining 'suite' without any fuss.

'Amit, I hope you are no longer angry with the "injustice" meted out to you. I expect to see some action from you now.'

'Sir, you have been my trainer. I will arrest Samant Pratap soon, just for you,' I replied cockily. I wanted to arrest Samant to regain my 'rightful' place in the bureaucratic circles. Not only would it boost my ego, it would also be a fitting answer to all my detractors.

Kumar Sir just looked at me with a faint smile. I had made the announcement as if Samant Pratap was one of the thousands of deals offered by Flipkart or Amazon. Just a click and presto, Samant Pratap delivered to your home! Of course, there was no online shopping at that time.

~

I reached my office. It was absolutely grotesque. A huge, ugly table stood in the centre with a number of plastic chairs in various colours arranged in front of it. Quite a few files wrapped in red cloth adorned the table. Particularly jarring was the SP's chair, draped with a huge towel. In many sarkari offices, the boss's chair is specially covered with a *tauliya*, a pristine white towel, symbolizing power! A *peekdaan*, or spittoon, was lying next to the table. I immediately decided the office required an overhaul. I needed a decent workplace.

I ordered for a furniture catalogue from Patna.

'Huzoor, we don't have the budget for such expensive furniture,' the head clerk told me disapprovingly.

'Don't worry. Just get a local carpenter and ask him to copy the designs. I am sure there must be a talented carpenter in Shekhpura. I have done this in all my earlier postings.' Satisfied with my instructions, I turned to work.

I summoned DSP Sharma and SHO Rajesh Charan to find out the exact situation in Shekhpura. Both unanimously said that arresting Samant Pratap was a Herculean task, but one Chandan Singh, a mid-level criminal and a rival of Samant, could be arrested immediately. His arrest would herald my arrival in Shekhpura. And true to his word, Rajesh produced Chandan Singh in front of me in less than twenty-four hours.

'*Sir, badka bhetnar criminal hai!*' said an elated Rajesh Charan. Bihar cops had coined an entirely new word, '*bhetnar*', for veteran!

I was not very impressed with Rajesh. Chandan's arrest with a country-made rifle and some ammunition was too easy, as if he had been waiting in his house for someone to go and get him. It often happens when a new SP joins a district. Some SHOs arrest a few petty criminals, called 'pocket' criminals, to impress their new boss. I was seasoned enough not to fall for this ploy.

Anyway, my target was Samant Pratap, not some small-time criminal.

Samant was one of the most dreaded ganglords in Bihar. His name was associated with the infamous massacres of the state, which had taken hundreds of lives. He had started out as a small-time goon, but had gone on to become the Veerappan of Bihar. It would require a manic obsession on my part to nab him.

9

The Making of a Butcher

Samant Pratap was an unusual child. While the other children in his village enjoyed playing hide-and-seek, *gilli-danda* and swimming in the pond with the buffaloes, Samant chased chameleons. He was fascinated by their changing colours. But the colour he liked the most was crimson. So he would chase the hapless reptiles and bludgeon them to death. The lizards would writhe in pain and die a slow death.

Samant derived a strange pleasure from the macabre. He was a born sociopath who could get violent at the drop of a hat. Other children did not dare come near him.

He grew up in a poor household in Nawada. His uncle got him a job as a tractor driver. But Samant realized early that that was not the life he would lead. He knew that he was destined to rule as a king. He started as a pickpocket and soon formed a gang of boys who committed petty crimes, extortions and thefts. The local villagers feared him. His reputation as a troublemaker grew steadily. Samant got his first big break when a fellow villager asked him to usurp a piece of farmland that belonged to a landlord. The fact that the landlord was quite wealthy and powerful did not deter Samant from grabbing the land.

Taking it as a direct challenge, the landlord summoned the most dreaded criminal of his own ilk, Sarveshwar Singh. Samant needed to be taught a lesson.

One night, Sarveshwar and his men entered Samant's house and dragged his father and brother out. Failing to find Samant, an enraged Sarveshwar fired indiscriminately at his house, injuring Samant's *bhabhi* in the process. When Samant returned home the next day from the brick kiln in the neighbouring village, he vowed to finish off not only the landlord and Sarveshwar, but their families too. It was not out of love for his family. He simply did not like to be challenged.

Samant knew he could not match the strength of Sarveshwar's gang in any way. He decided to join forces with Sarveshwar's adversary, Pankaj Singh, who also happened to be Sarveshwar's cousin, but did not see eye-to-eye with him. Both of them were embroiled in a bitter property dispute. Their hatred for each other had only grown with time.

'*Pankaj Bhai, aapka aur hamaara dushman ek hai* (Pankaj Bhai, we have the same enemy). We have to eliminate him,' said Samant when he visited Pankaj.

Though Pankaj detested Samant's clan, he loathed Sarveshwar even more.

'*Toh kaise karna hai* (So how do we do this)?' Pankaj asked.

'*Aapko maaloom hoga na* (You would know best). You tell me, where can we kill him? Does he follow any schedule? He must have some chink in his armour.'

'Sarveshwar is a bhakta of Bhairav Baba. A staunch devotee. Every Thursday, he goes to the Bhairav temple on Chamundi Hills, without fail.'

'Then he will have to be killed in the temple. *Uski bali chadhani hogi* (He will have to be sacrificed),' declared Samant.

~

The chanting was at its crescendo. Hundreds of bhaktas thronged the temple in Chamundi Hills, the abode of Maa Chamundi. It was a pilgrimage as sacred as any other. Samant, Pankaj and their gang blended in with the crowd of bhaktas. There was a sea of ochre, with almost all the pilgrims wearing different hues of this sacred colour. 'Jai Chamundi Maa, Jai Chamundeshwari'—the hills echoed with the chants of the bhaktas and the centuries-old temple shone with the light of beautiful diyas. Suddenly, the devotees stopped chanting. Sarveshwar had arrived to pay obeisance.

Once inside the sanctum sanctorum, Sarveshwar gestured to his bodyguards to move out. He needed to pray in solitude. The smell of the incense sticks wafted through the air. Sarveshwar closed his eyes and prostrated himself in front of Bhairav Baba.

All of a sudden, he sensed movement close by. He looked up from where he was lying on the floor. The pandit was shaking. Pankaj was standing over him. By his side was Samant. He shut the doors of the temple, smiling wickedly all the time.

Sarveshwar closed his eyes. He knew his time was up. Pankaj took out his pistol and aimed it at Sarveshwar's head.

But before Pankaj could squeeze the trigger, Samant dropped a huge stone that was lying next to the Shiva linga on Sarveshwar's head. Soon, the milk flowing over the steps of the temple turned crimson red. Pankaj could not see his own cousin's head reduced to a pulp. He vomited violently.

This was the beginning of Samant's rise as a dreaded outlaw. In a few years, he would be known as the Butcher of Nawada.

~

Samant had lofty ambitions. He needed to cement his position in the world of crime.

'Pankaj Bhai, let us gather some better weapons.' Pankaj looked at Samant and said, '*Theek toh hai*. Aren't our countrymade weapons good enough for our work?'

'*Arre, kuch bada socho* (Arre, think big). Having sophisticated weapons will put us in a different league,' retorted Samant.

'Okay, but where will we get those weapons from?'

'Oh, leave it to me. The weapons are available on the roads every night.'

~

Pankaj could not believe it. They were about to loot rifles from policemen. Samant, Pankaj and his men surveyed the streets. There was not a soul in sight. Only two frail home guards were patrolling in the cold, dark night. The home guards were shivering, their hands dug deep into their torn trench coats. Their rifles were slung casually on their shoulders. The gangsters quickly surrounded the two unsuspecting home guards and easily overpowered them. The poor home guards were totally outnumbered and unable to provide any resistance.

Samant inspected the rifles and smiled with glee.

'*Chalo, bhaago!* Let us go!' shouted Pankaj.

'*Kahe*, Pankaj Bhai? What is the hurry?'

Samant pointed his favourite desi katta at the home guards. The poor men stared at certain death.

Samant shot both of them even before Pankaj could open his mouth to protest. Pankaj shuddered. Samant bordered on crazy. He was obsessed with killing.

Now Samant's gang had police rifles too. Pankaj became increasingly wary of Samant. There was no doubt that Samant called the shots in the gang now. He was also quite intelligent, a quality he put to good use when planning criminal activities. And he was extremely dangerous.

When he realized that his expenses were increasing, Samant kidnapped the son of a bullion trader in Lakhisarai. The trader paid Rs 5 lakh to Samant. He dared not even inform the police, such was his fear of the gangster. Thankfully, the child was spared. Nobody in the gang could believe it. Maybe Samant was not in the mood that day. But the very next day, Samant killed the child's uncle—after the ransom had been paid and the child released. The butcher did not want to sully his image.

~

Nawada was a small, backward town famous for aloo, *baaloo*, or sand, and the name of a political leader that rhymed with both these words. Samant had no interest in aloo or potatoes, but he definitely wanted to get into the business of baaloo. Sand mining was very lucrative. Samant's business soon diversified into illegal mining. Of course, kidnapping and extortion remained the flagship business. His group functioned with the efficiency of a world-class company!

Soon, politicians with unsavoury reputations tried to entice Samant. His clout among his people increased day by day.

Kumarballabh was the local neta at the time. Samant and he belonged to the same clan.

'*Samant Bhaiyya, hamaare saath mil jao* (Samant Bhaiyya, come join us). You will go very far,' he said to Samant when he met him.

'Sure, Kumar Bhai, tell me, what can I do for you?'

'*Bas chunaav jitwaana hai* (Make me win the elections).'

'What will I gain from your victory?'

'Samant, it is always good to have political connections. *Tumhare dhandhe ke liye achcha rahega* (It will be beneficial for your business in the long run).'

Samant smiled. Kumarballabh was right.

To his men, Samant declared, 'We have to ensure that our man Kumarballabh wins the assembly elections. Money won't be a problem,' while fiddling with his desi katta. All the gang members nodded in unison.

Kumarballabh's only rival, Kesho Singh, was a '*dabangg*' leader in his own right. He belonged to the same clan as Sarveshwar and Pankaj. Samant's plans against Kesho were beyond Pankaj's tolerance. No doubt, Pankaj had been working with Samant Pratap for the last few months, but it had purely been a marriage of convenience. Samant had already become much more powerful than him. Kumarballabh's victory would firmly establish Samant as the kingmaker.

Pankaj's men were already very upset with him.

'*Tu doosre logon ke saath kaise mil gaya* (How come you have allied with a man from another clan)?'

'Just to take revenge on your cousin, you have betrayed our people. Shame on you!'

Pankaj was tired of being called a traitor. He had to redeem his honour.

~

Kumarballabh had called Samant over for a drink to review the situation. He said worriedly, 'Samant, we are in for a tough fight. Kesho Singh is quite influential in the *diara*, the riverine belt.'

'*Toh kya tareeka hai aapke jeetne ka* (So how are you planning to win)?' asked Samant.

Kumarballabh paused for a moment. He gulped the English whisky he was having in one go.

'*Kesho Singh ko maarna hoga* (Kesho Singh will have to be killed),' Kumarballabh looked Samant in the eye.

'Haha! *Ho jaayega* (It will be done). But I need a promise from you.'

'Anything for you, brother.'

'I want my bhabhi to become the MLA in the next elections.'

~

Kesho Singh was delighted. His *bahu* had just delivered a child, a boy.

'Finally, I have an heir. I will groom him to carry my political legacy forward,' thought Kesho.

Kesho had never loved his son, Akhilesh. He found him too weak and docile. Years of abuse and neglect by Kesho had made his son mentally ill. '*Kahaan sher ke yahaan yeh nalayak paida hua hai* (How come I have an imbecile for my son)?' Of course, the endless taunts did not help Akhilesh in any way.

On his way to his paternal village, Kesho kept dreaming about his grandiose plans for his grandson. Suddenly, his Tata Safari came to a screeching halt. Kesho's head hit the front seat.

'Boodbak! You idiot! Don't you know how to drive?' an angry Kesho shouted at his driver.

'Huzoor, I can't go further. The bridge has been blocked by a tree. Our men will have to get down to remove it.'

'*Toh hatao na* (So remove it),' said an irritated Kesho.

Two of his personal bodyguards got down reluctantly. The tree was huge.

'We need some more men. *Do-teen aadmi aur aao*,' shouted one of the beefy guards.

Two more men got down from the escort vehicle.

The four men tried to lift the tree trunk. Their combined strength finally moved the tree a bit. This is exactly what Samant had wanted.

The improvised explosive device went off as soon as the tree trunk was moved. The four guards were blown to smithereens. Their limbs and torsos flew in the air, landing several feet away.

Kesho was absolutely shaken. Fear gripped him.

'*Reverse le, bhaag*,' he shouted at his driver at the top of his voice.

The driver tried to reverse the SUV as fast as he could, but rammed straight into the escort jeep behind it. The jeep's driver simply could not move his vehicle. The other end of the bridge had been blocked by a Tata 407.

Samant and his men jumped down from the Tata 407. Kesho's two remaining bodyguards were sitting ducks. They were killed even before they could cock their rifles.

Samant casually walked towards the SUV. Kesho was drenched in sweat; he knew death was knocking on his door. Yet, he did not want to go down without fighting.

Samant tapped on the window.

'*Kesho, tera time khatam* (Kesho, your time's up),' laughed Samant.

In one swift moment, Kesho pulled out his pistol and pressed the trigger.

Samant was totally taken aback. He had not expected Kesho to carry a weapon.

But the pistol jammed. It seemed Kesho had not serviced his pistol for a long time.

Samant smiled. He knew luck was with him.

'*Aur le licenci tamancha* (Your licenced pistol is of no use).'

Kesho slumped forward as the shots from Samant's gun hit his chest.

Samant then pointed his gun at the driver's temple.

'What are you doing? I told you Kesho Sir's schedule. I followed all your instructions,' pleaded the driver.

'Then follow my final instructions. *Mar jaa* (Go die)!'

Samant laughed deliriously. His men looked at the carnage. Eight people had been murdered that day.

From that day, Samant Pratap became the undisputed king of Nawada and the adjoining areas.

Samant had built up a legend around himself. His barbarity knew no bounds. He also loved creating a spectacle out of his killings. Just like Bollywood potboilers, he would enter a man's house, drag him out in full public view, break his limbs one by one, then go for the teeth and, finally, bludgeon his head.

Samant rarely used a weapon—though he was surrounded by AK-47-wielding goons, he preferred desi kattas. Firing a desi gun gave him an inexplicable thrill.

With every murder, Samant's legend grew. The more daring his escapade, the greater the legion of admirers and followers he had. Bihar has always had a strange culture of hero worship. One has to be either extremely good or extremely bad to be adulated. For every famous IPS officer they looked up to, there was also a dreaded criminal like Samant that the people were in awe of. As more and more people, particularly unemployed youth, joined Samant's gang, his criminal empire also expanded. Samant had his finger in every pie, be it extortion, kidnapping for ransom or illegal mining. Politics was a natural progression for Samant Pratap. The local politicians flocked to him to support their candidates. Samant loved his role as kingmaker. So terrifying was he that the candidates he supported were elected virtually without any opposition. And anyone who dared contest Samant's candidates was simply eliminated—in the most macabre manner.

10

'Loha Hi Lohe Ko Kaat Sakta Hai'

Rajesh Charan, being the town SHO, used to come every morning to report to me. He had impressed all my predecessors with his personality and performance. But somehow, I never warmed up to him. There was something about him that I didn't find quite right. I have always had a fantastic sixth sense, a gift of being able to judge people very quickly. I hoped that I was wrong this time.

'Arre, Amit, so proud of you, my friend. *Yaar, Rajesh mera apna bhai hai* (Yaar, Rajesh is my own brother). Please treat him as your brother too,' an excited Anupam Charan, my batchmate, had said. It seemed he was expecting that I would be extra generous and cordial to Rajesh, now that I was his immediate boss. It was quite a natural expectation too.

~

'Sir, your house is being readied. I have instructed the contractor to use the best distemper. Does madam have any choice for the colours of the interiors?' asked a beaming Rajesh. He knew that his brother had called me. This was the time for him to earn a few brownie points. Politely yet firmly, I told him to concentrate on the policing aspects and leave the renovation work to the contractor.

79

The house was basically a two-and-a-half-room structure, with one bathroom. Since my family was about to join me, I used to visit it every evening to check on the progress of the renovation. The house was in bad shape, but I was hopeful of turning it around. This would be my one contribution to my successor—he could live in a small yet well-maintained house. The other contribution would be Samant Pratap's arrest. I was confident of both results.

Shekhpura was teeming with policemen in the aftermath of the twin massacres of both Ram Dulars and their families. Kumar Sir had personally deputed extra force in all the villages that might possibly be attacked by Samant. Many police parties were sent to raid all of Samant's possible hideouts. Some of his associates were arrested too, but somehow, I was not very impressed with the 'standard' police response to this situation. I knew that police operations would soon lose steam, and Samant would be hardly affected by the arrest of some petty gang members. His gang had to be eliminated this time, and that would happen only if some of his trusted lieutenants, like Horlicks, were arrested. Or Samant himself. Otherwise, the gang would grow again like the Hydra.

Samant had strong support from the local population, both out of clan considerations as well as the fear of retribution. The moment a police team left the police station, Samant got a message alerting him. Someone like him, who frequently held press conferences in the district with great impunity, would have very little difficulty in finding out the police's plans. Our department had his moles too.

I had to think like Samant if I wanted to catch him. At times, I certainly think that I could have been a successful criminal too. That is what one panditji, an astrologer whom my family regularly consulted, had predicted when I was a child. '*Mataji, aapka beta ya toh criminal banega ya police-wallah* (Mataji, your son is destined to become either a criminal or a policeman)! His stars are aligned in such a way that he will be associated with the world of crime.'

My mother had become quite worried about my future after my poor performance in IIT. I did not have a job and very few people had confidence in me passing the civil services exams. So she started showing my *janampatri* or horoscope to various astrologers. Needless to say, my mother was quite relieved when I joined the Indian Police Service.

~

My back and hip started hurting all of a sudden. 'Shit,' I grumbled before getting into the blue Gypsy.

I asked my driver to take me to the Kasar police station.

An unshaven man, his skin darkened by constant exposure to the sun, was waiting for me just outside the police station. Ranjan Kumar, the former SHO of Kasar police station, had been put under suspension by the Police HQ. It seemed as if he had aged a decade in the last week. The second massacre had taken place in his jurisdiction. I hobbled out of the Gypsy and somehow managed to stand straight. Ranjan was in civil clothes, because a policeman is not allowed to wear the uniform when suspended. He was in the police station to hand over charge of the *maalkhana*, the police depository, and all the cases.

Ranjan saluted me by whipping to attention, impressing me with his sense of discipline even in adversity. I feebly managed to return the salute.

I signalled to my bodyguard and my driver to leave—I needed to talk privately to Ranjan. Barely able to control my pain, I stood by the bonnet of the Gypsy. Ranjan was a little tense. Why would the SP come to see a disgraced, suspended SI?

'Ranjan, I want to know the exact reason for the massacre of Ram Dular and his family, every single detail.'

'Sir, I don't know much about it. It happened out of the blue.'

'I know that Krishna and Raju had beaten up Lakha a few days ago. The murder of five of Samant's men was the tipping point. That angered Samant enough for him to commit the cold-blooded murder of Ram Dular's family. Look, the government has posted me and the DIG here only to arrest Samant Pratap. It is our top priority. You have to help me in this mission.'

'But, sir, what can I do? I am just an ordinary SI, that too, suspended,' a resigned Ranjan muttered.

'Ranjan, I know your competence. You're a very capable officer with an excellent network of spies. And I know that you are on good terms with Raju and Krishna.'

'No, no, sir. Why would I know shady characters like Raju and Krishna?' Ranjan denied vehemently.

'I have been in the service long enough to know that certain people have to be developed as sources. If not a criminal background, these people will at least have dubious antecedents. I, too, have engaged such people to get information about criminals in my previous postings. Come on, do you think a normal, decent person would become a police informer?'

Ranjan kept staring at the ground, unwilling to speak further.

It was time for me to come up with an ace.

'Ranjan, you are under suspension. Strict disciplinary action will be taken against you. Your career is at stake. If you help me nab Samant Pratap, I promise you that I will get your suspension revoked and you will get your job back. With full honours.'

Ranjan's eyes lit up for the first time. I knew that he was short of money and his wife was suffering from depression. People around him had changed after his fall from grace. Who could know that better than me? I had gone through almost the same experience just a while ago.

'Okay, sir, I am with you. I hate Samant Pratap anyway and I know your reputation of standing by your subordinates. Tell me, what can I do for you?'

I just smiled and made a call to M.A. Hussain, the IG of the Bhagalpur zone. A strict, no-nonsense but idiosyncratic officer, he was known for taking tough stands.

'Sir, this is Amit Lodha, calling from Shekhpura. Yes, sir, I'm on the job. I assure you that Samant Pratap will be behind bars soon. Sir, I would be very grateful if you would accede to one request. I'm going to use the service of one officer to catch Samant. In the times to come, I might require a favour for him.'

M.A. Hussain listened to me intently. There was a long pause.

'Okay, Amit. I hope the favour you are seeking won't be bigger than the arrest of Samant.'

'Certainly not, sir. Quite a trivial matter.' I smiled as Hussain disconnected the line. Both Ranjan and I knew that M.A. Hussain was a man of his word. Reputation travels fast in police circles.

'I want to meet Raju and Krishna. Get them to my house in a day or two,' I told Ranjan.

'Sir, are you sure? I mean, they have dubious reputations and your meeting them might sully your image.'

'I know it's a risk. But I have no choice. *Loha hi lohe ko kaat sakta hai* (Only iron can cut iron)!'

11

'Aap Suspend Ho Gaye Hain'

Ranjan had worked in the Naxal district of Lohardaga in Jharkhand before coming to Bihar. On his posting to Shekhpura, he had expected a peaceful life. He had had enough skirmishes with Naxals in the jungles of Lohardaga. Little did he know that he would have the most harrowing experience in Shekhpura.

Ranjan was made the SHO of the Kasar police station in Shekhpura. Samant Pratap's influence was substantial and his word was law in the area under Ranjan's jurisdiction. After just two days of Ranjan joining as the SHO of Kasar, Samant sent an emissary.

'Huzoor, Samant Bhaiyya has sent his regards to you. We would be happy to provide you with newspapers and supplies of chicken, mutton . . . Anything you want, sir!' said the messenger with a smile.

'Don't you dare enter the premises of this thana again! I can very well afford to pay Rs 250 for a monthly subscription of the newspaper. Get out!' yelled Ranjan as he shooed him away.

Ranjan was now determined to put Samant behind bars. The offer he had made was an affront to the police department. But Ranjan soon realized that Samant was no ordinary criminal, considering all the things he heard about him. He was the undisputed king of all that he surveyed.

Ranjan weighed his options. He had limited manpower—just four constables. One of the constables was always on leave. Ranjan asked one of the earlier SPs for more force to conduct raids against Samant and his gang.

'*Ranjan, aap issi force se kaam chalaiye* (Ranjan, you will have to manage with this force). I am sorry, I don't have any spare jawans,' said the SP categorically.

Shortage of manpower had become a common situation in most police stations in Bihar towards the end of 2005. The new government then came up with the rather effective idea of getting ex-Army jawans to work on a contractual basis for the Bihar Police. The ex-Armymen came to be known as the Special Auxiliary Policemen (SAP), and they greatly augmented the strength of the Bihar Police.

Luckily, during the earlier assembly election, Ranjan had got a company of the Central Reserve Police Force (CRPF) officers to maintain law and order in his area. This gave him a chance to go all out against Samant. In fact, Ranjan narrowly missed catching Samant after a fierce clash. Soon, his reputation as a scrupulous and fearless officer travelled across Shekhpura. It was then that Raju and Krishna decided to approach him.

'Bada Babu, both of us have the same aim. The end of Samant Pratap,' said Krishna.

'Why do you want to help the police?' asked Ranjan with a little suspicion.

'Sir, I think Raju will tell you,' Krishna said, looking at Raju. Raju's eyes welled with tears.

'Sir, it is true that till a few months back, we considered Samant the messiah of the downtrodden. We also supported him as our leader. In the parliamentary elections, Samant exhorted all of us to vote for Rajneesh Don, a man from our own clan,' said Raju.

Rajneesh Don was infamous for leaking the question papers of all prestigious exams such as the SBI Probationary Officer's Exam and CAT, the IIM entrance exam. A number of doctors, especially, approached him to get their children admitted to prestigious medical colleges. After all, the doctors had made huge investments in their nursing homes and hospitals. How would their 'talented' children run those hospitals without degrees from good colleges? Rumour had it that he had helped a few subordinate government officials too. In fact, the Central Bureau of Investigation (CBI) had constituted a special task force to nab him. I also played an important part in his arrest since Rajneesh Don belonged to Nalanda. Such was his clout that he fought the 2004 parliamentary elections from Begusarai and got more votes than P.P. Jha, the former DGP of Bihar.

Raju continued, 'But Samant was one greedy man. Another powerful candidate offered him a bounty to sway the votes of our men in his favour. Samant readily agreed. My brother protested strongly. How could we go against our people?'

'Samant did not tolerate any dissent; he did not like anyone speaking against him. Raju's brother's dead body was found in the fields the next day. His eardrums had been punctured and his tongue had been cut,' Krishna completed the story.

Raju started sobbing. 'Not only has he murdered many of his own men, he has raped countless girls and women. And nobody dares lodge an FIR. That would be like signing your own death warrant.'

'Samant loves killing people. One more case only adds to his aura,' continued Krishna.

Ranjan was convinced that Krishna and Raju were the ticket to the capture of Samant Pratap. He asked them to provide all the information they had on him. 'Do whatever you can to finish him. I am here to support you,' said Ranjan.

A few days later, Lakha, one of Samant's henchmen, tried to molest Ram Dular's sister. An agitated Ram Dular sought Krishna and Raju's help. It was time the members of Samant's gang were taught a lesson. Lakha was caught unawares and thrashed badly. This 'success' emboldened Raju and his men. They looked for an opportunity to carry out an attack on Samant's group.

One day, Ram Dular informed them that some of Samant's close aides were making merry in Mannipur village. At an opportune moment, a few of Krishna and Raju's supporters climbed the terrace where the drunk gangsters were dozing after a night of revelry, and killed all five men in their sleep. Samant lost most of his important men in one go.

Samant seethed with rage. He decided a lesson had to be taught to Ram Dular.

~

Ranjan was about to have lunch when he got the call. '*Bada Babu, hum Samant bol rahe hain. Bahut shauk hai laashe ginne ka* (Bada Babu, this is Samant. You like counting dead bodies, right?). Go, there are a lot of bodies lying in Mannipur village.'

Ranjan felt like throwing up. He immediately left for the village.

The village was absolutely quiet. Not one person said a word. Everyone was dead scared. Samant had extinguished the lives of so many people in one night.

The floor of the wedding pandal was smeared with blood. Ranjan and his constables were horrified by the sight. The first body was headless. A woman and a child were sitting quietly next to it. Their tears had probably dried up.

Ranjan and his team started picking up the scattered bodies one by one and put them in the thana's Commander jeep.

After a few moments, Ranjan came across the body of an eight-month-pregnant woman. The lifeless body of a young boy, probably the woman's son, was clinging to the woman. Even a battle-hardened cop like Ranjan found it extremely difficult to control his emotions.

Within half an hour, the village was swarming with policemen. The SP and DM also reached the spot. 'Sir, let us remove the bodies. There might be a law and order problem tomorrow morning,' Ranjan requested the SP. In such cases, the people were known to demand compensation and action against the local administration before the bodies could be taken away.

The SP was too shocked to speak. Samant Karan had been promoted to SP from DSP just two days ago. He had been quite happy to have been made the SP of a district just a few months before retirement. But now all his joy had vanished; he was absolutely crestfallen.

Sensing that the SP was in no position to speak, the DM, an amiable person, intervened.

'No, no. Don't take the bodies forcibly. I have the people's support in Shekhpura. I'll talk to the villagers and send the bodies to Munger tomorrow morning.'

Shekhpura was so backward that even dead bodies had to be sent to the neighbouring district of Munger for a postmortem.

The chief minister (CM) was absolutely livid. A no-nonsense person, he had been elected for his promise of sushaasan or good governance. The massacre was a challenge to his government.

The CM, the Home Secretary and the DGP flew by helicopter to the sites of both the massacres. Huge crowds had gathered at both spots. The police had a tough time managing the crowds. Most of the protestors were Samant's supporters. They did not want to miss this opportunity to malign the police. So they started yelling, '*Bada Babu murdabad, murdabad!* Suspend

Kasar SHO Ranjan! He is responsible for all the murders!' on the arrival of the CM. The CM, a seasoned administrator, remained quiet at that time.

'Get the post-mortem of the bodies done here in the village itself. Call a team of doctors from the Civil Hospital, Munger. After that, ensure that the bodies are cremated properly,' the CM ordered.

As the CM was about to board the helicopter, one intrepid press reporter asked him, 'Sir, what action will you take against the district administration?'

The CM stared at him hard and said, 'Watch the news at 7.30 p.m. today. You will know.'

The DIG, DM and SP were immediately removed from their posts.

~

Ranjan had not slept the entire night. He returned to the police station late in the evening after almost twenty-four hours. He took off his blood-soaked uniform and put it in a bucket. Then he emptied an entire packet of detergent into the bucket.

He called his wife in Ranchi. He always worried about her as she kept having bouts of depression. '*Lagta hai hum ko suspend karenge* (I think I'll be suspended),' said a dejected Ranjan.

'*Karenge nahin, kar diya hai* (You have been suspended). The news is on all the channels,' replied his wife.

'*Chalo achcha hai* (It is good). I have not spent any time with you in ages. Let us go to Delhi for a holiday,' said Ranjan, as he felt all the weariness of the last few months finally hit him.

12

'You Are Eunuchs!'

I returned to the 'circuit house' and straightaway went to brief Kumar Sir.

'How was your day? I hope you have started working on the case,' said Kumar Sir, who was lounging in his vest and shorts. The heat was unbearable, and the humid weather made him perspire from head to toe. But not once did he complain. His presence in Shekhpura was reassuring. I briefed him about my meeting with Ranjan but did not elaborate much.

'Amit, I'd suggest that you visit the village too. You'll learn more about the massacre. Your visit will probably assuage the anger of the people and instil some confidence in them.'

'Sure, sir, will do.'

I saluted and retired to my room, dreading the presence of lizards and rats in the bathroom. But this time, I had a bigger surprise in store for me—a fully grown black cobra was silently slithering down the ventilator!

~

Much to people's surprise, I'm not afraid of snakes. I admire them for their grace, agility and stealth. I coolly called the guard to get an expert to take it away. I instructed them that no harm should come to it. The guard shook his head vigorously. Surely, he must have thought that I was a nutcase—a person terrified of lizards who was quite unfazed by the presence of a cobra in his room!

Soon afterwards, the landline rang. 'Hello, how are you? I'm so happy that all of us will join you tomorrow. Avi misses you so much. Aishwarya has also not seen her papa for so long!' said Tanu cheerfully.

Our house was almost ready and I had decided to call my family to Shekhpura. Tanu was being a fantastic mother, taking care of both the kids all alone. And she had been taking care of Manju Devi, the septuagenarian maid, too! Thank God the maid was still alive.

~

I reached Mannipur village after an arduous journey. The village looked deserted, probably an after-effect of the brutal murders. After all, the village had seen a wedding function turn into a funeral service. Being a police officer, I had gone to many crime scenes and was accustomed to seeing dead bodies, with wailing relatives all around them. It can be very disturbing for other people, but we tend to get used to it. We do our business the way a surgeon operates upon a terminally ill patent.

But this was an entirely different experience. There was a deathly silence, betraying the trail of blood that Samant had left behind.

I went to Ram Dular's derelict house and surveyed the courtyard. In the corner, an old, fragile woman was lying on a charpoy.

I took a stool and tried to strike up a conversation with her.

'Maaji, what happened that night? I'm really sorry for your loss.'

She gripped my hand and started shaking vigorously, as if in a fit.

'No, you are not sorry. My entire family has been brutally massacred. My son, my grandson, everyone. My *khaandaan*, my dynasty, is finished. All because of the inefficiency of the police. Can you get my children back? Has the police done anything except take the statements of a few people? Your policemen promised security to Ram Dular for the information he gave. Naturally, he was on Samant's hit list, but you did not protect him and his family. You let him die. You are all eunuchs.'

I couldn't take the tirade any more. The woman was being harsh to the police, but she had every right to vent her ire. As I visualized the night of the carnage, I wondered what it would be like if *my* children had been trapped in such a situation. I shuddered and turned to leave. I saw a small, frail child standing in front of me. His innocent eyes were still filled with the horrors of that fateful night. He was Ram Dular's nephew, the only surviving member of the family apart from the matriarch. I patted the boy's head and left the courtyard.

I tried to talk to the rest of the villagers. As expected, they all feigned ignorance, but fear was writ large on their faces. Their silence strengthened my resolve. An absolutely innocent family had been butchered for no fault of theirs. Just because one man had wanted to satiate his bloodlust. The saga of Samant Pratap had to be brought to an end. So far, I had been treating Samant's arrest as another ego trip, but the visit to Mannipur jolted me. It was my duty to bring justice to the people who had suffered at Samant's hands.

13

The Cable TV Connection

June 2006

Deeply shaken, I drove back to my house. I just thought how incredibly lucky I was to have my family with me. My thoughts were interrupted when I got home and heard my son, Aditya, squeal with delight when he saw me. I was reminded how, since he had been a baby, he would always gurgle with happiness when I put on my uniform and tug on my lanyard and the Ashoka Stambh. I have always found it absolutely surreal to have the Ashoka Stambh on my shoulders. It automatically gives me a feeling of immense pride and responsibility. Seeing my family reminded me that I had a responsibility towards them as well. I hugged Tanu and took our now six-month-old daughter, Aishwarya, in my arms. Again, I felt afraid of losing them all.

I took a round of our small house and arranged the furniture in perfect alignment. I have a case of obsessive-compulsive disorder. I always want everything in order in my house and office. But this quest for order and perfection helps me a lot in my profession. It helps me focus on cases with manic concentration.

~

Kumar Sir was reading a two-day-old edition of the *Times of India*. I remembered my friend Ramnathan telling me that getting even basic things was difficult in Shekhpura. At the time, I had thought that he was exaggerating.

But today, these small things didn't matter to me at all. Kumar Sir could observe a strange calm on my face. He sensed that perhaps the arrival of my family had lifted my mood. But it was more because of the focus and clarity I had now. I was determined to catch Samant, come what may.

'Amit, I have asked for additional forces so that we can patrol the villages more effectively. The extra force will help us conduct more raids,' he said. 'Sir, my gut feeling says that Samant is not in Shekhpura right now. He knows that it's not one SP looking for him; it is the government that is determined to catch him. I don't think we'll be able to catch him with conventional policing. Either we get a tip from an insider about his location or use the latest technology. The first option seems highly unlikely. He has an absolutely loyal local supporter base and, moreover, only a person on a suicide mission would leak information about him. We all know what he does to anyone who crosses him.'

Though Kumar Sir was a staunch believer of old-fashioned policing, he was equally open to new ideas. He never imposed his diktats on his juniors and that was one of his many qualities. In this case, he listened to me intently.

After a long pause, he said, 'Okay, do as you wish. But I hope whatever you do remains in the ambit of the law.'

He knew my reputation as a maverick officer. But he also knew that rules could be broken when you had an adversary who was a law unto himself.

~

There was no sign of the hustle-bustle that was usually seen outside the offices of the SP and the DM. It was quite shocking to see no people in the office, considering I had been used to hundreds waiting to meet me at my other postings. I entered my chamber and checked my new table and chairs. The carpenter had done a fantastic job. The furniture was even better than the original. I was happy with the office now. And there was no towel wrapped around my chair.

I looked at the board showing the crime statistics. Ironically, Shekhpura had one of the lowest crime rates in Bihar. And the biggest criminal in the state.

I called Ranjan.

'Ranjan, come over to my house tonight. Get Krishna and Raju with you. I need to know everything about Samant,' I said.

'Yes, sir.'

'I also need the mobile numbers of Samant and his closest associates, particularly Horlicks.'

'Sure, sir. I'll ask Raju and Krishna to get the details,' replied Ranjan. He was quite surprised at the demand for the phone numbers of Samant and his gang.

Ranjan reached my house at 1 a.m. Raju and Krishna followed him with great trepidation. It was the first time they were meeting an SP. They were also very worried that I might send them to jail. After all, they had been Samant's supporters till a few months ago, even though they had no criminal records.

'*Baith jaiye* (Sit down),' I signalled to all three of them.

They kept looking at each other.

'*Nahin, sir, theek hai* (No, sir, it's all right),' replied Ranjan. Like any junior officer, Ranjan was used to standing in front of his seniors. This is the unwritten code of conduct for policemen. Moreover, he was under suspension. Naturally, Raju and Krishna did not dare to even touch the chair unless Ranjan sat down.

I could sense their unease.

'Sit down, it's going to be a long night,' I said in a serious tone.

With a little reluctance, Ranjan pulled up a chair and sat down. Raju and Krishna perched themselves quite awkwardly on the chairs. They were still finding it difficult to believe that they were sitting with the SP of Shekhpura, and that too, in the SP's residence. They had dared not sit even in front of an SI.

'Tell me everything about Samant and his gang. I want to strike at the top. Who are his most trusted people right now?'

'Sir, luckily, his gang has weakened in the last few days. Some of the members have been killed. Chhotu Samrat, a very close associate, was put behind bars recently by Ranjan Babu. Of the top leadership, only Samant and Horlicks Samrat remain,' said Krishna gleefully.

'Sir, but Samant's gang is very dangerous. They can still wreak havoc. The recent massacre at Mannipur is an example. Though Chhotu is in prison, he has escaped from jail twice earlier. He is capable of doing so again,' interjected Ranjan. 'His last jailbreak was quite audacious. As we know, a number of undertrials are taken to court before a magistrate. Samant's gang knew the exact date and time at which Chhotu was to be taken to the Nawada court premises. Chhotu and his accomplices made an excuse to go to the toilet that day. I remember, it was 28 February 2004. You will not believe it, sir, but Chhotu and his company simply tore down the walls of the toilet and escaped from the back of the premises,' he continued.

'Are you serious? What do you mean he tore down the wall?' I asked.

'The court remains closed on the weekend. There is no security, not even a single person to guard the premises. Samant's men climbed into the court compound one weekend and broke the wall of the court lockup toilet to make a small hole. After they were done, they just stuck sheets of yellow paper over the hole to make it look like it was a part of the wall.'

'Chhotu just tore off the paper and escaped?' I was incredulous.

'Ji, sir, this is exactly what happened.'

Raju and Krishna looked at me with a faint smile.

My surmise was right. It would be almost impossible to capture Samant using standard police procedures.

We discussed Samant and his gang, the people who were part of it, his modus operandi, his supporters, etc. in detail.

Finally, I asked, '*Numbers ki list laaye ho* (Have you got the numbers)?'

Krishna handed me three neatly folded papers.

'*Sahi hai?* Have you checked?'

'Yes, sir, 100 per cent,' said Raju with full confidence.

I clutched the paper, which had the numbers of Samant, Horlicks and a few other members of the gang. I smiled. Now it would not be very difficult to play cat and mouse with them, I thought. I could not have been more wrong.

~

The mobile phone is arguably the most revolutionary invention of this millennium. It is almost impossible to imagine a world without this palm-sized gadget. It has made life incredibly easy—for criminals as well as the police. Often, even the most intelligent and tough criminals are caught because of their devices. However smart the criminals may be, their mobile phones can provide many clues to the police. I decided to use my knowledge of tracking mobile phones.

I dialled various service providers like Reliance, Airtel and BSNL and requested them to provide the call details of Samant and his gang's numbers. Soon, the fax machine ran out of paper. My table top was covered with hundreds of printouts and faxes. I realized very quickly that it would be futile to rummage through so much data. I decided to concentrate on Samant's, Horlicks's and some other members' call logs. I had to cut the trunk and the root of the tree of Samant's empire. Then the branches and leaves would fall on their own.

After separating Samant's and Horlicks' call details, I called the service providers to ask for the tower location of their respective mobile phones. Samant and Horlicks were not in Shekhpura. Horlicks was in Kolkata and Samant's location indicated he was in Ranchi. The printout revealed that Samant had been using his mobile phone quite regularly, and the calls were largely outgoing. Obviously, not many people, including his gang members, called him for frivolous talk. Even criminals had a clear hierarchy. Horlicks's records showed more call traffic. Both the brigands had SIM cards issued in fake names. Earlier, it was quite easy for criminals to get SIM cards without any verification by vendors. Of course, now the government has implemented stringent rules.

I called Ranjan again.

'Ranjan, talk to Raju and Krishna right now. Find out if Samant and Horlicks have any friends or relatives in Kolkata and Ranchi. Do they frequent these cities? Do they have any hideouts there?'

There was an urgency in my voice.

'Sir, I have my doubts. Samant and Horlicks don't have any contacts in those cities, as per my knowledge. However, I'll talk to Raju, Krishna and some other sources.'

Ranjan called after some time.

'Sir, no one in those cities.'

'Okay, I'll call you later,' I said as I disconnected the phone.

It was as I had expected. Samant and Horlicks were not novices. They wouldn't have gone to any known person's place to hide. It would not have been difficult for the police to track them down. I kept thinking about the various possibilities.

~

A couple of days later, my wife called me, 'Chun (my pet name), the *cable-wallah* has come to set up the connection. And let me know if anyone is going to Patna. My stock of diapers for Aish will be exhausted soon,' said Tanu.

I beamed with joy. Tanu had given me an excellent excuse to go home immediately. The Football World Cup was just a few days away. I thanked the inventors of cable TV. Those days, it was very popular. Dish or satellite TV had just arrived and the set-top box was decidedly more expensive than cable. Even the number of channels were rather limited. I would be able to see all the football matches live in Shekhpura on cable TV. So what if I couldn't get bread?

I invited Kumar Sir to lunch. This was our first meal in our house. Kumar Sir was quite happy to meet Tanu and my kids. I told him about the soccer schedule, particularly Brazil's fixtures. He reminded me of our game with Samant. It was a 'must-win' situation for us.

14

'Krazy Kiya Re'

'You know, Amit is an IITian!' some of my senior colleagues would declare with great pride. The fact that there were quite a few IITians who were doing very well in the IAS, IPS and other civil services did not help my cause at all.

I would start looking in the opposite direction to spare myself further embarrassment. How could I tell them that I had had no interest in academics when I was at IIT? That I did not know the 'E' of engineering?

To make up for my lacklustre performance at IIT, I started taking a great interest in computers and mobile telephony as an SP. In my last stint as a district SP in 2005, I had gone to Delhi to learn more about this field from the special cell of the Delhi Police. The special cell had a team of brilliant individuals of all ranks. They were aware of the latest international developments and had cracked many tricky cases. They acquainted me with the latest tool—call observation.

It was time to use this wonderful facility.

Call observation facility, or 'parallel listening', in common police parlance, is a simple but extremely effective weapon in the hands of the police. It enables the police to monitor any person's phone. Every single call, incoming and outgoing, can be heard. It is as good as putting that individual's phone in the hands of the police. Largely, this facility has been used by intelligence agencies to track down criminals or to listen in on the conversations of terrorists, mafia syndicates and so on. But as it happens so often, this facility has been misused too, sometimes for personal gain and political vendetta. The infamous Nira Radia tapes controversy is just one example, which led to accusations of misconduct by many senior journalists, politicians and corporate houses. The government is very particular about this facility, as any mala fide use can be a direct infringement on the constitutional rights of an Indian citizen.

In the state of Bihar, no less than the Home Secretary is authorized to sanction the use of the call observation facility by the police. Only police officers of the rank of SP or above can send a requisition to the Home Secretary. If the Home Secretary deems it fit, the mobile service provider will be directed to provide the facility to the officer concerned.

I called my personal secretary (PA), a rotund, balding person who had probably spent his entire life behind a typewriter and who was now equally adept at using a computer. The personal assistant or secretary is a unique creature in the bureaucratic jungle. He or she works tirelessly and seemingly enjoys typing reams of papers every day. Many of those papers are irrelevant and read by no one.

But every once in a while, a single letter can cause a lot of concern to a subordinate officer.

The PA is the eyes and ears of the SP, and his or her opinion can definitely influence the SP to some extent. All the subordinates keep the 'PA Babu' in good humour. Even the SP is wary of the PA lest they leak office secrets. Moreover, an unscrupulous PA can mar the reputation of the boss very easily.

'Ram Babu, type a letter to the Home Secretary immediately. I need to fax it right now.' Ram Babu had typed thousands of memos and orders, but that one requisition to the Home Secretary bewildered even him.

'Huzoor, what kind of a request letter is this? What is "call observation facility"?'

'Nothing, Ram Babu, don't fret over these matters. Not of much consequence,' I smiled at his ignorance, with a slight hint of arrogance, but more of relief that he did not know about this facility. If the SP's PA didn't know of it, then there was no chance of anyone else knowing about it. The chances were as remote as Andre Agassi having hair on his head.

The PA typed Samant's, Horlicks's and some other important gang members' numbers in one column. The adjacent column had my own official numbers, the phones on which I wanted to listen in on any conversations those two and others had. Instead of using Samant's and Horlicks's real names, I deliberately wrote down some fictitious names and some other false case details. I did not want any leaks, naturally.

I dismissed Ram Babu and called the Home Secretary, Anil Amar, a career bureaucrat—an officer who had always had important postings throughout his tenure.

'Sir, good afternoon. This is Amit from Shekhpura.'

Before I could say my next sentence, Amar cut me short.

'Amit, I hope you are working seriously to finish Samant and his gang. We have great expectations from you. It was I who suggested your name for Shekhpura considering your past performance.'

'Thank you, sir,' I said, slightly mockingly. I knew I was the fall guy.

'Sir, I have just sent you a letter requesting the call observation facility. Please pass an order urgently.'

The Home Secretary was taken aback.

'Sir, the sooner you sanction the facility, the sooner we can arrest Samant,' I said politely but firmly.

The savvy officer that he was, Amar immediately sanctioned the facility.

~

I saved Samant's and Horlicks's numbers in my official mobile phone. I knew their names would keep ringing in my head till I arrested them.

After a few hours, I saw a number flashing on my mobile screen. It was Samant Pratap calling someone. I pressed the green button on the mobile to start the parallel listening. The game was on now. Advantage Amit Lodha.

'*Arre, bhai, kaisan ho? Ki haal chaal hai?* (Hey brother, how are you)? The dogs must be looking for me. But can dogs ever hunt a lion? Haha! Let them run around. The lion will come out only when it wishes to. After all, he is the king of the jungle. Samant Pratap is the king. Haha!' said a boastful Samant, absolutely intoxicated with his power and brute authority.

'Sahib, still, be careful. There's police all around,' said a meek voice. Samant disconnected.

I immediately sent an email to BSNL, the service Samant was using, and asked for the call records. When the details came in, I found that Samant had called one Sujit Kumar. He was a simple shopkeeper with no criminal record. Apparently, Samant had called him to get a general feel of the situation in Shekhpura. He liked to talk to commoners once in a while. It imposed his rule over them and added to his aura. The tower location showed that Samant had moved to Hazaribagh.

A lion never leaves his territory, only mice do. For all his bravado, Samant was clearly jittery, even if a little bit. That was good news.

Horlicks's mobile was switched off. I got a little worried. Did I have a number that was not Horlicks's? Or did he know about my surveillance plans? I hoped for the best and went home.

~

I was woken up by the phone ringing loudly. I groggily looked around for my mobile phone.

'Shh, shh, what are you doing? I had put Aish to sleep with such difficulty. You have woken her up again,' said Tanu, a little angry.

The sound of the phone was drowned out as the baby started wailing. I saw the screen blinking between the sheets and grabbed it. The screen flashed Horlicks's name. The mobile clock indicated it was 4.10 a.m. I felt a thrill of excitement, yet cursed Horlicks. These damned villagers started their day quite early, unlike us city folk.

'*Kaisi ho jaaneman, meri bulbul* (How are you my love, my sweetheart)? I have been missing you so much,' crooned Horlicks. I didn't know a dreaded sharpshooter could be such a hopeless romantic.

'I also miss you so much, darling. I am waiting for you to come soon,' said a female voice, sounding very seductive.

'*Jaanu*, I'll come. I'm just taking it easy. These policemen must be sniffing after me like a pack of hounds. *Aur suno* (And listen). You look exactly like Aishwarya Rai from the song "Kraji Kiya Re"!'

'*Dhatt*, I am even more beautiful than Aishwarya Rai!'

Their romantic gibberish went on for a good twenty minutes. I could not sleep a wink after listening to that. Surprisingly, our own Aish had blissfully gone back to sleep and Avi had also slept through the night. I waited for the morning. I could barely contain myself till the Airtel office opened.

~

I got the call details of Horlicks's number by 10.40 a.m. From the conversations I had discovered that the woman's name was Sulekha Devi and she was in Mahawat village, Shekhpura.

I called Ranjan to my home immediately. I pushed the printout of the call details towards him. 'Do you recognize any of these numbers? Can you analyse the call records?' I asked him.

Ranjan looked at me sheepishly and said, 'Sir, I am sorry, but I can't understand anything. I am seeing a call record for the first time.'

I could understand. In those days, subordinate policemen, particularly those working in rural areas, did not have much knowledge of mobile phone tracking. Even a simple thing like a call record was given by the service provider only to the SP or an officer authorized by the SP.

'Okay, forget it. Tell me, who is Sulekha Devi? She lives in Mahawat village, apparently. It is Horlicks's village too.'

'Oh, Sulekha Devi! She is Horlicks's bhabhi.'

'Are you serious? Is he having an affair with his own bhabhi?'

'Sir, I am not surprised at all. These things are quite common in rural areas. I have also heard that everything is not okay in Horlicks's marriage.'

'Any chance of him coming back to Mahawat?'

I was just hopeful that Horlicks would visit her. After all, many men have fallen because of their dangerous liaisons. History is replete with such examples.

'Not a chance, sir. He knows that the police are looking for him.'

'What about his wife, Shanti Devi? Where is she?'

'Sir, she and her kids have also been missing after the massacre. We have no idea of their whereabouts, though Raju tried his best.'

It was natural for Shanti Devi to go underground. The Shekhpura police had been raiding their house and other relatives' places regularly.

~

Just a few hours later, Horlicks's number flashed on my screen again.

'*Baal butroon kaisan hai* (How are the kids)? How are Chintoo and Rani doing? I am sure Chintoo must be studying hard. Have you started making him read the newspapers? Get him some Angrezi newspaper; he has to clear the civil services exams. He should become an IPS officer,' said Horlicks.

'*Haan, padha rahein hain* (Yes, I am making them study). Chintoo is studying hard. He is reading the newspaper regularly. You could ask about my well-being too,' replied Shanti Devi in an irritated tone.

I just could not believe it. A hardcore criminal, a murderer, wanted his son to become a police officer!

The call was short and terse. I guess Horlicks was more interested in talking to his girlfriend than to his wife.

I could have interrogated Sulekha and practically everyone who was in touch with Samant and Horlicks, but decided against it. I did not want to alert Samant and Horlicks at all. I just needed to bide my time, and I would definitely find out their exact hiding place.

~

I put on the television to kill some time while Tanu nursed Aish. On one of the music channels, I saw Aishwarya Rai sashaying to the foot-tapping number 'Krazy Kiya Re'. It was the same song Horlicks had mentioned to his bhabhi.

Seeing the song on screen suddenly prompted me to say, 'Tanu, don't you think you have put on weight, particularly around your waist?'

Tanu remained quiet for a moment.

'Why don't you try giving birth to a baby? Let us see how well-maintained you remain after delivery, that too a C-section,' she retorted.

I knew I was being a jerk. I switched off the TV and lay spreadeagled on the bed. Deep down in my heart, I loved my wife madly. And she knew it.

~

After a few hours, Samant's name appeared on my phone screen. I activated the call observation.

'Samant, I hope you are safe and sound. Now listen carefully. The new SP is very intelligent. He is some engineer from some IIT-YIT. I'm warning you. Switch off your mobile phone,' said a stern, dignified voice.

'Netaji, thank you for your concern. I have seen so many SPs come and go. The present SP is a kid, *bachcha hai*. I can handle him easily,' retorted a confident Samant Pratap.

'I am warning you. Switch off your phone. I don't know what exactly the SP is doing, but I have received information that mobile phones can be tracked. He does not believe in conventional policing. It makes me suspect strongly that he must be using some new technique to catch you.'

The voice went silent.

~

Samant wondered how the police could track him using his mobile phone. He was constantly on the move. Nobody knew about his whereabouts, not even his most trusted lieutenants, not even Horlicks. He would never be caught. After all, he was the king; so what if he was in exile right now? But somehow, his heart was beating faster. He was sweating too. He shrugged and cursed the scorching heat.

15

'Dekhte Hain'

'Sir, ADG Sir wants to talk to you,' said my PA. It was the ADG A.K. Prasad. He was known as HMV—His Master's Voice—as he was an absolute 'yes' man.

'Lodha, how's it going? The boss is monitoring your performance on a daily basis. I have told him that you are working hard. You know you are not in his good books, but I am trying to get your career back on track,' Prasad said.

I knew very well that it was Prasad who was instrumental in my not being in the 'good books'. Prasad had once called me to get one of his nephews posted as the SHO of an important police station in Nalanda. Like any young, inexperienced IPS officer, I had blurted out at the time, 'Sir, with all due respect, Rakesh Kumar is highly inefficient. I can't post him as an SHO.'

There had been a deathly silence on the other end of the line. After a few seconds, probably after he had swallowed his ego, Prasad had banged the phone down. He would remember this ignominy for a long time.

I did not think twice about the incident at the time, but after some years of experience, I realized that I was right in my thinking but wrong in my approach.

Now, I would listen to a senior officer or a politician and just say, '*Sir, dekhte hain* (Sir, I'll see).' That is the best way to ward off any unjustified demand.

'There's no need to be Sunny Deol,' is what IG HQ, Lima Inchen, a genial Naga, had told me during my early days as an SP. 'Just listen to people, be it politicians or seniors. Be polite; no need to be unnecessarily aggressive. These altercations look good only in movies. Finally, be practical. There are certain requests that are genuine, so accede to them. And wherever your conscience pricks you, simply put your foot down. Soon, you will build a reputation. Things will be smooth for you after that.'

I could not have got better advice, that too, during my early years in the service. Later on, many MLAs, with whom I had had spats earlier because of my brazen attitude, confided that at times, they knew they had made unjust demands. But they had no option. People would camp in their offices asking them to call me, the SHO or other officers for favours. As elected representatives, they were always answerable to the public. It did not matter if there was no electricity or the roads were in a pitiable condition in their constituency. What mattered to the public was how powerful the local MPs, and particularly the MLAs, were in influencing the SP or the DM to favour them for their own personal benefit.

'*SP Sahib, hum kya karein* (SP Sir, what do we do)? A politician's job is very difficult. Everyone has great expectations from us, even if they have not voted for us in the election. People camp in our office. Outside our residence. Even when we know that we're making an unreasonable demand, we have to call you,' a local MLA had once explained to me earnestly. 'Sometimes, due to immense pressure, we even have to see you personally. Earlier, you used to bluntly say to our face that you won't listen to us. This caused us a lot of embarrassment.'

'Yeah, I understand,' I said with a wry smile.

'But nowadays, your attitude is much better. You patiently listen to our demands and nod. And the best one-liner is—*dekhte hain*. That solves our problems. It's a win-win situation for both of us. We fulfil our obligations and you take a decision you deem right, but later.'

I had learnt these lessons in diplomacy quite early. I developed a reputation for being a polite, yet no-nonsense officer. Many times, in fact, an MLA or a politician's request turned out to be genuine. It was just that a regular person was too scared to meet the SP directly. So he would approach the MLA to meet us and put up his point. Sometimes, we vilify our politicians too much. It is a few of our own seniors who are more difficult to handle.

Now I wish I had chosen my words carefully in dealing with ADG Prasad during my initial days. He harboured a grudge against me. I really don't know if it would have made any difference. I remembered my first meeting with him.

'*Kaun jaat* (Which caste)?' Prasad asked.

'Sir, I don't understand,' I stammered, totally confused.

'What is your caste?' he asked in English this time.

I was at a total loss for words. Later, I found out that he had been looking for a groom for his daughter!

16

The Traitor

The call to Samant from 'Netaji' had me really worried. I found the number from Samant's call details and promptly put it on observation too. The SIM card was, of course, issued under a fake name and address.

Netaji's number was not a very busy one. Surely he was someone important and elusive. Who could it be? How did he know that I might be tracking Samant's mobile phone?

I asked Ranjan about Netaji and got my answer: 'Sir, Netaji is Samant's own uncle. He is the ex-MLA of Nawada and was instrumental in Samant's escape from Nawada Jail.' Obviously, it would have been futile to question Netaji. Moreover, Netaji's suspicion of my plans would have been confirmed.

I wondered how well-connected Samant was. I thought of booking Netaji under some law, but decided against it. It would be very difficult to prove any criminal offence against him. Just talking to a criminal was not an offence in itself.

After a while, Samant's phone showed some activity again. I listened to the incoming call.

'*Pranaam bhai. Kaisan hain? Samant Bhaiyya, suniye na! Do–chaar ko aur maarenge toh achcha hoga* (How are you? Samant Bhaiyya, listen! It will be good to kill some more people). This

SP too will be transferred or even suspended,' said a voice from the other side.

I was shocked beyond words. I knew this voice very well. How could I not recognize it—this voice briefed me every morning about the situation in the district!

It was Rajesh Charan, the town SHO. The man who was supposed to be a trusted officer had turned out to be a back-stabber! I was seething with rage; I had never been betrayed so badly. Right from day one, I had had a bad feeling about Rajesh, but never in my wildest dreams did I foresee that he would be Samant's mole in the police department. And he was plotting my own firing from Shekhpura!

I called Kumar Sir and told him about Rajesh's treachery. Calm as always, he took it in his stride. 'Not entirely unexpected. Rajesh belongs to Samant's clan. And anyway, it's each to his own today. Rajesh knows that Samant was once powerful politically too, and that his time may come again. And of course, Samant must be greasing Rajesh's palms with a handsome amount.'

I reached home and dashed to the bedroom. Tanu just put her finger on her lips and signalled for me to remain quiet. The kids were taking a nap.

I stayed outside and kept thinking about Rajesh Charan's treachery. I was furious and wanted to bang his head against a wall. Tanu came out and seeing that I was agitated, gave me a glass of Rooh Afza to soothe my nerves. She talked to me till I had cooled down. My wife has always been a great source of support to me, the anchor who has given me the kind of stability I needed to go from strength to strength in my career.

As my anger simmered, I realized it was good that I had come to know about Rajesh's character so early on. I didn't want to imagine the damage I would have suffered if I had shared any crucial information or strategy with him.

I vowed to teach that scoundrel a lesson. It's because of a small percentage of black sheep like him that the police department gets a bad name.

But there was no need to take any action against Rajesh right now. Let him not suspect anything. Maybe his conversations with Samant would give me a clue at some point. I could not afford to let my plans go haywire. But I made a promise to myself that I would ensure that Rajesh was stripped of the police uniform the day I arrested Samant. And I would give Ranjan the chance to wear his uniform on the same day. Thank God the number of Ranjans outnumbered the number of Rajeshs!

For all the criticism heaped on the police—mostly unjustified, some justified—it is one department that works 24/7, 365 days a year. The Indian police is efficient and effective, considering the very meagre resources it has. The police-to-public ratio in our country is among the lowest in the world. One has to visit an average police station, particularly in the rural areas, to see the pitiable infrastructure. The station in-charge is supposed to patrol his area, raid the hideouts of criminals, escort VIPs and carry out a plethora of duties with the meagre resources available. Only Superman could perform better!

Yet, in times of crisis, the police raise the bar and surmount any problem. Hats off to the Delhi Police for solving the Nirbhaya rape case. The most barbaric of all crimes saw country-wide demonstrations, protests and candlelight vigils. I wish the citizens had been equally forthcoming in taking Nirbhaya to the hospital. After Nirbhaya lay naked on a road for hours on a freezing cold December right, it was a PCR van of the Delhi Police that took her to the hospital. And then, in spite of no support and tremendous pressure, the police cracked a virtually blind case. Every single rapist was arrested within days of the tragic incident. All of them were tried and convicted by the highest court of the country. The case was solved only by the fierce resolve, intelligence and sheer hard work of a bunch of dedicated policemen who remain unsung. They are the heroes who always bring a glimmer of hope even in the darkest times. I am lucky to be a part of a service that has some outstanding leaders and thousands of unknown officers and constables who put duty above everything else.

17

Nature's Call

'Amit, I will be reaching Shekhpura tomorrow to take stock of the situation,' boomed IG R.P. Keshav's voice on the phone.

'Sure, sir, we will prepare for your visit.'

The visit of the IG from the Patna HQ was going to be an important event.

Kumar Bharat had gone to Patna to meet his family and get some new clothes. He had been living out of a suitcase, braving the heat and the rats. I decided to instal a cooler in his room in the meantime.

Back at my house, I shifted the fax machine and desktop computer to my drawing room. I decided to send all the requisitions to the Home Secretary and to the mobile service providers myself. I started writing the letters by hand as I was quite poor at typing. My staff was surprised, but I did not want to take any chances. I could not trust anyone after Rajesh's betrayal. Least of all my PA.

~

'Samant, you stubborn idiot! I had told you to switch off your phone. This SP is on to something. Don't tell me later that I didn't warn you,' said a mysterious voice and disconnected the phone. Samant Pratap stared at his phone. Netaji might be right, he thought. He switched off his phone.

While this conversation was going on, I was talking to Kumar Sir and missed Samant's call. I saw the screen flashing Samant's name seconds before I could connect to his call. I cursed myself and hoped that nothing important would have been discussed. Unfortunately, as I would realize later, that one missed call proved costly for me. It would take me a lot of hard work and lady luck to locate Samant again. I shrugged and started preparing for the IG's visit.

~

It was an unusually dark night. The fact that there were no street lights made driving on the pothole-filled road quite a difficult task. It was pouring heavily. The conditions would have made even legendary Formula One racers jittery. But it was an everyday ride for a Bihar Police driver. The bodyguard was feeling helplessly sleepy, his head bobbing up and down every now and then. The rain had made it quite cold outside. The driver and the bodyguard had covered their ears with a *muretha*, a scarf popular in the area. Vikram, the driver, had also switched on the heater. The heater made a buzzing sound, but it did not bother the passengers in the car. The IG, R.P. Keshav, was sitting in the back seat of the old, white Ambassador, his personal favourite. A beacon-fitted Ambassador was the ultimate symbol of power. Only the top echelons of our country were entitled to it at the time.

R.P. Keshav commanded the driver in his baritone, '*Driver, gaadi roko* (Driver, stop the car).' He got down to relieve himself. The unusual cold was playing havoc with his bladder. It was an unwritten code that the driver and the bodyguard would remain at a distance in such a situation. This time, both of them chose to remain seated in the car. Who would get out of the car in such cold weather?

The IG walked a little distance away from the car to move out of the sight of his staff. Heck, one needed privacy to answer the call of nature. It started thundering then, with the raindrops falling faster. Keshav finished his business quickly and started pulling up the zip of his pants. From the corner of his eye, he saw the Ambassador driving away. What the hell was Vikram Singh doing?

The Ambassador picked up speed along the road, the IG's flag fluttering in the wind. The IG's mobile phone was lying on the back seat, in silent mode. Bhajan Ram, the bodyguard, had fallen asleep, and Vikram was concentrating on the road ahead. It was a very treacherous and bumpy journey. He had to ensure that Sahib had a comfortable ride.

A few minutes earlier, both of them had heard a sound, and they assumed it was the IG closing the door. None of them looked back, another unwritten code when Sahib is in the car. And they drove, totally oblivious of the fact that their boss was desperately trying to stop the car, totally drenched in the rain.

Keshav was at a loss for words. He just could not fathom why the car had left without him. He patted his pockets, desperately hoping to find his mobile phone. Keshav cursed using the choicest of Bihari swear words on realizing that he had left it in the car.

He started walking. It was pitch-dark, and the road was wet and slippery. The car kept moving towards Shekhpura, the red beacon flashing on top.

Keshav kept walking, his safari suit totally drenched, his ego bruised. He hadn't felt so helpless in his entire life. A senior police officer, an IG, bereft of all his accoutrements—it was unthinkable. But worse was in store for him.

'Kharaunja Police Station' read the familiar red and blue board, typical of all police stations in India. Keshav's eyes brightened. He was in familiar territory again. He quickened his pace and marched towards the police station, much like the way he had done during his training days two decades ago.

A sentry was sitting in one corner, listening to some Bhojpuri songs on his mobile phone. An ASI was going through some FIRs in the light of the lantern. Two battered-looking people were crouching in the lock-up. There were sundry other things lying on top of each other, ranging from utensils, clothes and cycles to televisions, all seized during various raids.

'Hey, who's on duty?' roared Keshav. The ASI and the constable jumped out of their chairs.

'*Kya baat hai, bhai?* Why are you shouting? Don't you know this is a police station?' shouted the constable over the blaring Bhojpuri song.

'I am the IG of the Police HQ,' snapped Keshav, expecting the constable and the officer to stand at attention on his command.

Instead, both of them looked at each other, totally confused. Suddenly, one more constable came in.

'*Kaun hai, bhaiyya* (Who are you)?' asked the constable.

'You idiot, how many times will I tell you? I'm the IG!' shouted Keshav, unable to control his fury.

'*Hum ko boodbak samjhe ho* (Do you consider us fools)? Which IG would be standing drenched in a police station at midnight? Where is your car? Your staff? Do you have any I-card?'

'Let's put him in the hawalat. Nowadays, there are so many rogues masquerading as IPS or IAS officers,' said the ASI.

Keshav's confidence vanished, quickly giving way to fear. The two inmates of the lock-up looked at him expectantly, hoping to have some good company inside. After all, how many times do you see a well-dressed, sophisticated man in a lock-up? So what if he was drenched from head to toe?

At that moment, the SHO entered the police station. He had just finished his night round. Worriedly, he blurted out, 'Jai Hind, sir. I didn't know you were coming by.' He was least expecting an IG in his police station. The IG is too senior an officer for lesser mortals like the SHO.

Keshav finally heaved a huge sigh of relief. 'Thank God, at least the SHO recognized me,' he muttered to himself. The SHO wiped his brow, worried if everything was all right. He had worked hard to control crime in his area. Little did he know that everything that could go wrong had gone wrong just minutes before, in his own police station.

'Get me a vehicle and send me to the Shekhpura circuit house. And remember, not a word of what happened today goes out!' hissed Keshav.

'Ji, huzoor,' a perplexed SHO replied. He would come to know of the catastrophe later.

~

The next morning, Keshav came out to inspect the guard of honour. Already in a foul mood, he admonished the poor guard for the most trivial of faults.

'Your shoelaces are not right! Your bayonet is not aligned properly,' yelled Keshav.

Everyone could sense that the IG was in a nasty mood. In the corner, I saw the bodyguard and the driver of the IG trembling with fear, just like lambs waiting to be slaughtered. I was quite surprised. In the government services, particularly the police, staff like the driver and the bodyguard often behave in a very haughty and arrogant manner. An SP's driver will behave like a super SP on the road. During those days, he would honk non-stop to clear the road and if, God forbid, any mortal tried to overtake him, then that person had had it. Similarly, the bodyguard was known to get rough with people. He would just pick you up and hoist you away. So if someone wanted to take a picture with the 'Sahib' he would do it at a grave risk. Of course, things have changed a lot now. Today's young superintendents and deputy inspector generals of police don't mind a selfie once in a while.

Keshav's bodyguard and driver looked like they were waiting for the guillotine. I still wonder what action the IG must have taken against them.

But Keshav was a thorough professional. He quickly forgot about the incident and analysed the situation in Shekhpura. He left after he had heard our plan and patted us on the back. He was quite sure that Samant's time was limited.

18

Bhujia

Avi was playing with his toys on the floor, with Tanu trying to feed him. I was quite surprised that a four-year-old child could eat a thing like lauki easily. 'See, even he doesn't make faces. You know, all green leafy vegetables are good for health. Sometimes I wonder if you are the kid in our home. You throw so many tantrums. And look at your unhealthy eating habits,' Tanu chided me, pointing at the bhujia packet in my hand. I ignored her and had another spoonful. I loved the taste and put a small bit into my daughter's mouth. She also gurgled with happiness, savouring the tangy taste.

'Stop it! What are you doing?' Tanu shouted and snatched the packet from me. Before I could seize it back, my phone screen showed 'Horlicks Samrat calling'.

I pressed the green button to accept the call and start listening in. It seemed that Horlicks's call had dropped. In the ensuing melee for the bhujia packet, I pressed the green button again inadvertently.

Horlicks picked up the phone and said in a typical Bihar tone, *'Hallo, hallo, kaun?'*

I froze and immediately disconnected the phone.

'Oh shit, what have I done?' I cursed myself.

By pressing the green button twice, I had redialled Horlicks's number. Obviously, to start the parallel listening, I had to press

the green button, which was akin to accepting a call. By the time
I pressed the green button, Horlicks's call had got disconnected.
When I pressed the green button again, this time it dialled
Horlicks's number!

Horlicks was equally bewildered. He called Netaji.

'Arre, saala, the SP called me just now. Why would he call
me?' asked Horlicks.

'I told you, switch off your mobile phone,' said Netaji, and
then the line went dead.

Obviously, Horlicks had stored the official number of the
Shekhpura SP in his phone. Almost all professional criminals
have the numbers of important officers and officials, particularly
the SP, DM and the local SHO. This is not surprising in the
state of Bihar.

I had no time to waste. I wanted Horlicks to feel that I
actually wanted to talk to him. That would remove any suspicion
from his mind.

I called Horlicks again and spoke in a deep baritone, trying
to act as officious as possible.

'Horlicks, hum SP bol rahe hain.'

There was a hushed silence at the other end.

'Pranaam, sir,' said Horlicks, barely believing that he was
talking to the SP of Shekhpura.

'Horlicks, you know the government is absolutely
determined to finish Samant and his gang. Your gang's end is
inevitable. I would suggest that you surrender. I'll make you
a government approver. You can lead a normal life. And you
never know, Samant might be killed in a shoot-out with the
police too.'

Silence again.

I remembered that Horlicks was very keen on his son
becoming a police officer.

'Horlicks, if you help us and tell me the whereabouts of Samant, I'll help you and your family to any extent. Think of it. The government will help in your children's education, their careers. Who knows, your son could become an inspector of police. Why only that, your son could be an IPS officer. Imagine him as the SP of a district.'

I did my best to appeal to his emotions, hoping that he might break down. I also hoped that I had not gone overboard.

After another pause, Horlicks spoke up.

'Sir, I wish I had met you earlier. But now it is too late. Samant is like my brother. I wouldn't have told you his location even if I knew. I haven't spoken to him for quite some time.' He paused and then continued, 'I guess this is my destiny. Shooting people and maybe one day getting shot by the police. Pranaam, sir.'

I waited with bated breath for his next move. I hoped that Horlicks had taken the bait.

After some time, I saw he was making another call.

'Netaji, the SP called me just now,' an excited Horlicks blurted out, barely able to conceal his excitement. '*Arre, kya raub tha aawaaz mein* (Arre, the SP had so much authority and gravitas in his voice). I hope my son, Chintoo, also becomes an SP some day.'

I smiled, reflecting on how even criminals are in awe of policemen. Such is the power of the uniform! I also felt a little sad and sincerely wished Horlicks's son could indeed become a police officer one day. After all, if the opposite had happened, with Dawood Ibrahim becoming a terrorist despite having an extremely honest, ethical policeman for a father, why not this?

'Shut up, you moron! Don't get carried away by the SP's sweet talk. I have repeatedly told you to switch off the phone,' shouted Netaji.

Horlicks just looked at the phone screen, lost in thought.

'My son, Chintoo, could be a policeman.'

He wiped the tears from his eyes and tucked his pistol in the back of his trouser band.

'This SP seems to be quite a nice person,' mused Horlicks.

19

'Bol Bam'

2 July 2006

Samant's mobile phone was now switched off. I ran his IMEI number every day, but it was clear that he had not put any other SIM card in his phone. Even Raju and Krishna were clueless. I was getting desperate. Where could Samant and Horlicks be? Unlike the stock market, where I had bought penny stocks, in the world of crime, I was aiming for the bullseye by going after two blue chips—Samant and Horlicks. I had to force them out of their hideouts.

~

Meanwhile, Horlicks's romantic conversations had become too excruciating for me to bear. To add to my woes, Reliance Communications had come out with a scheme of free unlimited calls between Reliance numbers. Horlicks and his girlfriend both had Reliance connections and were using this scheme to the utmost. Now their talks, which were full of sexual innuendos, had become seemingly endless. To make matters more difficult for me, Horlicks kept changing his location. He moved frequently between Kolkata, Ranchi and a number of other towns.

'*Jaaneman, tum bilkul Katrina Kaif jaisi ho* (Dear, you look just like Katrina Kaif),' cooed Horlicks.

'Who is Katrina Kaif? I have never heard of her,' said his girlfriend.

'*Oh, nayi heroinwa hai* (Oh, she is a new heroine). You are as attractive as her!'

'*Hai*, you are so naughty. Each time a new heroine. *Achcha*, tell me, when will you come?'

'Not now, *jaan*. The police are looking for me. Let the dust settle, then we will have our honeymoon.'

The last few conversations between Horlicks and his bhabhi clearly suggested that Horlicks was in no mood to meet her. I would have to find him, but that was possible only if he stayed in one place.

I remembered my conversations with Tanu on the telephone at the beginning of our relationship. We would also coo sweet nothings and, after every two sentences, say, '*Aur kya chal raha hai* (What else is going on)?' to prolong our conversation. It's a different matter now that we talk more about calling a plumber to fix a leaking pipe.

We also used to discuss the menu for lunch or dinner over the phone, which even today is ultimately decided by Tanu.

'*Suno*, what will you have for dinner?'

'Sweetheart, how about some noodles?'

'No, it is not good for health. It is made of maida.'

'Then put some vegetables in it. It will improve the taste.'

'*Nahin*. I have decided. We will have some karela. Bitter gourd is good for the skin!'

I don't know why she bothers to call.

Even though listening to so many phone calls a day was tiring, I eagerly looked forward to listening to Horlicks and Samant's important conversations. But there were some other personal calls that were extremely irritating. My mother had decided that my younger brother had become old enough to get married. She called one day and said, '*Beta, Nikky ko ab settle ho jaana chahiye* (Son, Nikky should get married now). I have included your number in all the matrimonial advertisements and websites like Shaadi.com.' As a result, prospective in-laws would call constantly to discuss the matter. My ears were already ringing from listening to the gangsters' calls, and now my mother had compounded my woes. I got several calls from all over the country, which bothered me tremendously. Through the process, I also came to know that Shaadi.com was set up by some of my seniors from IIT Delhi. I cursed them too.

The people looking for a match for their daughter would often have a host of meddlesome questions. 'SP Sahib, we would be happy to have an alliance with your family. By the way, where exactly are you posted? What, Shekhpura? Where is it?' asked one girl's father.

'Sir, I am a government officer. I am supposed to work in all parts of India.'

Before I could anything else, he said, 'But we won't like our daughter to stay in small places,' and put the phone down. He did not even give me a chance to say that my brother had an MBA and would work in big cities. And, of course, he didn't live with me. I also wondered why Tanu had never bothered about my postings to remote areas.

~

My only hope now was Shanti Devi, Horlicks's wife. I had put her number on observation too.

'I am sure Chintoo must be studying hard. Have you started making him read Angrezi newspapers, the *Tames of India* particularly? He should become an IPS officer. I will see his progress when I come over in a few days.'

'*Haan, padhta hai* (Yes, he reads the papers). *Woh Tames of India wallah bhi,*' replied an irritated Shanti.

'*Suno*, Bitiya should also concentrate on her studies.'

'*Arre, abhi toh teen saal ki hai* (Hey, she is just three years old). Should I send her to college?' taunted Shanti.

Every second day, Horlicks stressed on the education of his son in his calls. He really wanted his son to become a cop. Though his daughter was very young, he was bothered about her studies as well. I was quite intrigued. I had to find out how Horlicks became a criminal. How could such a family man become a dreaded outlaw? And why was he having an extramarital affair?

~

I found out that Shanti's location had remained the same for quite a few days now. I felt that it was only a matter of time before Horlicks visited his family. She was in Deoghar, a town in Jharkhand famous for the Baidyanath temple. Ironically, a sinner like Horlicks Samrat had chosen a holy town to hide his family.

Horlicks had no relatives in Deoghar, according to Raju and Krishna. His conversations made it clear that his children were attending school in Deoghar. His family could not have stayed in a hotel for so long. He definitely must have rented a house, which meant Shanti was living somewhere in the heart of a densely populated town. Looking for her and the children would be like finding a needle in a haystack.

I immediately called Ranjan.

'Come to my house right now. Get Raju and Krishna with you.'

~

'All of you have to go to Deoghar. Shanti Devi is definitely living in a rented house there.'

'Sir, Deoghar is a holy town. It is very densely populated, teeming with pilgrims. How will we find Shanti?' asked Ranjan. Raju and Krishna nodded in agreement.

'The Airtel people have told me that Shanti's mobile phone location has been in the Nandan Pahad area for the past fifteen days. Scout the area in the radius of that cell tower. It will be difficult, but not impossible.'

Nandan Pahad, where the cell tower was, lay between Deoghar Sadar and the Jasidih railway station.

Ranjan and company did not look sanguine at my suggestion.

'I know it will take a lot of hard work, but I am hopeful of a positive result. Tell me, do you recognize Shanti Devi?' I said, trying to make them feel more hopeful.

'Sir, I know Shanti quite well. She fought the MLA elections in my thana area some time ago. Of course, Raju and Krishna also know her.'

'Does she also know all of you?'

'No, sir. Luckily, she doesn't recognize any of us,' said Ranjan.

'We will take a few of our boys to help us find her,' said Raju.

'No, you are not going to involve anyone else. This operation has to be kept a secret,' I said firmly.

'Right, sir. I will also need a weapon for my personal safety. Horlicks is quite dangerous. Could I keep my service pistol?' requested Ranjan.

'No, Ranjan, I can't allow that.'

A suspended policeman is not supposed to carry any official weapon—it is against the rules. 'On paper, you can't arrest Horlicks as you are under suspension. So you need someone to legalize your operation. I will depute a policeman to go with you. He will make your mission more official, should you require any such help. Any particular person you trust?' I asked Ranjan.

'Sir, Havaldar Shiv Narayan. He is very loyal to me. He worked under my command in the Kasar police station.'

'Okay, take him along. Just ask him to submit an application for leave to me before he goes with you. Nobody should know that he is working with you.'

I knew I was taking some big risks, but nothing mattered to me then. I was willing to go to any lengths to nab Samant and Horlicks.

Havaldar Shiv Narayan Ram was quite a God-fearing man. It was probably an effect of his name. But I knew he was a brave and loyal soldier of the police department. He was very excited to hear from Ranjan. He submitted his leave application and left for the Kiul railway station. After a few hours, he met Ranjan, Raju and Krishna, who had been waiting for him there. In his bag was a carbine, a light automatic rifle, which he had folded. He was also carrying a hundred rounds of 9 mm ammunition.

It was the month of Shrawan. Thousands of *kanwariya*s or devotees walked for almost a hundred kilometres carrying the holy Ganges water in their *kanwar*s. The entire route to Deoghar reverberated with the chants of '*Bol Bam*'.

Ranjan and everyone else in the Bolero looked at each other and said in unison, 'Bol Bam!'

20

'Bagal Mein Hai, Huzoor'

'Chun, the constant buzzing of your phones disturbs the children. I have great difficulty getting them to sleep,' said Tanu earnestly. I decided to shift out of the bedroom.' I detested the thought of sleeping on the carpet in the drawing room, alone. A lizard could always crawl over me. Yet, I decided to overcome my fear. I could not afford to miss any call. I shifted to the drawing room and slept on the carpet. It was good for my back too. I kept the mobile phones beside my pillow. I ensured the batteries were fully charged before I slept.

I had learnt my lesson after redialling Horlicks's number that day. I stopped using my official mobile phone and started taking Horlicks and Samant's calls on other phones bought specially for observation. I also made sure I installed the call recording facility in all the mobile phones. Mobile phones then weren't as advanced as they are now. My clunky Nokia and Samsung handsets were the most popular phones at the time.

Soon, I was unable to handle Horlicks's call traffic. I started calling Ajit every night and giving the phones to him.

'Please listen to all the conversations. I can't understand many Bhojpuri words; they are Greek to me. Tell me if there is anything relevant for me.'

Meanwhile, Ranjan and his team checked every nook and corner of the Nandan Pahad area. They did not meet with any success and returned to Shekhpura.

A few more days passed. I asked Ajit every day if he had heard anything relevant that could help locate Horlicks. Ajit would say nothing and just look down. I was getting increasingly restless.

~

'Amit, meet Manish. He's a businessman from Lakhisarai. He will tell us Samant's location,' said Kumar Sir, introducing me to a young man fresh out of college.

'Namaste, sir. It will be my privilege to be associated with you in this noble mission. Samant is a scourge that has to be wiped off the face of the earth,' said Manish. I was not particularly impressed by his grand filmi dialogues.

'Why would you help us? Do you have any personal animosity with Samant?' I asked him, my eyebrows arched.

'*Sir, bas desh ki seva karni hai* (Sir, I just want to serve our country),' Manish replied with folded hands. Sensing my cold response, Kumar Sir glanced at Manish and asked him to come back later with some tangible information.

'Sir, who's this guy? How will he get us Samant?'

'Amit, I've known Manish for quite some time now. He's helped us arrest some criminals earlier.'

'What kind of criminals? And what would he gain out of this? Why would he risk his life?' I said, still suspicious of Manish. I was anyway quite confident about being able to track Samant and Horlicks using mobile technology.

'Oh, the criminals were petty, not in Samant's league. Nevertheless, he helped us. We gave him some money from the

SS Fund. And more than that, he likes cultivating relationships with officers. It helps him.'

I knew that nobody would help us for free. Practically every Tom, Dick and Harry wanted to bond well with government officials, particularly police officers. It increased their social standing, and they could throw their weight around using their 'connections'.

'Amit, there is no harm in trying Manish out. We're not going to lose anything.'

Later we would almost lose our lives for acting on a tip from Manish.

~

Tanu was finding it increasingly difficult to feed Aishwarya anything. It seemed she had taken after her father. She avoided everything nutritious and ate anything that was unhealthy. To divert her from the bland taste of cereal and porridge, Tanu started taking Aish to the garden and assembling all my staff around her. So the sweeper, the cook, the washerman and even the rifle-wielding guard would surround Aish and then sing and dance for her. The sweeper would act like a monkey. The cook would dance, gyrating his pelvis in the most risqué manner. This way, Tanu could feed Aish all the nutritious food she wanted while my staff entertained our daughter. Aish took a particular fancy to the 'super-hit' Bhojpuri song '*Tu lagawelu jab lipistic, hilela Arrah district*' sung in the harshest of voices by our sweeper. I was extremely irritated by this, but it seemed to be the only song she would have her meals to. What made me angrier was that she would start crying the moment I would sing Kishore Kumar songs for her. Even an infant did not appreciate my singing talents. This ritual was quite a scene every day.

The staff started waiting for Aish's mealtimes because of the entertainment it brought them as well.

~

I was sitting with Kumar Sir, watching a match between Argentina and Uruguay. The football was quite listless—nothing apart from plenty of boring passes.

Kumar Sir's phone rang while the match was on.

'Sir, I have found out Samant's location. He's in Lakhisarai district!' Manish said excitedly. Kumar Sir looked at me with a faint smile. He was always in control of his emotions, his face almost always deadpan. He was the perfect foil for my exuberance. 'Manish has found the location of our target. I have called him over,' he said, narrating the conversation to me.

I was still sceptical. How could he have found the location so easily? We waited for Manish to arrive.

After an hour, he entered my house, covered in mud and drenched in sweat. The excitement on his face was obvious.

'Namaste, sir. *Mooh meetha karaiyega*. I deserve a treat after you nab Samant. Both of you will become heroes of the Bihar Police.'

'Manish, how do you know Samant's location?' I asked him, cutting him short and making no effort to mask my distrust. He looked at me incredulously.

'Sir, I met him today afternoon. I rushed straight from Simri village in Lakhisarai to tell you. Can't you see my feet, my clothes? I'm covered in mud!'

He still didn't make any impression on me. Manish took out his mobile phone and showed me a picture.

'Sir, this is Samant's picture. I took it today. Now I hope you are convinced.'

The picture was unmistakably Samant's, but it was a bit too perfect. How could someone take such a clear picture of a wanted fugitive without making him suspicious? Did Samant pose for Manish? In fact, memory told me that the picture was an old one, perhaps published in the local newspaper, *Hindustan*, a fortnight ago.

'Draw a map for us. How many people will be required? What kind of arms is Samant carrying?' I asked.

Manish confidently drew a map of the village, pinpointing the location of Samant and his gang.

Kumar Sir gave a wad of notes to Manish, which he eventually accepted happily with a perfunctory, *'Sir, iski kya zaroorat hai* (Sir, you didn't need to)!'

I called the sergeant major and directed him to send fifty constables in half an hour.

'Amit, we'll leave at 9.30 p.m. sharp. I will not brief our men till we reach Simri village in Lakhisarai. Otherwise, our operation details might get leaked. Have a light dinner.'

I was in a bad mood. Sir was putting too much faith in Manish. But I was still not convinced. 'Why would Samant meet you? How did you get access to him so easily?' I asked Manish. I could see that my questioning was making him quite uncomfortable.

'*Sir, mera vishwas kijiye. Bhagwan ka diya sab hai mere paas* (Sir, please believe me. I already have everything I could ask for). God has been kind to me. It's just that I want to help the police as a responsible citizen.'

He looked at Kumar Sir and continued talking. 'I posed as an arms supplier to see him. I've helped the police nab some other criminals also in the same way. Kumar Sir can vouch for me.'

Kumar Sir folded the map Manish had drawn and put it in his pocket. Even he was a little doubtful now. I could sense it. He left for the circuit house to get ready. I switched on the TV to watch the next football match, which was getting quite exciting. It was about to be decided by a penalty shoot-out. I knew I would miss the last moments of the match, but perhaps something more thrilling was going to happen that night.

I took my Austrian-made Glock pistol and loaded nine bullets into the magazine. I put the remaining bullets into the spare magazine. I kissed Tanu and sat in the Tata Sumo. Kumar Sir asked the driver to drive to Lakhisarai. The fifty-odd constables followed us in a minibus and a Tata 407.

It started drizzling on the way.

After an hour and a half, our convoy reached Pipariya police station. The head constable and the ASI on duty were quite surprised to see so many policemen in the police station.

'How far is Simri village? How are the roads?' asked Kumar Sir. The ASI was in his lungi and vest. The poor guy must have just gone to sleep after a tiring day. He was about to run off to change his clothes but I stopped him.

'Don't waste our time. Quickly, give us a guide to take us to Simri.'

The ASI knew that some big operation was being launched against an important criminal. Otherwise, a DIG-rank officer wouldn't be standing in his police station so late at night, with so many armed jawans.

The ASI called the chowkidar and directed him to escort us to Simri village. The chowkidar is a typical low-wage employee of the government. He is supposed to be the eyes and ears of the police. During the Raj, it was quite an important post, despite being low in the hierarchy. But over time, the authority of the chowkidar has dwindled to almost nothing. Nobody bothered about him here, neither the villagers nor the policemen. He was reduced to doing menial work in the police station.

Our chowkidar was an emaciated, gaunt, middle-aged man, which made his eyes protrude even more. It was obvious that he was having a bad time financially. Often, chowkidars would get their salaries quite late in those days, sometimes even three months after the due date. Things are much better now as the government has ensured online disbursement of salaries.

'So you know Simri village? We have to get there in the shortest possible time.'

The chowkidar looked at Kumar Sir with a blank expression, unable to muster any excitement for the late-night adventure.

'Arre, sir, I will take you there by boat. We will reach in half an hour. We just have to cross the Kiul river. *Us paar hi toh jaana hai* (We just have to go to the other bank).'

'Okay, then I think we will require two boats for our men.'

I started to feel excited. I always yearn for adventure. The thought of crossing a river by boat, that too at night, was quite an interesting proposition!

The banks of the Kiul, a tributary of the Ganges, were quite close to the police station. The ASI hailed two *mallah*s or boatmen. Rudely woken from their sleep, the mallahs showed little interest in taking us across.

'*Bhaiyya, kitna loge* (Bhaiyya, how much will you charge)? Don't worry, we will pay you handsomely,' said Kumar Sir.

The mallahs were pleasantly surprised.

'Huzoor, we'll take you for free. You do so much for the public. Can't we do even this much for you?'

All of us smiled, humbled by the lovely gesture.

The boatmen readied the boats and removed the anchors. Now Kumar Sir assembled all the jawans and briefed them about the operation. He could not risk waiting. Simri was right across the river.

'We are going after Samant Pratap. Be very careful. You all know how dangerous he is. Also, be cautious—there should be no casualties in the crossfire. The villagers should not be harmed.'

The police party was taken aback. Samant Pratap! That name was enough to instil fear in anyone. After all, he had escaped from Nawada Jail after killing a policeman, killed an ex-MP in his house and was known to have murdered scores of other people. But our demeanour and steely resolve soothed the nerves of the jawans. Their body language changed.

'Are you all ready? Check your weapons,' commanded Kumar Bharat.

'Yes, sir,' the banks of the Kiul reverberated with the collective shouts of the policemen. Such is the effect of inspiring leadership.

The men quickly checked their weapons, the British vintage .303 rifle. Only our personal bodyguards had carbines. The much vilified Enfield .303 rifle is an excellent weapon for the police. Its single-action bolt mechanism ensures controlled firing, suitable for facing mobs. You don't use an assault rifle like the AK-47 to spray bullets on a rampaging crowd. It would leave scores of people dead, something the police never wants.

But that night, we were not facing a bunch of rioters. We were supposed to fight one of Bihar's most feared and lethal gangs. If Samant actually was in Simri. I still had strong doubts.

All my excitement soon fizzled out. The Kiul was in spate, the waves striking the boats menacingly. I feared that the boats would capsize. I was a good swimmer, but swimming leisurely in the pool is entirely different from swimming in a gushing river. To top it all, it started raining heavily. I looked at Kumar Sir.

Even if he was worried, he did not show it. He ordered all of us to get on to the boats. I also got in hesitantly, next to the keel. The mallah pushed the boat into the water. It started swaying in a dizzying way. I felt my gut clenching. All the jawans seemed frightened. We were so close to the shore, yet the boat was rocking violently. What would happen when we rowed deeper into the river?

I got my answer the very next instant. A sudden jerk capsized the boat. I was tossed up, suspended mid-air, weightless for a fleeting moment, and then thrown into the water. Almost all the jawans lost their balance and fell into the ice-cold river. Luckily, the water was only waist-deep, or else many of us would have met our watery graves. We quickly scrambled out.

Kumar Sir was in a state of shock. He was about to get into the other boat when he saw all of us tumble into the water. He immediately stopped the men from getting into the other boat and signalled for them to pull us out. Our uniforms and weapons were drenched. The operation was over before it could start.

But Kumar Sir was not one to give up. He asked all of us to gather around and check our weapons.

'We can't go by boat now. Is there any other way of reaching Simri village? By road?' he asked the chowkidar.

I could not believe my ears. We could have died if we had been in the middle of the river. The weather was not cooperating and we were not even sure if Samant and his gang were in Simri. Silently, I questioned Kumar Sir's judgement. He looked at me, understanding what was going on in my mind.

'Amit, we have come so close to the village. What if Samant is actually in Simri? Will we be able to forgive ourselves if we miss him? Without even trying?'

I did not want to argue with him, that too in front of so many jawans. The very foundation of the success of the police is following the command of your senior officer. A strict hierarchy is maintained to instil discipline. This is true for all uniformed forces. After all, if a soldier does not obey the orders of his general, how will wars be won?

'*Sir, ek toh aur raasta hai* (Sir, there's one more route). We will have to walk down. The road has been damaged in a number of places because of the rain,' said the chowkidar.

I cursed him. Could he not have kept quiet?

Most of the jawans tied their boots together and hung them around their necks and shoulders. We folded our trousers up till our knees. All of us removed the magazines from the weapons and shook the water out of the barrels. The rifles were in working condition. On Kumar Sir's command, we started following the chowkidar.

The entire area was pitch-dark. It had started raining heavily. The jawans switched on their torches. Many of us slipped on the muddy tracks.

'Ouch, holy shit!' I muttered as I fell on the muddy sludge. My uniform was soaked with grime. I got to my feet. The sole of my 'imported' sneakers had come off. So much for an expensive brand.

'How far is the village?' asked Kumar Sir after what felt like a lifetime.

'Sahib, it is close by. *Bagal mein hai* (It's right here),' replied the chowkidar. He had been repeating this one line for the last one and half hours. For a villager like the chowkidar, walking long distances on foot did not matter much, and the distance wasn't measured in kilometres.

Day was about to break. It had stopped raining now.

'Sir, Simri village is right in front of you,' he finally said.

Kumar Sir and I waved at the police party. Everyone halted. We gestured to the jawans to load their rifles. We all cocked our weapons as silently as possible. We separated into three parties to surround the village.

We had taken just a few steps in a crouching position when we saw a few villagers walking towards us. They were carrying *lota*s and cans. They were going for their ablutions. We relaxed our poses. Obviously, people can't go about doing their morning business so casually if a ganglord of Samant's repute is hiding in the village. The villagers were also quite shocked to see so many policemen swarming their village.

Our adrenaline levels, which had risen, suddenly dropped. My intuition, honed by years of experience, clearly told me that there was not even one criminal in the village, let alone Samant and his entire gang.

Nevertheless, Kumar Sir still asked the police team to cordon off the village. He and I personally led the search party inside the village. The men and women were doing their morning chores. Some were milking the cows, while others were filling up water at the tube well. They all stopped momentarily, amused and surprised to see so many men in khaki. Our men started checking the houses, much to the indignation of the residents.

'We are looking for some criminals. Please cooperate with the police,' I said sternly.

'Huzoor, nobody has come here. Ours is a *sharifon ka gaon* (a village of respectable people). This is the first time the police has come to our village,' an old man told Kumar Sir. He had a look of disappointment on his face. He knew the villager was telling the truth. Life was going on as normal in the village. That would have been impossible in Samant's presence.

After a while, we assembled our teams and did a headcount. The jawans checked their weapons and ammunition. We were tired now. I saw a few tractors parked outside some houses. We asked the tractor owners to drop us to the police station. Our legs did not have the energy to walk 19 kilometres, which is how far we had travelled through the night. Strange are the ways of the human body and spirit. If Samant and gang had been in the village, we could have fought for hours and easily walked back after the encounter. The euphoria of a successful operation subdues most physical discomfort.

On our way back, we were shocked to see scores of dead snakes on the track! The poor reptiles must have been trampled under our boots.

We reached the police station by 10 a.m. Kumar Sir's sombre mood clearly indicated the result of our mission. The SHO dared not ask us if we wanted chai–paani.

Suddenly, my personal mobile phone rang. The screen flashed my friend Vipul's name.

'Amit, my friend, how are you?'

This call was the last thing I needed at this time.

'Vipul, I'm busy with an operation right now. I will call you later.'

'Okay, we are at the airport. I just wanted to tell you that Pondi is going to Frankfurt to work with McKinsey. *Achcha sun*, we are planning to have a party before Pondi leaves India.'

It was one of those days when I was in no mood to entertain anybody. I disconnected the phone. So Rohit Pandey was joining McKinsey. And I was out in the badlands of Bihar chasing a fugitive.

Once again, the image of Ram Dular's nephew flashed in front of me. Why the hell was I thinking about other people's lives, their successes? I had chosen the IPS over an MBA or business. I reprimanded myself for thinking about such petty issues. My resolve to arrest Samant strengthened further.

In the car on the way home, I dozed off. Kumar Sir sat in a pensive mood.

At home, I scrubbed my body for almost an hour. The sludge and grime seemed to have stuck to all parts of my body. But I was glad that my arthritic condition had not troubled me last night. I had some brunch and went off to sleep again. I don't know how long I slept. I woke up to some pain in my ankle. When I half-opened my eyes, I saw the cook massaging my ankle. I immediately sprang up and moved away.

'Huzoor, you must be exhausted. *Thoda aapka deh dabaa dete* (I just thought I must massage your body),' Girish, my cook, said earnestly.

I was already least impressed with his culinary expertise. He could hardly make an omelette properly, and now he was trying to twist my body into seemingly impossible angles. Getting my body massaged by my pot-bellied cook was surely a recipe for disaster.

~

I called on Kumar Sir in the evening.

'Amit, I also had my doubts about last night's operation. But we must keep trying. Samant will definitely get news of the raid. It will keep him on edge. We must not let him relax.'

In a way, he was right. Old-fashioned policing was still relevant in the time of mobile phones and computers. Moreover, by leading the operation himself, Kumar Sir had shown the seriousness of his resolve. He had shown exemplary leadership. The top leadership of the police, particularly officers who lay down their lives fighting Naxalites and terrorists, often remain unsung. We must always remember the bravery of officers like Hemant Karkare, Ashok Kamte, Samant Salaskar and Tukaram Omble, who died fighting for our country.

'Sir, I have to teach that rogue Manish a lesson. He took us for a ride, literally,' I said.

Finally, Kumar Sir smiled.

'Forget him, Amit. He just wanted some easy money. We are cheated by so many people. It's part and parcel of our profession.'

I was not as large-hearted as Kumar Sir, however. I made a note of his name and offence in a corner of my mind. Right next to Rajesh Charan.

21

The Headbutt

9 July 2006

It was the final of the World Cup. Italy was facing France.

The cable transmission would often stop during the very frequent power cuts in Shekhpura. I did not want to miss the match, so I specially sent a few litres of diesel to the cable-wallah.

'Come what may, don't disrupt the cable connection today. Switch on the generator. There is an important match,' I commanded him.

There was frenzy in the Berlin stadium. We could feel the excitement as we watched the live telecast on our TV. Kumar Sir had also joined us.

'*Jaldi aao*, Zinedine Zidane has headbutted the Italian defender. There is total chaos on the football field!' shouted Tanu, banging on the door.

That was the infamous headbutt that is engraved in the memory of all football fans. Marco Materazzi, the Italian player, had said some nasty things about Zidane's sister. Unable to control his anger, Zinedine Zidane had hit Marco hard. Not only did Zidane, the most celebrated player of that time, lose his head, he lost the World Cup too. He was shown the red card. France lost the match to Italy 5–3 in the penalty shoot-out.

While this pandemonium was happening in Berlin, I was in the bathroom and one of my mobile phones was ringing.

I rushed out and instinctively picked up the phone, ignoring the madness happening on TV. It was Shanti Devi calling someone.

'*Haan, note kar liye address?*' said Shanti.

She had just given her address to someone. I had been listening to thousands of useless calls for the last thirty-five days, my ears ringing constantly from doing so for hours. I had been waiting for this one important conversation that would give me Horlicks's or Samant's location. And now I had missed that vital clue by a few seconds. Since the call recording started only after I received a call, the initial part of the conversation could not be recorded either.

'Oh God, please don't be so cruel,' I prayed.

My prayers were answered immediately. The person who had called Shanti spoke again.

'Bhabhi, I have noted the house number but missed the colony's name. Can you repeat it?'

'Satsang Nagar Colony. *Kar liya note?*' said Shanti.

'*Haan. Theek hai, Bhabhi. Pranaam.*'

I jumped with delight, as if I had won some lottery and all my stock market losses had turned to profits. I controlled my urge to detain the person with whom Shanti had spoken. That would have certainly alerted her. Anyway, I had to wait till Horlicks himself reached the house. I immediately called Ranjan to my house. I asked him to get Raju and Krishna too. Tanu and Kumar Sir wondered what was making me so happy.

~

Ajit came in and told me of Ranjan's arrival. I hurried out to the veranda.

'Ranjan, Shanti Devi is living in Satsang Nagar Colony, Deoghar. You have to go there to find her. Raju and Krishna, you have to go along with Ranjan.'

'Sir, how will we find her?' asked Ranjan.

'See, Satsang Nagar Colony must be a small area. Ranjan, Raju and Krishna, all of you know Shanti Devi by face. Every colony has a *subzi mandi*. She will definitely come to buy vegetables. The moment you see her, follow her. Don't arrest her. I repeat, don't arrest her. Remember, our target is Horlicks.'

'But, sir, how will we find her in the subzi mandi? We cannot keep sitting in a vegetable market all day,' interjected Krishna.

'Good question. That is exactly what you will do. All of you will pose as vegetable sellers and sit in the subzi mandi. Your disguise will also prevent Shanti Devi from recognizing you, if at all she knows you by face.'

All three of them had shock written all over their faces.

'Sir, you can't be serious,' they said in unison.

They knew their protest would have no effect on me. A resigned Ranjan asked me, '*Sir, aaj ka din thoda ashubh hai* (Sir, today is not an auspicious day). Can we not go on Tuesday?'

I just looked at him and arched my eyebrows. I thought I would have the same effect as Aamir Khan had on his subordinate police officer when he asks a similar question in the super-hit movie *Sarfarosh*. Alas, I was no Aamir Khan. They just looked back at me expectantly.

'No, every day is good for the police. Don't believe in these *faaltu* (useless) superstitions. You will leave right now,' I said angrily.

Ranjan flirted with the idea of staying in a hotel overnight on the way to Deoghar so that he could move on a more auspicious day, but remembering my anger, decided against it.

22

Beauty Kumari

'Sir, a girl called today while you were in the office. In fact, she has been calling for the past one week,' my telephone operator told me on my arrival from the police lines, where all the constables reside and all the resources, such as vehicles, are kept.

I was a little surprised. 'Who is she? Did she want anything?'

'Sir, she must be a local girl. She said that she was a huge fan of yours,' said the telephone operator.

'Okay, let me talk to her the next time she calls,' I said with a straight face, trying my best to hide my excitement. After all, who does not like some adulation, that too, from the opposite sex?

Just minutes later, the telephone buzzed.

'*Sir, woh hi ladki hai* (Sir, it is the same girl),' said the telephone operator.

'Okay, transfer the call,' I said.

'*Hello, sir, main aapki bahut badi fan hoon* (Hello, sir, I'm a huge fan of yours). I like you so much,' gushed a young girl, her voice a little shrill.

I ignored the shrillness of her voice, flattered by the compliments.

'What is your name?'

'Oh, sir, my name is Beauty Kumari. Could I come and meet you? It will be a dream come true.'

'Sure. I am a bit busy nowadays, but you can see me in my office on Friday.'

'Oh, thank you so much, sir!'

'I have fans even in Shekhpura,' I mused.

Years of growing up as an extremely shy and gawky boy and studying in a boys' school meant that I never got any female attention. During those days, people were quite conservative. Any girl older to me was a 'didi', an elder sister. For anyone younger to me, I was a 'bhaiyya', an elder brother. With girls my own age, I really did not know how to react. So the best course was to avoid them by turning the other way or looking through them, as if they did not exist. I employed the same attitude in the initial years at IIT. I simply did not know how to have the most basic conversation with a girl. Even if a girl asked me for a pen, I would either be very shy or overexcited, thinking, 'Oh, she has talked to me!' Or else I would be rude, inadvertently. There were only thirty girls in IIT Delhi in 1995. And for some reason, the girls' hostel was situated at the opposite end of the campus. For a person like me, who did not attend classes at all, seeing a girl was as rare as sighting an alien.

It was only in the last year at IIT that I became friends with some of my classmates. However, I had not matured enough to understand that a girl could just be friendly, without being your girlfriend.

Later, I started getting some attention from girls. Soon, I had an inflated sense of self. I cultivated a fake accent and memorized some really cheesy one-liners. It all worked. At least, that is what I thought. By the time I reached the Lal Bahadur Shastri Academy, Mussoorie, I had developed an entirely different idea about myself. I started believing that I was some kind of a stud. I tried to make up for all my lost *jawani ke din*.

After marrying Tanu, I somehow matured a little bit, but still had those juvenile ideas about myself. It probably was a defence mechanism to overcome the complex I had developed over the years.

I entered my house in a very happy mood. My staff could clearly see the joy I was radiating. 'Tanu, why did you marry me? You got so many proposals,' I asked, beaming.

Tanu was putting Aish to sleep, rocking her slowly in her lap. Without even looking at me, she replied, 'Simple. Because you are an IPS officer.'

My balloon burst instantly. I had expected her to say that she found me very handsome, smart, witty and so on.

Fuming, I marched out of the room. At least Beauty Kumari found me impressive.

23

'Aloo Le Lo'

Satsang Nagar Colony was a colony typical of any small town in India. The houses were close to each other, often encroaching on government land and into each other's spaces. A number of houses had put *toka*s or wires on electric poles to illegally draw power. The drains were clogged and overflowing. The roads were narrow and full of potholes, with hundreds of pedestrians trying to survive against a barrage of autos, rickshaws and cattle.

The small subzi mandi was chock-a-block with vegetable and fruit sellers. There was an almost equal number of cows trying to eat from the *thela*s and the garbage. The cows even tried to put their mouths into the customers' bags. Their efforts were sometimes successful. Some startled customers would drop their bags on being chased by the cattle and the bovines would have a field day.

Ranjan looked at Raju and Krishna. He just could not help himself—he burst out laughing. They were all looking the part, dressed as vegetable sellers standing next to a thela. After a momentary pause, Raju and Krishna joined in, laughing hysterically, their bellies moving up and down in a rhythmic motion.

By sheer chance, Havaldar Shiv Narayan had a relative who sold potatoes in the subzi mandi of Satsang Nagar. He had requested his relative to let Raju and Krishna assist in selling the vegetables.

'*Thoda kaam seekh lenge yeh dono* (These two guys will learn some work from you),' said Shiv Narayan.

'*Chalo, theek hai* (Well, all right). But I won't pay them anything,' said the potato seller reluctantly.

Both of them sat near the thela with sacks full of potatoes. Never in their wildest dreams had they imagined they would be selling potatoes one day.

'*Aloo le lo, aloo le lo,*' shouted Raju and Krishna in unison. The thela owner looked at them with disdain.

Ranjan sat at the tea stall close by. He hoped to see Shanti soon. The initial jokes and buffoonery had quickly grown old, and Ranjan and company wanted this charade to end soon. Standing in the sun for a full day and selling potatoes was a demanding job.

But two days soon passed. Raju and Krishna managed to sell almost all the potatoes but there was no sign of Shanti.

Ranjan called me that night.

'Sir, we have been waiting for the past two days, but have not seen Shanti.' There was exasperation in his voice.

'I know you must be tired. Policing is not as glamorous as people think. Have patience. She has to come to buy vegetables sooner or later. Tomorrow is going to be our day,' I said confidently. I had a good feeling about this. For the first time in many days, I slept soundly.

The next morning, I was relaxing in bed. Avi sat in my lap, moving his toy truck all over my body.

My phone rang.

'Sir, I can see Shanti. She has just come to buy some stuff for her house,' Ranjan spoke in a hushed tone. The trained policeman in him managed to control his excitement.

I put Avi on the floor and moved towards the garden, my heart beating really fast. This was the moment I had been waiting for.

'Keep a safe distance from her. She should not see you or get suspicious.'

'Sir, Krishna and Raju are with me. What is your order?'

'Just follow her from a distance. Find out where she lives.'

I waited for Ranjan to call again. Every second felt like an eternity.

'Sir, sir, we lost her. She just vanished.'

'What? What the hell are you saying? How could you lose her?'

I tried my best to keep my cool.

'Sir, we were right behind her. Give us some time, we'll try to find her.'

I looked towards the sky and closed my eyes. I was still hopeful of a miracle.

~

'Sir, we tried our best. We could not find her,' Ranjan said when he called again, his voice trembling with disappointment.

'Relax,' I said, feeling strangely calm. The gods were just testing me a little; I had to be patient.

'Tell me where exactly you lost her. Describe the area, the locality.'

'Sir, it's a residential area with houses on both sides of the street. The residents seem to be largely middle- or low-income people. The street ends after 300 metres.'

It was a cul-de-sac, a street with a dead end. My brain started working in hyperactive mode. The closed street meant that Shanti was definitely living in that small locality. She must have entered her house just before Ranjan and Raju could see her again.

'Ranjan, immediately find the local newspaper vendor. Find out from him if any family has shifted in recently. Also ask the vendor if that family has two kids. If the new residents have subscribed to an English newspaper, then they must be Shanti Devi and her kids. Not many people in that locality are going to read English newspapers.'

Luckily for us, there were only two *newspaper-wallah*s in that locality.

I waited and waited. After around two hours, Ranjan called again. This time, he sounded gleeful.

'Sir, you were right. A family of three did shift to this colony just about a month ago. The paper-wallah regularly delivers newspapers to their house. The lady of the house creates a huge ruckus if the vendor forgets to deliver the English newspaper for even one day. In fact, that is the only household that takes an English newspaper in that locality.'

'Which newspaper have they subscribed to?'

'Sir, the paper-wallah is saying it's the *Times of India*.'

I had a big smile on my face. Horlicks's obsession with making his son read the English newspaper had given away the location of his family's new hideout. I was almost certain that it was Shanti who was the new resident of Satsang Nagar Colony.

'Sir, what to do now?'

'Just take the exact address of the house from the vendor. Then station yourself near it to keep watch. The moment you see Shanti Devi again, call me.'

I just could not eat. I was in no mood for anything, not even playing with my kids. I was too anxious.

It was in the evening that I got the next call from Ranjan.

Now Ranjan was unable to control his excitement. I could sense the energy in his voice. How our emotions kept changing!

'Sir, I have seen her. She just came out to hang out her laundry.'

'Are you sure?'

'Sir, I couldn't be surer. What do I do now?'

'Go back to your hotel and rest. You should be absolutely fresh to catch Horlicks.' Somehow, I was sure that he would be visiting Deoghar to meet his family soon.

24

'Suttal Hai'

It was Friday. I was sitting in the office taking care of some routine matters.

'Sir, a girl has come to see you,' said the orderly.

'Send her in,' I said, signing some files.

A girl walked in with a middle-aged man. 'Hi, sir, I am Beauty Kumari. Remember, we spoke on the phone?'

I looked up in horror. The girl was the exact opposite of her name!

Before I could say a word, Beauty commanded her father, 'Papa, can you step outside? I have to speak to Amit Sir in private.'

Much to my surprise, the man walked out without any protest. I did not know what Beauty planned to do. She suddenly jumped across the table and held me by my arms, shaking me. Her grip was quite strong.

'*Sir, aap mujhe bahut achche lagte ho* (Sir, I like you very much). I want to marry you. I have no problem becoming your second wife. I will adjust with Didi.'

I was in absolute shock. I somehow gathered my senses before Beauty Kumari could manhandle me further.

'Guard, guard, Ajit, Ajit, come quickly,' I shouted at the top of my voice. My bodyguard, Ajit, and the orderly came running in to see me sweating in my seat, and a girl sprawled on the table. Ajit and the constable did not know how to react. They were not trained for this kind of a situation.

'Ajit, take this girl out of my office chamber immediately. Ensure that she never comes within even 500 metres of me. Ever. In fact, why only her? I don't want any girl close to myself again,' I said hysterically.

'*Sir, shaant ho jaiye* (Sir, relax),' he said, offering me a glass of water.

I gulped it down, still breathing heavily.

'Sir, the nature of your job is such that you have to meet everyone. You can't say that you will not see a girl or a woman. From now, for your safety, we will also depute a *mahila* constable in the office.'

I stayed silent. Ajit saluted and left me alone. I could hear the laughter outside. It was Ajit. The other staff joined him.

It was a lesson for me. No more beauties for me. So what if my wife did not give me the time of day? Till today, a lady constable or officer is always deputed to my office to escort any female visitors. You never know when a seemingly innocuous encounter may be disastrous for your life—professional and personal.

~

Horlicks had been chatting with his bhabhi for an hour. I really didn't understand how someone could derive so much pleasure from talking on the phone. Maybe it was the freedom with which Horlicks could converse with his girlfriend or maybe he just needed an outlet for his suppressed feelings. Whatever it was, Horlicks seemed to experience a new high each time he talked to her.

As was his ritual, Horlicks immediately called Shanti Devi after finishing his lovey-dovey conversations. It had been a long time since he had seen his children. He did not show any affection for Shanti Devi, but he seemed to be really fond of them.

'*Haan, sab theek* (Is everything all right)?' asked Horlicks.

'*Sab theek hi hoga* (Everything should be fine). How does it matter to you if we are alive or dead?' replied Shanti harshly.

'Okay, enough. Give the phone to Babua,' pleaded Horlicks.

'*Kab aa rahe ho, Baba* (When are you coming, Dad)? We have been waiting for you for so long,' said Chintoo.

'*Aa rahein hain na, jaldi hi. Ek do din mein* (Soon. I'll be with you in a day or two). I miss you a lot.'

Till the going is good, life is all glamour, guns and girls for a criminal. But when the police make things tough, life is hell. One is always on the run. Horlicks sounded like a tired man now. No wonder he did not want the same life for his children. Chintoo and Rani deserved a better future. He was desperate to see them.

I was equally desperate to catch him. The news that he was reaching Deoghar energized me tremendously.

~

I immediately called Ranjan.

'Our target is reaching Deoghar very soon, maybe in a day or two.'

'Sir, this is great news!' Ranjan sounded quite happy. He had shown remarkable patience so far.

'Sir, what if Horlicks shoots at us? We cannot rule out a gunfight or a scuffle with him,' Ranjan continued.

I just listened.

'The SHO of Satsang Nagar has to be informed about our plan, just in case we have a problem. We might need the support of the local police.'

'Okay, but you don't have to tell the local police much about Horlicks. Any leak of information could cost us.'

'Sure, sir. Manoj, the SHO of Satsang Nagar, has trained with me. I have good relations with him,' said Ranjan.

When a criminal has to be arrested in the jurisdiction of another district, the local police have to be taken into confidence. They are informed of the arrest and entries are made in the station diary. If the transit period is twenty-four hours or more, the arrested person is produced before the local court too.

~

Two days later, my mobile phone started vibrating under my pillow. It was Shanti Devi.

'*Haan, aa gaye hain. Suttal hai* (Yes, he's here. He is in deep sleep). He must be very tired after such a long journey.'

I was thrilled beyond words. Shanti Devi had just told me the location of her husband. Horlicks Samrat was in the house!

I immediately called Ranjan.

Ranjan did not pick up the phone. I tried again. No answer. I was getting really restless, even shaking a bit. It was the same feeling one has when appearing for an important exam. This was one test I could not afford to fail.

'Ranjan, Ranjan, pick up the damn phone,' I muttered.

I was engrossed with the thoughts of Horlicks. I had shifted back to my room by then as I could not get over my fear of lizards. I climbed over the children and got out of bed. I looked for my slippers in the dark and almost tumbled over a stool kept near the bed. Aish started crying in her sleep. Tanu took her in her lap and started consoling her.

She realized immediately that I was in the middle of something really important.

I went out into the open. Our house was very small. I just had to take a few steps and I was in the small garden we had. Still, I had the second largest house in Shekhpura. The DM had the biggest house. He had usurped the house of a senior engineer!

It was nippy outside early in the morning.

Ranjan was still not answering my call. I knew he must be sleeping after a tiring day. I thought of calling Raju and Krishna, but before I could act on it, my phone buzzed. It was Ranjan.

I regained my composure again. Even if an officer is worried, he has to appear quite relaxed and confident in front of his subordinates.

'Ranjan, Horlicks is in his house right now. Go and get him.'

I did not elaborate, nor did Ranjan ask me any questions. Ranjan was a seasoned policeman. He knew exactly what to do. I was confident he would find Horlicks.

~

Raju and Krishna rubbed their eyes and jumped out of bed. All three of them got ready quietly. Havaldar Shiv Narayan, an early riser, was already dressed. All of them checked their weapons. Shiv Narayan was the only one with a legal weapon. In fact, he was the only one lawfully entitled to arrest Horlicks. Raju and Krishna were 'ordinary civilians' and Ranjan was a suspended policeman.

Ranjan called the SHO of Satsang Nagar.

'Manoj Bhai, I have come here to arrest a man wanted in a case of cheating and forgery. Na, na, nobody important. I might require the help of your police force. *Do–chaar aadmi de dena* (Keep two to four constables ready). Just in case. Okay, thank you.'

~

The seedy hotel in which they were staying was quite close to Horlicks's house. It was, of course, a strategic choice. They quickly reached the colony. The sky was slowly changing hue as the sun rose. Ranjan and the other three men did a reconnaissance of the house again. The first floor house had windows with grills. One could jump from the balcony to escape, but at the peril of breaking one's legs on the road below. Only Akshay Kumar could land on his feet from that height. Ranjan posted one constable under the balcony and made another constable stand near the staircase to block any escape attempts. Confident that Horlicks's exit routes had been sealed, Ranjan silently moved upstairs. Shiv Narayan followed him at a distance, moving gracefully.

Raju and Krishna waited in their Bolero.

Ranjan was about to knock on the door. That was the only option to get into the house. He hoped that an unsuspecting Shanti would open the door as Horlicks was fast asleep. But first, he took a chance and gently pushed the door. And it opened, just like Alibaba's cave! Ranjan tiptoed inside. His heart was beating fast. Just next to the entrance, he heard a female voice singing a bhajan in the bathroom. It must be Shanti Devi, getting ready for her morning rituals. Ranjan gently drew the bolt and locked her from outside. He could not believe his luck—it was almost too easy. But it is true—the harder you work, the luckier you get. He deserved it after all the hard work he had put in.

It seemed that Horlicks's children had just left for school. Shanti Devi had simply not bothered to lock the door. On the bed was lying the man we were looking for so desperately. Horlicks Samrat was sleeping like a log, totally oblivious to the intrusion in his house. Shiv Narayan and Ranjan looked at each other, making it a moment that would remain imprinted in their memory.

Ranjan put his hand over Horlicks's mouth and shook him. Horlicks got up with a jerk. He could not believe what he was seeing. His eyes grew wide with shock, his mouth covered by Ranjan's hands. For an instant, he thought that Ranjan would shoot and kill him.

Horlicks closed his eyes. So this was the end. The faces of all the people he had killed flashed before his eyes.

'Oh God, please take care of my children. Let them fulfil my dreams,' he thought.

He waited for the trigger to click.

When the fatal shot did not come, he opened his eyes to find Ranjan trying to tie his hands, that too, with his wife's sari. How stupid of him! Horlicks wrestled out of Ranjan's grip and punched him hard. He started looking frantically for his gun. Why the hell had he not kept it close by? How could he be so casual?

Ranjan was still trying to recover from the hit, but Shiv Narayan was agile and alert. He hit Horlicks's head with the butt of his carbine. As everything went black, Horlicks swayed where he stood. It was enough for Ranjan to hold him down and tie his hands. He then stuffed Horlicks's mouth with Shanti's blouse. Finally, he blindfolded him with a black gamchcha, a cloth Shiv Narayan always kept with him to beat the heat. Meanwhile, Shanti had finished her bath. Unable to come out, she started banging on the door. Horlicks tried his best to break free from his bonds. His best bet was his wife, but she was locked in. Ranjan and Shiv Narayan pushed Horlicks downstairs.

Krishna and Raju were delighted, their eyes expressing a joy beyond explanation.

'Let's move fast. A crowd might assemble. People are slowly coming out of their homes,' Ranjan gestured to Raju and Krishna to keep quiet. Any sound from them would have given away their identities to Horlicks.

Krishna could not control his urge. He slapped Horlicks hard. Tears welled up in Horlicks's eyes under the blindfold.

25

'My Husband Is the "Famous" Criminal of Bihar'

'*Sir, pakad liya*. We've caught him. Further orders?' Ranjan said in a calm, composed manner totally belying the drama that had unfolded a few moments ago.

I heaved a sigh of relief and ran in.

'What?' asked a half-asleep Tanu.

My smile said it all. She jumped out of bed and collided with the same stool. Both the kids were woken up and they started crying. And this time, Tanu did not bother.

'Good news?' she asked.

I just kissed her on the forehead. She hugged me tightly.

Ranjan was patiently waiting for my instructions. He understood the importance of that moment.

'Excellent, Ranjan. Very proud of you. Get him to Shekhpura quickly.'

'Thank you, sir. All because of your guidance,' responded Ranjan, using the stock reply of any policeman when congratulated.

~

Ranjan called Manoj.

'Thank you, Manoj Bhai. I am grateful to you for giving us your constables. The guy was a bada criminal, a notorious person called Horlicks Samrat. He was wanted in a number of murder cases in Bihar. I am taking him back to Shekhpura.'

SI Manoj was a little taken aback, but he had his hands full at the time. He did not react very strongly to the news.

The constant banging on the door and shouting by Shanti Devi alerted her landlady, who rushed upstairs and opened the bathroom door. Shanti Devi was shocked to find that her husband had been forcibly taken away by some intruders. She immediately called me.

'*Sahib, hum Deoghar se Shanti Devi bol rahe hain* (Sahib, this is Shanti Devi calling from Deoghar).'

I was absolutely shocked.

'Who? Why have you called me?' I gathered my senses and replied.

'Sir, I am the wife of the "famous" criminal Horlicks Samrat. You have been looking for him,' she said earnestly.

I was quite amused. To Horlicks's wife, her husband was a 'famous' personality.

'Sahib, some people took him away just a few minutes ago. Tell me, were they your men? I am a little worried about his safety.'

'I am not concerned about your husband. I am the SP of Shekhpura, not the SP of Deoghar. How will I know what is happening in Deoghar?' I said authoritatively and disconnected the phone.

Phew. That was interesting. Even Shanti had my number. And she had the gall to call me and inquire about the safety of her husband.

Unfortunately, she was not going to give up so easily. She called the SP of Deoghar. '*Madam, hamaara husband ka kidnap ho gaya hai* (Madam, my husband has just been kidnapped). Please help me,' requested Shanti. She narrated the incident to the SP.

The SP, Amrit Kaur, was quite tired. Shanti's phone had probably woken her up too early. Like most SPs and SHOs, the nature of her job frequently kept her awake till late at night, often till 2 a.m.

However, Amrit Kaur immediately swung into action and called Manoj, the SHO of Satsang Nagar. A kidnapping was the last thing she wanted in her already troubled district.

'Bada Babu, there has been a kidnapping of one Horlicks Samrat in your jurisdiction. Immediately block all the roads. There have been too many crimes of late in our district. I won't tolerate any slackness on your part. If you don't recover the kidnapped person, I will suspend you.'

'Madam, the person is a dreaded criminal. He is wanted in dozens of cases in Shekhpura and Nawada. A team of Shekhpura police was camping here for the last few days to nab him,' said Manoj, hoping that it would assuage the SP if she knew that it was an operation of the Shekhpura police.

Amrit Kaur was absolutely infuriated.

'Why did you let the Shekhpura police take him away? Horlicks Samrat's arrest would have been a big achievement for us. Get him back at any cost or you lose your job,' an angry Amrit ordered Manoj.

A worried Manoj immediately called Ranjan.

'Ranjan Bhai, return immediately. My SP Madam is very upset with me. And why didn't you tell me earlier that you were looking for Horlicks Samrat?'

'Manoj, revealing Horlicks's identity would have jeopardized our secret mission. We are on our way to Shekhpura now.'

Now Manoj got a little angry. He felt cheated by Ranjan.

'Come back immediately. We have already blocked the road to Shekhpura. I will be forced to lodge a kidnapping case against you if you don't return.'

Ranjan was in a fix. He immediately called me and explained the new, totally unwelcome development. I was also flummoxed by this sudden twist in the story.

I quickly dialled Amrit Kaur's number.

'Good morning, ma'am. I am Amit Lodha, the SP of Shekhpura. My team has just arrested a dreaded criminal, Horlicks Samrat, from Satsang Nagar Colony in your district. Ma'am, I would be grateful if you could send him to Shekhpura as soon as possible.'

'Yeah, sure, Amit. I will just interrogate him for some time and find out if he was planning to commit any crime in Deoghar.' Amrit Kaur did not sound very happy with my call. I was also not completely convinced by her explanation. Why would Horlicks commit any crime in Deoghar?

'One more thing, ma'am. Please keep Horlicks's arrest a secret. We don't want anyone to know that he's in our custody. The media should not know about it.'

'Okay.'

'Ma'am, I repeat, strict secrecy has to be maintained. We have to interrogate Horlicks to find out the location of his other gang members. If they come to know of Horlicks's arrest, they will be alerted. They will definitely change their hideouts.'

I could not have made myself clearer. Amrit Kaur was two batches senior to me. She was experienced enough to understand the gravity of the situation.

I called Kumar Sir to break the news.

'Sir, we have arrested Horlicks. Ranjan and his team got him in Deoghar.'

Kumar Sir was happy. This was a much-awaited good news and I was glad I could give it to him at a trying time. He was in Patna to attend to his son, who was ill.

'Well done! Interrogate him and let me know the details.'

'Sir, nobody apart from you and the SP of Deoghar knows about the arrest, for obvious reasons.' I told him that Amrit Kaur had called Horlicks for questioning.

'Okay, I understand. I will come tomorrow.'

26

'Sahib Gusal Mein Hai'

Horlicks's arrest called for some celebration. I asked my cook to make some aloo paranthas and munched on some bhujia while playing with Aish. She looked at me eagerly, waiting for me to give her some bhujia. I obliged. She squealed with delight.

Ajit came rushing in.

'Sir, the ADG wants to talk to you. The wireless operator just conveyed the message.'

The ADG was not too fond of me because of the grudge he harboured against me from my Nalanda days about not appointing his nephew. And I disliked him for not liking me. It was a case of ever-increasing hostility towards each other.

I matured later when I realized that all the ill feelings were only causing me pain and nothing else. Sometimes, instead of reacting, it is better to let go.

I dialled the number of the ADG's residence. A.K. Prasad was known for his effeminate voice. 'Hello,' said a feminine voice on the other end.

'Good morning, sir. This is Amit from Shekhpura.'

'*Sahib gusal mein hain* (Sahib is in the bathroom).'

'May I know who is on the line?'

'I am the ADG's wife. Please call after ten minutes.'

'Okay, madam. Sorry for bothering you.'

Madam's voice had a striking similarity to that of the ADG. I smiled and dialled the number again after some time.

'Hello, ADG's residence.'

'Good morning, sir. This is Amit. You had asked me to call you.'

'Oh, uncle. Papa is doing puja. Can you please call in a few minutes?'

This time, it was the ADG's daughter. She also sounded like him.

After a few minutes, I dialled the number one more time. This time, I did not want to embarrass myself by addressing Madam as 'sir'.

'Hello,' cooed an effeminate voice again. Instinctively, I assumed it must be a lady on the other side.

'Madam, could I speak to ADG Sir?'

'*Lodha, hum ADG bol rahein hain* (Lodha, this is the ADG speaking).'

My cheeks turned pink with embarrassment.

'Sorry, sir. I thought it was Madam,' I said meekly.

The ADG ignored my apology. Either he was used to this identity mix-up or he assumed I was deliberately making fun of him.

'You did not tell me that Horlicks Samrat has been arrested,' he said. I was surprised.

'Sir, I was about to tell you,' I lied. 'But how did you come to know?'

'Don't you watch TV? Horlicks's arrest is being broadcast on all the news channels. The SP of Deoghar, that lady, she has just now held a press conference. She is claiming that Horlicks's arrest is a big achievement for the Deoghar police.'

I remained silent.

'Were you not working on this case? Isn't that why you were posted to Shekhpura?'

'Sir, it was my team that arrested Horlicks. I had deliberately tried to keep his arrest a secret, so that we could gain some information about Samant.'

The disappointment in my voice was obvious.

'Okay, now you get him and interrogate him properly.'

I turned on the TV. Horlicks's face was on all the channels. A beaming Amrit Kaur was telling the media how the Deoghar police had meticulously planned the arrest of the dreaded criminal of Bihar, Horlicks Samrat. I felt absolutely devastated. Amrit Kaur had not kept her promise. Now Samant would come to know about Horlicks's arrest. He would be doubly cautious.

I called Ranjan, angry at his incompetence.

'Why did you let this press conference happen? Why did you not tell me? Now all our hard work has gone down the drain.'

My euphoria had vanished. How could things have changed so quickly?

Ranjan was equally sullen.

'Sir, we were asked to wait outside the SP's office for some time. The staff told us that the formalities would be completed soon. We didn't know that the SP would hold a press conference. In fact, the Deoghar police have asked us to get a transit remand to take Horlicks to Shekhpura.'

I was unable to control my anger. I called Amrit Kaur. She did not pick up even after I called three or four times. I knew she wouldn't answer my calls now. I dialled her office.

'SP's office, Deoghar,' said a voice at the other end.

'PA Sahib, I am a journalist calling from Aaj Tak. Could I speak to SP Madam? I need to get a live bite for my channel.'

An excited Amrit Kaur came on the phone.

My voice quivered with rage. I spoke to her in a stern voice, 'Madam, what have you done? You have undone months of our hard work. How could you be so unprofessional?'

I did not bother that she was senior to me.

'No, no, Amit. It's not like that. I can explain.' The joy in Amrit Kaur's voice had vanished. 'You know, there has been a spate of crimes in Deoghar. The people's confidence in the police is quite low. We were looking for some kind of big achievement to show to the people that the Deoghar police are working hard. I hope you can understand. We will send Horlicks as soon as you send your team. We've finished the formalities.'

I banged the phone down. This happens often—there are times when the crime graph of a district suddenly rises, despite the best efforts of the police. The public's confidence in the police dwindles, and the police department faces a lot of backlash. Just to divert the media's attention or to create better public opinion, the police desperately look for some big achievement. They work hard, but they also have to appear to be working hard. Horlicks's arrest was that one silver lining the Deoghar police was desperately looking for.

I immediately dispatched SI Abdul Aziz, an officer well-versed in legal formalities, to get Horlicks Samrat from Deoghar. He had one more important quality. He did not ask many questions.

27

The Interrogation

Ranjan followed the Shekhpura police party escorting Horlicks Samrat from Deoghar to Shekhpura at a distance. Raju and Krishna sat quietly in the car, gazing out of the window. Nobody wanted to take any chance with Horlicks.

SI Abdul Aziz kept looking back every now and then to check if Horlicks was secure. If he was mystified by the arrest, he did not show it. However, he did ask Ranjan what he was doing in Deoghar.

'Sir, I was asked by Bada Sahib to come to Deoghar to verify if the arrested man was actually Horlicks,' Ranjan had replied cheekily.

Bada Sahib or the SP is the ultimate boss of the district police. Abdul Aziz did not ask any more questions. It was none of his business. His job was to get Horlicks safely to Shekhpura. The twelve commandos in the two jeeps were sufficient to tackle any escape attempt.

'Sir, we are about to enter Shekhpura district,' Ranjan called to inform me.

'Okay. I have sent Ajit and my personal guards also to further escort Horlicks to the Chewara police station. I will get there after some time. All of you lie low for now.'

Chewara was far from Samant's stronghold and we were at a lower risk there of any potential attempt by gang members to free Horlicks. After all, he had escaped from jail earlier as well. 'And Ranjan, well done! But remember, our job is not finished yet.'

'Yes, sir,' he replied.

~

Ajit and a few commandos were waiting for Aziz at the Shekhpura border. SI Abdul Aziz smiled when he saw Ajit. It was a glorious day, not only for the Shekhpura police, but also for the Bihar Police. Ajit looked at the man whose very name instilled terror in the hearts of people in not one, but four districts. The man who had killed so many people—men, women and children—did not look anything like a killer. He could have easily passed off as a simple, nameless, faceless person, like millions of other people who live in our villages, our cities. Horlicks did not even raise his head. He was looking down, sullen and meek. Ajit checked his handcuffs. He could not take any chances. He knew how dangerous Horlicks was.

The SHO of Chewara, Anuj Kumar, was a veteran policeman. He had dealt with many hardened criminals in his career. A bullet injury in his left thigh was the result of an encounter with the notorious Sultan gang, a testimony to his bravery and commitment. He took great pride in his job. So what if he had a slight limp?

But he was not prepared for the surprise in store for him. In walked a haggard Horlicks Samrat, the terror of Shekhpura. He rubbed his eyes in disbelief. Was it actually Horlicks, the killer who had been a bane for the police for the last five years? The same Horlicks who could have been an excellent sniper in the Army, but for circumstances?

Ajit pushed Horlicks inside the lock-up. The entire police station became alert and attentive. When I arrived, I entered Anuj's chamber and asked him to get Horlicks out of the cell. I was not surprised by his absolutely normal appearance. Real-life criminals look quite ordinary, unlike their screen cousins. Even policemen do not have a larger-than-life swagger. We are just ordinary folks with an extraordinary passion.

Horlicks came out and folded his hands.

'Pranaam, sir,' he said.

That was the beauty of Bihari culture. Biharis always speak with great respect to everyone. They use 'aap' for everyone, even those much younger. Though Horlicks and I were almost the same age, I wondered how our paths had diverged so sharply. I wondered what goes on in the human mind to turn a regular family man into a notorious criminal.

I got up, sized Horlicks up close and shoved him hard. He lost his balance. He started crying. It was my standard procedure when I met a hardened criminal. This was my way of showing them who the boss was.

'*Beta ko SP banaana hai* (You dream of making your son an IPS officer). Does your son know who you are? He'll be ashamed of you when he grows up.'

Tears started flowing freely from Horlicks's eyes now.

'Now, tell me, where is Samant?'

'Sir, I really do not know. Even if I knew, I wouldn't have told you.'

Ajit picked up a lathi. I glared at Ajit. He realized his mistake.

I had had a very bad experience once during my training days.

Young, probationer IPS officers are posted as SHOs to understand how a police station, or thana, works. I too was posted to Bero, a remote police station in Ranchi. Just a few days after my joining, a house was looted by some criminals. I made it a matter of personal prestige to solve the case.

'*Sir, pakka Gaurav Sahu ne kiya hoga* (Sir, it was definitely Gaurav Sahu)!' said SI Harishankar, my trainer at the Bero police station.

'How do you know?'

'Arre, sir, he has a history. Look at his crime record. He was seen loitering around the crime scene a few days ago,' replied Harishankar.

I tried my best to use the investigative techniques taught at the NPA, but to no avail. There was no fingerprint-lifting kit in the police lines, and even if I had picked up the fingerprints, there was no database to match them with. I did not find any other clues.

In my desperation, I raided Gaurav Sahu's house and found him sleeping peacefully. Naturally, he pleaded his innocence. I also had my doubts about whether he was actually involved in the loot. Sometimes, a person is branded a criminal even after one petty offence. Gaurav, a young boy, had a series of entries against his name in the police dossiers, none of them conclusive of his actual guilt.

I interrogated him for hours, but he kept on pleading his innocence. I tried to break him mentally too. My frustration knew no bounds. But by then, Gaurav was totally exhausted and he soon fainted.

Harishankar looked at me in horror.

'*Sir, yeh kya ho gaya* (Sir, what has happened)?'

'*Sir, mar gaya kya* (Sir, is he dead)?' inquired a visibly worried Head Constable Munshi.

'I don't know,' replied Harishankar.

The entire staff of the police station vanished.

I felt terrified as I knelt to check on Gaurav.

'Oh God, don't be so cruel,' I pleaded fervently. I did not want my career to end even before it had started.

I shouted for help, but none of the policemen responded.

For some reason, Inspector Ram Singh still kept standing in front of me. He was probably too petrified to run away.

'Inspector Sahib, help me. Come on,' I commanded him.

The inspector moved as if he was in a trance, but his help was enough for me to lift Gaurav and put him in the back of my ramshackle Gypsy.

I drove the Gypsy as fast as I could, straight to Ranchi. On my way, I narrowly missed mowing down a child and colliding with a truck. My Gypsy bumped over the countless stupidly designed speed breakers or *thokar*s all along the road. I didn't care.

'*Paani pilao, Ram Singh* (Give him water, Ram Singh)!'

Ram Singh did not say a word. He was probably imagining himself facing serious consequences for this man collapsing on our watch.

I kept praying throughout the one-and-a-half-hour drive to the Rajendra Medical College Hospital (RMCH), Ranchi's best hospital. Ram Singh and I put Gaurav on a stretcher and rushed towards the emergency trauma centre.

'Please, doctor, this is an emergency. This man is battling for his life. Please do something,' I pleaded.

The doctor, a young man, possibly an intern, was quite baffled.

'How did it happen?'

'This guy fainted when we were questioning him.'

The doctor checked Gaurav's vitals.

'Doctor, I am an IPS officer. Please save his life. I will be grateful.'

The young intern looked at me. I was not in my uniform. He just nodded and took Gaurav inside.

After an hour, the doctor came out with his senior. The elderly doctor put his hand on my shoulder and spoke with great affection.

'Beta, be careful in the future. You have a long career ahead.'

I just nodded and shook his hand. I promised myself I would steer clear of even slightly intensive interrogation.

~

Ajit looked threateningly at Horlicks and said, '*Bata kahaan pe hai Samant* (Tell us where Samant is). We will finish your entire gang.'

The questioning continued for quite some time, but Horlicks did not give up any information. At the end of the day, I called off the interrogation.

'Anuj, I am sending some more jawans from the police lines. Convert the police station into a fortress. Also keep a watch on Horlicks. He should not be allowed to cause any harm to anyone. Especially to himself.'

28

'My Son Will Become a Police Officer'

Horlicks lay on the cold floor in the lock-up of the Chewara police station. He closed his eyes and remembered the day his life had changed forever.

He had shut his shop early that afternoon. He had to meet the principal of Jawahar Navodaya Vidyalaya. He wanted to reach the principal's office as early as possible, considering how difficult it had been to get an appointment.

He was really excited that his son, Chintoo, might get admission to a good school. Being illiterate himself, he had worked hard to make sure his children didn't lack for anything. He would often think to himself, 'My son is so intelligent. He will fulfil all my dreams. He will become a big man, bada aadmi. He will become a policeman, an SP.'

Born to a poor family, Horlicks was always ridiculed by others in his village because he was not educated and could barely write his name. The fact that he was slight and scrawny also meant that people did not give him a lot of respect. He was so skinny that people would say, '*Isko Horlicks pilao* (Give him some Horlicks)'. And so the name stuck. Horlicks harboured the dream of getting into the police as it was the ultimate symbol of machismo for him. He used to look at all policemen with awe, particularly the SP.

Horlicks even appeared for the constable recruitment test for the Bihar Police.

'Chalo, bhai, leave this ground. Don't you know you have to be a matriculate at least to become a constable?' asked the DSP in charge of recruitment.

'And even if you had a PhD, we couldn't have selected you. Your chest measurement and height do not conform to the physical requirements,' said the sergeant major, sympathetically.

Horlicks felt thoroughly dejected. 'I'll make my son a policeman, an IPS officer. He will be the boss of the district police,' he vowed.

The school in his village was not good enough. The Navodaya school would be a great stepping stone for Chintoo's education.

A little distance from the school, he heard someone say, '*Chal, paise nikal* (Come, take out your money)!' It was Bhikhu Sharma. Two more burly guys surrounded Horlicks.

'Bhikhu, please. This money is for my son's education. Please let me go,' pleaded Horlicks.

Bhikhu was the village goonda. A tall, muscular guy, he towered over Horlicks.

'Bhikhu Bhaiyya, I beg of you. I sold my buffalo to arrange this money. Please let me go.'

Bhikhu slapped Horlicks hard and snatched the money bag from him. A dazed Horlicks tried to cling to the bag. He was too weak to offer any resistance.

Bhikhu dragged him along. The other two goons rained punches and kicks on Horlicks.

'You weakling, your son doesn't deserve any education,' Bhikhu said, kicking Horlicks hard in the stomach.

All of a sudden, Horlicks shrieked and jumped on Bhikhu. Before anyone could realize what was happening, he bit down hard on Bhikhu's ear, making him scream in pain.

Horlicks did not stop till he had chewed off the entire earlobe. Bhikhu writhed in unbearable agony.

The two goons could not believe that a thin, timid fellow like Horlicks could wreak such havoc. They managed to get Bhikhu up and fled.

Horlicks picked up the bag and started moving towards the principal's office.

About half an hour later, Horlicks was accosted by two police constables.

'*Aaja, jeep mein baith ja* (Come, sit in the jeep). You are under arrest for attempting to murder Bhikhu Sharma,' said the policeman.

'But, sir, I am innocent. Bhikhu was the one who attacked me,' shouted Horlicks.

They replied, 'No one remains innocent after chewing off another person's ear. We have to follow the law.' His protests went unheeded, and he was soon put in Nawada Jail. And that is where he would meet Samant Pratap, the terror of Nawada.

Samant treated Horlicks like his younger brother. Finally, there was someone who treated Horlicks with respect. It wasn't long before he vowed to serve Samant with absolute devotion and loyalty. After escaping from Nawada Jail, Horlicks quickly realized that he was really good with guns. He started enjoying his kills. It gave him a high.

'Nobody will dare laugh at me. I am no longer weak,' he proclaimed.

Soon, he transformed from a meek, shy person to a dreaded killer and became Samant's most trusted man.

But some questions never went away, 'What have I done to myself? Will I be able to face my children when they learn the truth?'

He had become an excellent sharpshooter, but failed as a father. And somewhere deep down, he desperately wanted to redeem himself.

29

'Shekhpura Police Zindabad!'

16 July 2006

I reached home partly happy, partly disappointed. While I had succeeded in breaking one half of the Samant–Horlicks *jodi*, I was miffed that I still knew nothing about Samant's whereabouts. I knew Horlicks was telling the truth. He did not know Samant's location. We had been listening to his calls for almost forty days. Not once had he mentioned Samant's name.

I switched on the TV. There was a Bollywood *masala* movie on one of the channels. The cop in the movie danced on screen and had a great time chasing and arresting criminals. I smirked and wished the lives of real cops could be so much fun.

~

Kumar Sir reached the next day and called a press conference detailing Horlicks's arrest. There was frenzy; my office was swarming with media persons.

A very small place like Shekhpura had hardly any proper journalists. The *press-wallah*s got meagre salaries as there was nothing newsworthy in Shekhpura except the activities of Samant's gang. To make ends meet, most of the reporters had side businesses that ranged from running *kirana* shops to selling mobile phones. There were stringers too, who provided news and footage to the popular news channels for a certain price.

The stringers had a field day at the press conference. They got their camcorders, obsolete cameras—anything that could help them record. It was not every day that news from Shekhpura made headlines all over Bihar. The stringers made good money for the news of Horlicks's arrest.

'The Shekhpura police have arrested Horlicks Samrat after a painstaking operation. Samant's arrest is inevitable and his gang will be annihilated. I congratulate Amit Lodha and his team on this success,' Kumar Bharat announced to the media.

The press wanted to ask a lot of questions. Naturally, like everyone else, they were also flummoxed. How had Horlicks been arrested? What exactly was the operation? Who all were involved in the arrest? Should the policemen not be felicitated for this stunning success?

Kumar Sir left the office deliberately. He did not want to overshadow anyone. He knew it was our moment. More importantly, he knew that I was quite good with the press and could always use them to the advantage of the police.

'Sir, who are the people involved in the arrest of Horlicks? How was the operation planned?' were the questions thrown at me.

'Sorry, I can't reveal the names of the police personnel. It may jeopardize our mission. The operation was meticulously planned and brilliantly executed. Of course, with some inside help.'

'Inside help? You mean, someone from Samant's gang has helped you?' someone asked excitedly.

'Oh no, nothing like that. It was just a slip of the tongue.'

'*Arre, nahin*, sir, we will not tell anyone. Tell us the name of the person. Someone must have given you a tip-off. Otherwise the police could not have nabbed Horlicks so quickly. After all, Horlicks and Samant have been wanted for more than five years now.'

I had been quite sure the journalists would take the bait.

'You know, it is somebody very important in the gang, someone very close to Samant, who is helping us. We have promised him absolute clemency for his help. Please don't publish this information. This news should not go out of this office. I know I can trust all of you.'

'Yes, sir, absolutely. *Hum pe bharosa rakhiye* (Trust us).'

'Of course, I trust you people,' I said, smiling.

I knew this was the first thing the journalists would tell everyone the moment they left my office. I wanted this rumour to spread quickly. The gang members would start suspecting each other. They would start looking for the mole in their group. Fear would creep into the ranks and, as a natural consequence, Samant would become jittery. I wanted him to become paranoid.

I knew I would succeed with my trick. Everything is fair in love and policing.

'And one more announcement. Shekhpura will be liberated before 15 August. Samant will be behind bars before Independence Day.'

I spoke with the utmost confidence, bordering on arrogance. It was deliberate. There was pin-drop silence in the office for a moment, and then pandemonium broke out. Everyone had now been told that Samant's arrest was not just a possibility, it was imminent.

After the press-wallahs left the office, there was absolute commotion outside the Shekhpura police station. People from all over the town had gathered to get a glimpse of the notorious criminal of Shekhpura, Horlicks Samrat. Everyone was gathered around in a hushed silence. When they saw him in the lock-up finally, someone had the courage to shout, 'Shekhpura police zindabad!'

Every policeman beamed with pride. Except Rajesh Charan. He was a worried man now.

30

'Mard Hai to Aaja!'

Samant's mobile had been switched off for twenty days now. I wondered how I would get to him.

My question was answered soon—by the man himself! My official number flashed Samant's name, but this time he was calling me directly.

'*SP saale! Tujhe ghar mein ghus ke maaroonga* (I'll enter your house and kill you)!'

Samant was seething with rage. He showered the choicest of abuses on me.

'You bastard, Horlicks is my brother. How dare you interrogate him?' he started yelling like a madman.

'*Tera baap hoon main*. What will you do? Tell me your location. I will come and kill you right now. *Darpok aadmi*, you take pride in killing women and children. Come and fight like a man. You have met an *asli mard*, a real policeman,' I replied.

Whew! I was amazed at myself. I really enjoyed mouthing all these heavy-duty dialogues. Watching all those Bollywood potboilers had definitely rubbed off on me.

Surprisingly, I heard Samant sobbing. I was quite amazed that a heartless beast like him was showing emotion. It meant he was feeling vulnerable. I could not be happier.

Samant abused me some more and disconnected the phone. He had probably run out of expletives.

I thought back to my first day in IIT Delhi. How much I had changed from a '*fuddu*' to a fiery officer! I remembered standing outside the Nilgiri hostel with my suitcases and mattress. Two burly, uncouth-looking guys had gestured to me, '*Abe o fachche*, come here!'

I had looked around, quite confused.

'*Oye fachche*, we are talking to you,' they said as they waved at me again.

'*Chal, intro de* (Come on, introduce yourself),' said one of them with a snide smile.

'My name is Amit Lodha. I am from Jaipur. I have . . .'

One of the guys slapped me hard on my cheek before I could complete the sentence.

'Is this the way you speak to a senior? You will address us as sir. Give us your intro again.'

'My name is Amit, sir.'

I got slapped again.

'So you are Amit Sir,' shouted the seniors. This torture went on for a few minutes. I was on the verge of tears. It gave both of them a lot of sadistic pleasure.

'Haven't you met Sudhakar Sir?' they pointed to a short, muscular bodybuilder smoking a bidi in a corner. He was absolutely naked except for a tiny red *langot*, a loincloth, around his groin.

'*Wish kar sir ko*. Sudhakar Sir is the most senior student here. The course is for four years, but this is Sudhakar Sir's sixth year. He is our guru!'

I expected a few slaps from Sudhakar too, but he took pity on me. He just smiled and shooed me away. I found out that he had been failing continuously for the last two years. The other two rowdy seniors were brilliant students—one of them was JEE All India Rank 6!

I really wondered if I had come to the right place. Was this what IIT was really like? The ragging for the next fifteen days was quite bad, but undoubtedly, it toughened me up.

~

I immediately drove to the Chewara police station. I got Horlicks out of the lock-up. He seemed to have recovered from the sustained rounds of interrogations. We continued questioning him for hours, though I knew he would say nothing. But my purpose in questioning Horlicks was different this time.

So I waited. Finally, after a few hours, I got the call.

'*SP, kitna tang karoge mere bhai ko* (SP, how much will you trouble him)?' Samant said, pleadingly. 'I won't spare you. I will come after you and your family,' he continued, switching now to cursing and threats. Somehow, all the expletives sounded like sweet music to me. I knew that he was badly shaken.

'Samant, I'm waiting for you. The pleasure will be entirely mine,' I replied. This time, I avoided any histrionics.

Just five minutes later, I got a rude shock.

My phone buzzed again. Samant was making a call. 'Arre, Kailash Babu. What the hell are you doing? What kind of SP have you posted in Shekhpura? *Humko marwaiyega kya* (Do you want to get me killed)?' said Samant, livid with anger.

'*Arre, hum kya kare* (Arre, what can I do)? It was the government's decision to post this Lodha fellow in Shekhpura. *Bahut badmaash hai*. He doesn't listen to anyone. I cannot do anything. And do not call me ever again. You will get me in trouble too.'

I could not believe my ears. I had just heard Samant Pratap, the most wanted fugitive, talking to Kailash Samrat, one of the most senior police officers in Bihar!

I simply did not know how to react. This was blasphemous.

I called Kumar Sir and told him about the conversation. Uncharacteristically, even he showed a bit of surprise.

'He and Samant belong to the same community. And remember, Samant was close to many powerful people just a few months ago. *Hota hai*. Though extremely rare, these things happen. Every department has some black sheep.'

'Yes, sir.'

Of course, even if I wanted to nail the senior officer, I had no proper evidence. The call record of the official's number would have shown Samant's call as an incoming one. The officer could very well have claimed that his official number was in the public domain. Any person could call him. And anyway, Samant's SIM card had been issued under a fake name. Technically, I simply could not indict Kailash Samrat, just like Netaji.

First, Rajesh Charan, and now Kailash Samrat. I just could not trust anyone. At all.

But it seemed like Samant was not done calling people yet.

'*Hum kya kare, sir?* What do I do, Netaji? They have Horlicks now. Oh, my brother!' Samant sobbed again.

The dignified, polished voice paused for a moment.

'Samant Bhai, I had warned you so many times earlier. Just switch off your damn mobile phone.'

Samant remained silent and then cut the call. He had kept his mobile phone switched off for the past so many days. Or had he?

Well, not exactly. As I would later learn, he had got a new phone with a new SIM card. He had been cautious. That is why he did not call me using his new number. That would have been an instant giveaway. He kept pondering for a few minutes. 'How was Horlicks arrested? What mistake had he made?' Samant would probably never know the answer.

31

'Jai Chamundi Maa'

'How was Horlicks arrested?' Samant kept wondering. He was as surprised and shocked as anyone else. Even he had not known Horlicks's whereabouts since he left Shekhpura.

Samant started becoming suspicious of his gang members. A number of rumours were floating around in Shekhpura and Nawada, particularly after the press conference. They were good enough to make Samant paranoid.

'Did someone betray Horlicks? Could it happen to me again?'

He had been betrayed once before. A few years ago, he had been arrested because of Pankaj Singh.

Pankaj had decided that Samant had to be eliminated. But he was always surrounded by his men. Moreover, if the assassination attempt failed, Pankaj knew Samant wouldn't spare him. Pankaj was desperate to get him out of his way. He had been relegated to the background in his own gang. And his own men had no respect for him.

He wondered how he could get rid of Samant, and ultimately decided that there was only one way to finish him off—the police.

So he hatched a plan. 'Sir, Samant Pratap is going to visit his *rakhail*, his mistress, in Nalanda tonight. Yes, sir, it is confirmed. Please note the address,' said Pankaj in a call to the police station.

The SHO raided the sleazy hotel around 1 a.m. Samant gathered his clothes and quietly moved out with the police.

'Wait, let me handcuff him properly. He is too dangerous,' said the SHO.

Samant looked the SHO in the eye and spat.

'Bada Babu, I know who the bastard is who betrayed me. Tell him I will kill him soon.'

The SHO did not react. He did not know who had made the call, and he did not care. What mattered was that Samant was finally behind bars.

~

With Samant out of the way, Pankaj tried his best to increase his control over the gang, but he did not have Samant's charisma. Soon, his group disintegrated. Samant's community did not have any loyalty towards Pankaj. People like Lakha, Laddua and Raushan, some prominent gang members, waited for Samant to come back. Their wait did not last very long, as Samant broke out of jail not much later.

'Find that traitor, that bastard. I'll tear his heart out and drink his blood,' growled Samant. He had become even more beastly, more dangerous, after his escape from jail.

'*Bhai, mil jaayega* (Bhai, we will find him),' said Lakha.

Pankaj had been on the run ever since Samant's daring escape from Nawada Jail made headlines in Bihar. He knew that Samant would come looking for him.

~

The small 'nursing home' of the quack was not very difficult to find. All the gullies of Nawada were plastered with advertisements for the 'Khandani Hakim', an expert in 'men's problems'.

Pankaj was inside, hopefully waiting to consult the quack. After all, the quack had promised that Pankaj would regain his 'manhood' soon. The quack had managed to procure some rare *jadi booti*, or herbs, which promised to show instant results.

Suddenly, someone tapped his shoulder.

'*Kaise ho, Pankaj? Bhool gaye? Aao, tumhare gupt rog ka ilaaj karte hain* (How are you, Pankaj? Have you forgotten me? Come, let me treat your men's problem),' said Samant, his eyes smiling wickedly.

A bewildered Pankaj tried to run away but was restrained by the strong arms of Lakha and Raushan.

'Samant, Samant Bhai!' said Pankaj softly, shaking with fear. He remembered the murder of his cousin, Sarveshwar, in the Bhairav Mandir.

Samant gestured to Horlicks. Lakha covered Pankaj's mouth while Horlicks stabbed him deep in the abdomen and twisted the knife. Pankaj's intestines ruptured instantly and blood spurted out. Samant caught hold of Pankaj's *janeu*, the sacred thread, and started strangulating Pankaj with it.

'*Niklo, chalo, kaam ho gaya* (Let us go, our work is done),' said Raushan.

Samant looked at Pankaj. He could sense his life flowing out. He kicked him hard in the stomach. Pankaj grunted one last time. His lifeless body lay on the floor. The hakim was so scared, he soiled his dhoti. Samant laughed wickedly and left the clinic.

~

As Samant reminisced about Pankaj's murder, he remembered how it had been a satisfying kill.

But who had dared to betray him now?

32

'Phone Kyon Nahin Baj Raha Hai?'

Life in Shekhpura changed suddenly. There was a restless energy in the air that jolted the town out of its stupor. Everybody was waiting for the inevitable—Samant's arrest. That was the only thing everyone was talking about everywhere, be it at the barber shop or tea stall.

It seemed as though the Shekhpura police had been infused with a new energy. The policemen were basking in their glory, their pride visible in their attitude and demeanour. At the same time, Horlicks's arrest triggered a wave of panic among the ranks of Samant's gang. The rats had started to abandon ship even before it had sunk. Many of them turned themselves in to the police. Petty crime almost vanished from Shekhpura. I could now concentrate all my energies on my target.

~

I was sitting in the garden at my home. 'Sir, Chintamani Sahib has come to meet you,' said my orderly.

Chintamani Sahib was a very powerful and influential man in Bihar.

I wondered why he had come unannounced, that too, to my house. I had seen some officials flatter Chintamani no end. He, of course, enjoyed all the attention.

I saw Chintamani walking at a brisk pace towards me. He signalled to his bodyguard to stay back. In the garb typical of many politicians, he was wearing a crisp white kurta and pyjama. I was a little embarrassed. I had not had time to even change my shorts and T-shirt.

'Namaste, Chinatamaniji, how are you?'

Chintamani adjusted his glasses and smiled warmly. I could sense that he was mighty pleased.

'*Amitji, bahut badhai* (Amitji, congratulations)! I knew that you would arrest Horlicks.'

'Thank you, Chintamaniji.'

'I knew your reputation. It was I who had recommended your name for Shekhpura. You know, there was great resistance. Your own senior was not in favour of you being posted as SP anywhere.'

I knew he was right, but only partially. I was also posted to Shekhpura so that I could be the fall guy in case things went wrong again.

I also knew that Samant was a big thorn in Chintamani's side. Both belonged to communities that had a history of animosity. Samant was the messiah of the backward people, whereas Chintamani was the new-age leader of his clan. The disbanding of Samant's gang would pave the way to Chintamani's complete stranglehold of the area. He would then reign unchallenged.

Chintamani continued, 'Amitji, if you arrest Samant, I hope you get a very good post.'

I immediately snapped back. 'Chintamaniji, are you trying to entice me? You think I'm doing all this for some kind of prize posting?'

Chintamani's smile vanished. He was taken aback by my hostile reaction. No doubt, only a few months ago I had wanted to be in a big district. A relatively big, prestigious and challenging district is a coveted posting for any SP. But this was not the way I wanted it. And now my mindset had changed. I was no longer the old Amit. After my chance encounter with Ram Dular's nephew, trivial things like postings had stopped mattering to me. I felt like I had to nab Samant for Ram Dular's family.

Chintamani made a hasty retreat. I was happy that I was still capable of showing spunk and was living up to the ethos of the IPS.

~

Life at home was blissful. The weather had become quite pleasant because of the imminent rain. Tanu used to take Aishwarya out in the garden and give her a bath in an inflatable water tub. The staff was still singing and dancing around her. Aish loved all the attention. Meanwhile, I gave my attention to her famous namesake by watching her movies between listening to phone calls throughout the day.

I kept waiting for my phone to ring. Ring it did, but not for what I wanted.

'Hello, I am Richa Chawla calling from Delhi. I am calling in reference to the matrimonial ad you have posted on Shaadi. com.'

I was exasperated by these calls, yet I had to make polite conversation, lest one of the callers became my sister-in-law in the future.

'How much does your brother earn? See, I have been a finalist of *MTV Roadies*. I expect a certain standard of living, okay?'

I thanked Richa and smiled at the prospect of my mother having a contestant of *MTV Roadies* as her bahu.

'We are sorry. Our daughter spends more than what your brother earns. I don't think it is an equal match,' said the father of another girl. I patiently heard all this and managed to get through all these calls.

But my patience was now giving way to frustration. There was no activity on Samant's phone. A few days ago, he had dialled only a couple of people from his original number—SP, Shekhpura, that is, me, Kailash Samrat and Netaji. Now his mobile phone was switched off again. I had to find a way to trace him.

'*Tanu, phone kyon nahin baj raha hai* (Tanu, why are my phones not ringing)?' I asked my wife desperately.

'Why did you announce that you'll arrest Samant before 15 August? *Shekhpura ko azadi!* What was the need for such grandiose dialogues?' chided Tanu.

'It was a deliberate ploy. It's a game I'm playing with Samant. I need to break him down psychologically,' I replied. Now I needed to take the mind games up a notch.

33

The 'Encounter'

The day after Chintamani's visit, I called Rajesh Charan to the office. His usual confidence was missing. Charan saluted me nervously.

'Rajesh, I have sent a team of my trusted policemen to arrest Samant. I am hopeful of hearing the good news any time. Since you are the town officer in-charge, I expect you to see that no law and order problem arises. Keep Samant's supporters under control,' I said, without batting an eyelid.

Rajesh turned pale and asked me, 'Sir, who all are in the team?'

'Oh, that's a secret. Some of your own brave colleagues.'

Just then, my phone rang.

'Oh, excellent. Super news! Proud of you, my boys! Dump the dead body in the Ganges. All of Samant's sins will be washed away.'

I got up from my chair and raised my arms in jubilation.

'Rajesh, get some sweets. Samant has been killed. He fired at our boys and we shot him in retaliation.'

Rajesh was sweating profusely now.

'*Sir, badhai ho* (Sir, congratulations)!' he stammered.

I dismissed him.

After a few minutes, Ajit entered my chamber and stood at attention.

'Jai Hind, sir,' he said with a smile.

'Good job! You called my mobile at exactly the right time.'

'Sir, let us hope Rajesh falls into our trap.'

I looked at him and grinned. I had started enjoying this game of hide-and-seek. It was only a matter of time before he was caught.

All hell broke loose in Samant's gang. Every phone under observation had only one conversation going on—whether Samant had actually been killed by the police.

A few months ago, the gang members would have laughed at the mere suggestion of the police even coming close to Samant. But now they believed that he could be killed in a clash with the police. The fear of the police was palpable. The tide had turned totally in the last few days.

'*Sahib ko maar diya kya* (Have they killed Sahib)?'

'Has Samant Bhai been killed in a police encounter?'

'No, no. Someone told me that he escaped.'

'I think he has been badly injured. He got hit by three bullets.'

'I think he is critical. He has lost one eye.'

Our ploy worked only partially. Though Samant's supporters were very jittery, none of them knew anything about Samant. They were equally in the dark.

34

'Network Nahin Aa Raha Hai'

Once I got home, I went over the case again in my mind. Samant's mobile phone was switched off. He had not put any new SIM card in his handset. I had even run the IMEI number many times, but got no results. But there was one aspect I hadn't focused on yet. Samant knew quite a lot about the way I had interrogated Horlicks. Someone had been telling Samant all the details.

Even if he had gone incommunicado, he had to remain in touch with someone. Someone he trusted with his life. Samant must be desperate to know what was happening in Shekhpura. He must be even more anxious right now as he was cornered and isolated.

But then, I had not heard any relevant conversation even mentioning him for the last so many days. We were already monitoring the calls of many of his associates. I kept turning these details over in my mind when I realized that we had put only the numbers of his gang members on observation. What if he was talking to some other people, some other supporters who did not have police records?

Samant had kept his original number switched off for the last one month, or used it very rarely. After he was warned about the possible tracking of his phone, he must have changed his mobile phone and SIM number, in all probability. But why would his family members, his friends and supporters change their numbers? I realized I should put the numbers of those people on observation. At least a few of them must be using the same numbers.

I immediately dialled the BSNL office and asked for the call details of Samant's original number for the last three months, as I had gone through only tower locations so far.

In half an hour, the faxes started rolling out. I had kept quite a few extra fax paper rolls. Soon, they were all exhausted. Tanu lay down with the children and put them to sleep.

Our bedroom was littered with fax papers. I started going through every single call. It was a very tedious process. I went through the call details of March and April, sitting down with a red fluorescent marker. I started circling the numbers Samant was frequently in touch with, both incoming and outgoing.

The papers were getting scattered, so I switched off the fan. The voltage was quite low, as always. The AC was taking its own sweet time to cool the room. My little boy, Avi, slept soundly, but baby Aish started throwing tantrums. Her dress was soaked in sweat in just a few minutes. Tanu picked Aish up and started rocking her in her lap.

After every half an hour, I took a break. As Tanu was still up, we joked and laughed at silly things or reminisced about the beautiful memories of our still young romance. We played with our children and smiled affectionately. I had never felt happier. Here we were, sitting on the floor in our nightclothes, both of us enjoying every moment. This was our world. Nothing else mattered.

But I had to keep working on the task at hand. After I painstakingly circled countless numbers on the sheets, I categorized them according to the frequency with which they appeared. All of it wasn't completed that night. It took me almost three days to zero in on about ten numbers that were most frequently in contact with Samant. Today, an SP's office has a special cell to monitor all calls and sift through data. We have advanced software to provide answer to any query, any permutation and combination, within minutes, if not seconds.

I looked at my handiwork with great satisfaction. I sent all the numbers to the Home Secretary's office for permission to put them under observation. I also bought five more mobile sets with the SS fund. My table was full of mobile phones and my secret service fund was being depleted.

The permission for parallel listening came quickly from the Home Secretary's office. Things get much easier when you start getting results.

With Horlicks's arrest, I had been spared the torture of listening to his idiotic romantic conversations. But now I had so many more numbers to listen to.

I gave one mobile set to Ajit to keep a tab on. Ranjan also got his share of mobile phones. I kept two more new phones with me. Those sets were earmarked specifically for the numbers Samant called most often.

I had done the hard work. Now I waited for the results. I had not been this anxious even for the UPSC exam results.

A week passed. All the new numbers were under observation, but we gathered no worthwhile information.

~

My mobile phone was vibrating. I took it out from under the pillow. I was delighted. Samant was calling someone from his old BSNL number. There was an activity on Samant's phone after so long. I could not have been happier. I moved to the other room quickly without colliding into anything.

'*Sanjay, kya chal raha hai* (Sanjay, what is happening in Shekhpura)?' asked a worried Samant.

'Bhaiyya, why have you called? *Hum ne mana kiya tha na* (I had told you not to). And why are you using your old phone?'

'Arre, bhai, the new Airtel SIM was not working. So I just thought of trying your number using my old BSNL number. *Iska network aa raha hai* (This one has network).'

'Everything has changed in Shekhpura. The police have become very active. Horlicks's arrest has been a big setback. The SP works very secretively. It's almost impossible to find out his next move.'

'Hmm. You are right. Could you find out who the traitor is?'

'Nahin, bhaiyya. It could be anyone. Suraj, Laddua, I don't know. Anyone can betray us. You have to be very careful. I hope nobody knows where you are.'

'No, no, nobody knows my location. I can't trust anyone. But how long will I keep hiding? There has to be an end to this.'

Both Sanjay and Samant kept quiet. I knew there was only one end to it. Samant's arrest.

I checked the clock. It was 4.47 a.m. Even at such an early hour, when dawn was just about to break, Samant was under stress. It seemed I had robbed him of his sleep.

My day could not have started better. It was clear that Samant was still using his old phone too, though only for emergencies. I was happy that I had continued keeping his old BSNL number under observation.

I called Ranjan immediately.

'Have you heard of any Sanjay? Anyone by this name who's close to Samant?'

'Sir, Sanjay is a very common name,' said a sleepy Ranjan, 'but I'll try to find out.' He must have cursed me for never letting him rest peacefully.

I waited for the clock to strike 10 a.m. I immediately called Sharmaji, the jovial GM of BSNL, Patna.

'Sharmaji, sorry for bothering you. I need the call details and location of a number. I have sent the number to you by SMS. You can note it down too.'

'Yes, sirji, I saw your SMS. You sent it quite early—I think around 5 a.m. The number is 9413@#$343, isn't it?'

'Yes, Sharmaji. Please, I need the details ASAP.'

'You will get it in your inbox in ten minutes. Please tell me when you arrest Samant Pratap.'

I was a bit surprised.

'How do you know?'

'*Arre, sir, hum bhi toh Bihar mein rehte hain* (Arre, sir, we live in Bihar too). We keep reading about your work in the newspapers. Moreover, everyone in my office knows you too. No other SP calls us almost every day. I am sure, with your zeal, you will arrest Samant soon.'

I thanked him and felt absolutely reinvigorated. I turned on my laptop, munching on the burnt toast I liked, with a liberal dose of butter. My inbox showed an email from BSNL.

Samant's BSNL number did not show any activity, apart from the one call that he had made in the morning to Sanjay. So it was obvious that he was using an Airtel number now. This is what he had told Sanjay too. Another column of the Excel sheet showed his location as MP Raj or Maheshpur Raj in Pakur. I wondered if it was his temporary hideout or a permanent location. And who was this Sanjay fellow?

Almost all the numbers I had painstakingly identified, and which were under observation, were issued against fake identities. It was quite common in Bihar during those days. SIM card distributors hardly ever checked the bank details, driving licence, etc. In fact, some of the vendors specialized in issuing cards to dubious people. A whole racket flourished.

Luckily, Sanjay had got that SIM card in his own name. We checked his background. He was a simple schoolteacher with absolutely no police record. I dug around a bit and found out, through my sources, that he had looked up to Samant as his elder brother, right from his childhood. His loyalty to Samant was unwavering. It did not matter that Samant was a beast now.

I immediately put Sanjay's number on parallel listening too and monitored each call over the next three or four days. Sanjay's conversations did not even have a mention of Samant. I started thinking hard. There had to be another way Sanjay was talking to Samant.

~

Paulo Coelho wrote in his bestseller *The Alchemist* that if you desperately desire something, the entire universe conspires to help you achieve it. This was definitely coming true for me. Finally, one of Sanjay's conversations revealed how Samant was communicating.

'Hello, Sanjay Bhaiyya. *Sahib se baat kaise hogi* (When can I talk to him)?' the woman's voice was familiar now, as if I had known her my entire life.

In a feudal state, any person of some importance immediately assumes the title of 'Sahib'. Even many men preferred to be called 'Sahib' by their wives.

'Shanti Bhabhi, can't you be patient? Let Samant Bhai call. Then I'll make you talk to him. And why have you called me on this number? I had specially given you another number.'

'Arre, *kya kare*, both the numbers are saved under your name. I think I dialled your original number by mistake. Next time I will call on your "special" number. *Kasam se.*'

Once again, lady luck had smiled on me. Shanti Devi would be the reason for Samant's fall. She had already helped us with Horlicks's arrest. I promised myself that I would personally thank her the day I arrested Samant.

I asked for the call details of Sanjay's number and circled Shanti Devi's number. I was surprised that she had another number, apart from the one I had been observing ever since she had been in Deoghar. This meant that either she had had one more SIM or she had bought a new one.

I got Shanti's new number and had a feeling that I had seen it somewhere. I took out the list of the new numbers I had made. I glanced through the list and found the same number! Shanti Devi had been in touch with Samant for a long time. In fact, I had inadvertently put that number also under observation.

I quickly called Ajit.

'Ajit, I had given you one mobile set for parallel listening. Have you heard anything of relevance?'

Ajit looked at me sheepishly.

'*Sir, ek aurat baat karti hai* (Sir, a woman keeps talking). I could not make out much. She mostly talks about useless things.'

'Get the phone immediately and give it to me,' I said.

I wish I had tracked the calls on that number myself and not given it to Ajit. What if I had missed some important conversation?

But there was no point crying over spilt milk.

35

'How Do I Turn Off the Gas?'

I charged the mobile that I was using to track Shanti's number and waited. After a few hours, Shanti called.

'*Hello, Sanjay Bhaiyya, kab baat karvaayenge* (Hello, Sanjay Bhaiyya, how long do I have to wait)?'

'Bhabhi, I told you to be patient. He will call by 5 p.m. today. You stay home. I'll call you.'

I instantly called Sharmaji and gave him Shanti Devi's number.

'Sharmaji, please give me the call details of 9413***877.'

'*Itni si baat* (Such a small thing)? It will be done right away,' replied Sharmaji.

I needed to find out Sanjay's 'special' number from Shanti Devi's outgoing logs. I scanned the records and found the number in the next ten minutes. Luckily, that was a BSNL number too. It was going to be a busy day for Sharmaji.

I checked my watch. It was already 3.40 p.m. I needed to put Sanjay's new number on parallel listening right away. I dialled Sharmaji again.

'Sharmaji, I need a personal favour. I'm sure you will not disappoint me.'

'Arre, sir, anything for you. *Aadesh karein* (Please command).'

Sharmaji was in a good mood, as always.

'I need you to put a number on parallel listening right now. I am expecting a call on that number in the next one hour.'

'Okay, sir, it will be done,' said Sharmaji, with his usual cheerfulness.

I felt relieved.

'Thank you so much, Sharmaji. I am very grateful to you. Please do let me know if I can be of any help to you ever.'

'No, sir. No need to thank me. Just arrest that fellow. It will be a big service to the people.'

'Surely, Sharmaji.'

I have always believed in developing relationships and have benefited tremendously from my excellent relations with people. I had never met Sharmaji, yet we had developed a bond just from talking over the phone. Both of us were sincere and true to our jobs. That was probably the reason for our rapport.

~

At 4.57 p.m., my mobile phone rang. It was Sanjay's number. I pressed the green button. I thanked Sharmaji in my heart for his tremendous help.

It was the same husky, rasping voice that had threatened me just a few days ago. I would never forget Samant's voice.

'*Sanjay, kya khabar? Shanti bagal mein hai kya* (Sanjay, how is everything? Is Shanti around)?'

'Pranaam, bhaiyya. Things will be all right once you come back. Shanti Bhabhi has been desperate to talk to you. I will take the phone to her. Just stay on the phone.'

In an instant, I understood Samant's modus operandi. It was a simple yet intelligent trick. Whenever Samant wanted to talk to anyone, he called on Sanjay's phone. Then Sanjay would take it to that person. Samant and Sanjay had both bought new SIM cards, obviously under false names. Now that I had Sanjay's 'special' new number, I would get Samant's 'special' number soon.

No one, absolutely no one, knew about those two numbers. There was no question of the police tracking them. Samant must have somehow come to know that the police could determine many details from a mobile number. He was intelligent enough to understand that the police was keeping a watch on a number of his associates, friends and relatives.

His days in Nawada Jail must have exposed him to the methods of the police. Netaji had also warned him in no uncertain terms. He had to be extremely careful after Horlicks's arrest. He knew that the police was after him like a pack of bloodthirsty hounds.

What he did not know was that I was working alone, like a tiger. And I was now obsessed. My only aim in life was to put him behind bars.

Samant was a worthy adversary. Both of us had taken entirely different paths to get here, and were facing each other head-on. While I had grown up as a meek, under-confident adolescent and then gone on to study at elite institutes where I had developed character, Samant was a sociopath, an arrogant beast. He loathed the upper echelons of society. He had always been uncouth. When I had reached my professional peak as the SP of Nalanda, Samant's terrifying reputation as a ganglord had grown just miles away in Nawada at the same time. Many times, both of us had made headlines together in the newspapers— Samant for killing people and I for saving victims. Even the number of people we had killed and saved was nearly the same.

I heard Shanti Devi come on the line, absolutely animated.

'*Kya, Sahib, kab se wait kar rahi hoon* (What is this, Sahib? I've been waiting for so long). You call so rarely nowadays. I miss you so much.'

'*Meri jaan*, I also miss you so much. Let me take care of that bloody SP Lodha. Then I will come and take you in my arms. Forever.'

Samant was having an affair with Shanti Devi! This was more than a Bollywood scandal.

I immediately called Sharmaji and asked for the call details of Sanjay's number. The email popped up on my laptop screen in ten minutes. I moved the cursor down the Excel sheet to one row: 4.57 p.m., when an incoming call had lasted six minutes, twenty-four seconds. This was what I was looking for. I saw a number in the adjacent column. Finding the ten digits was like being handed the lucky numbers of a jackpot. I was thrilled beyond words. Now that I had Samant's new number, I was back in the game.

I called the Airtel office for this number's call details. Simultaneously, I sent that number to the Home Secretary's office. Within a few hours, I was firmly in the driver's seat. I had almost every detail I needed to start hunting down the man again.

The call details were startling. The entire record had only one number in the outgoing and incoming columns, that of Sanjay. Samant was being extremely careful. Sanjay had a new SIM card too, just for talking to Samant. Purely by chance, Shanti had called on Sanjay's original number and led me to these new numbers.

Samant called Sanjay regularly, mostly to talk to Shanti, it seemed. She was back in her village after Horlicks's arrest. She was still surprised that the police could arrest Horlicks from their house in Deoghar. How had the police reached there? Who could have leaked the address? But she sounded happier here. From the conversations I had eavesdropped on and the information I had gathered, it seemed like she had never loved Horlicks, but only lusted for Samant. I would later come to know that Shanti was attracted to Samant's violent tendencies and bad boy antics. Horlicks was too straightforward a person for her as he did not have Samant's charisma. And who knows, she might even be aware of the affair between Horlicks and Sulekha!

From the details I received from Airtel, it was clear that Samant's location was constant. The Airtel SIM was in the Tower C area of Nalhati in Birbhum, West Bengal. This intrigued me because his BSNL number had shown his location to be Pakur just a few days ago. How could he be in two places?

I woke Ranjan up from his sleep again. He had just returned from Ranchi after tending to his ill wife. His wife's manic depression was increasing day by day. The doctor had attributed her condition to loneliness. A policeman's life is tough, but it is even worse for his family. An average policeman spends most of his time away from them. The postings are usually in far-flung areas which do not have basic amenities. Unfortunately, because of the nature of the job, the distance between a policeman and his family often increases in more than one way.

I briefed Ranjan about the new developments. He sounded happy to hear of the progress. He could see that I was pursuing Samant with all my might, that I had become obsessed. He knew that I would win this game and also that he was playing a very important role in it. Raju and Krishna were the foreign players in this franchise, just like those in the IPL now.

'Sir, we will leave for Birbhum tonight. It is a very densely populated town. We will have some difficulty in communicating as the local language is Bengali. It will take us some time to get information about Samant's location,' he said when he realized what I had in mind.

'What do Raju and Krishna have to report?'

'Sir, Samant does not have any acquaintances or relatives in Pakur or Birbhum. They are also surprised by his choice of hiding places.'

'Ranjan, Samant is totally rattled right now. He knows he can't trust anyone. Naturally, going to an entirely new location and living incognito makes sense.'

'Yes, sir.'

'Drive safe, Ranjan.'

Ranjan smiled and sat in the Bolero.

~

'Listen, Chun, I have put some milk on the gas to boil. Could you please turn off the gas?' Tanu shouted from the bathroom.

I got up lazily and walked to the kitchen. I looked at the stove and examined the knobs. The milk was getting hot, nearly boiling, but I suddenly realized I did not know how to turn off the gas. I panicked as the milk was almost on the verge of boiling over. I ran to the bathroom and banged on the door.

'Tanu! Tanu!' I shouted hysterically. The kids looked at me with amusement.

'What? Why are you banging the door?' Tanu asked, wiping the soap from her face.

'I don't know how to turn off the gas. Should I turn the knob right or left?'

'What? You still haven't turned it off? The milk would have spilled over by now.'

She put on her gown and ran to the kitchen. There was milk all over the stove. Disaster had struck. Tanu looked at me with mock anger.

'So much for your IIT engineering.'

This really pissed me off. 'Don't you make fun of me. And they don't teach you how to boil milk in IIT!' I shot back.

She just smiled at me and wrapped me in her arms.

36

'You Have Won a Nokia Mobile Phone'

Nalhati is a small town in the Birbhum district of West Bengal, located near the Bengal–Jharkhand border. According to Hindu mythology, it is here that the *nala*, or throat, of Goddess Shakti had fallen. The Shaktipeeth Nalhateshwari temple is thus named after it. Ranjan and company camped in the vicinity of the temple.

'It is proving to be very difficult finding Samant in Nalhati, sir. I'm a bit confused too. How can Samant be in two locations at the same time? You told me that his BSNL mobile phone showed Pakur as the location, while the Airtel phone's location was Nalhati on the same day, at almost the same time,' said a perplexed Ranjan.

Ranjan's question was quite valid. I had thought about it earlier too. I asked my PA to get an enlarged map of Bengal and Jharkhand.

'*Sir, Shekhpura mein kahaan se map milega* (Sir, where would we get a map in Shekhpura)? We don't get even the basic things here.'

I called Ranjan again and asked him to go to Pakur. It was a much smaller town in Jharkhand. If at all Samant was there, it would be easier to locate him.

The record of his conversations with Shanti confirmed that Samant was static. He must have rented a house or he was staying at some very close associate's place, I surmised.

That day, I came back home early for lunch. There was not much work for me to do.

It was an interesting paradox. I had practically no crimes to solve, but I was chasing the most wanted criminal in Bihar. I decided to take a short nap and lay down on the carpet in the drawing room. My back had started hurting again, and the pain was particularly bad in the hip joints. I just hoped it would subside in a day or two, as always.

I had hardly shut my eyes when my phone buzzed. It was a very excited Ranjan at the other end.

'Sir, sir, I have to tell you something very interesting.'

I waited with bated breath.

'Sir, the two tower locations of Airtel and BSNL . . .'

'Yes, yes, go on,' I said.

'Sir, the tower locations are overlapping in a particular area. My wife called me a few minutes ago on my BSNL number. My mobile phone showed Tower C of MP Raj, Pakur. Then the call got disconnected. I tried to call her back, but the call kept dropping. I borrowed Raju's phone and was about to dial my wife when I saw that the screen said "Airtel Tower A, Birbhum". I rechecked both the mobile phones; they showed the two different towers that you had made me note down, but at the same location.'

My back pain almost vanished because of the happiness coursing through me.

It was simple logic. I could not believe that this had not occurred to me earlier.

Apparently, Samant was living somewhere at the border of Birbhum and Pakur. His BSNL SIM was in the immediate range of Tower C of MP Raj of Pakur and the nearest Airtel tower was in Nalhati Birbhum, just a few kilometres away across the border from Pakur. A mobile phone tower's range is almost 30 kilometres. The two towers must not be very far from each other. Naturally, the effective radiuses of the Airtel and BSNL towers overlapped in a certain area. Samant was right in that zone. Now we just needed to zero in on him. But even that area was big enough to make it difficult to find Samant.

I had already found out that Samant's new Airtel SIM card had been issued in the name of one Pankaj Saini, a resident of Dumaria village, Pakur.

I asked Ranjan if Raju or Krishna knew any of Samant's associates by that name. They answered in the negative.

I then instructed Ranjan and Krishna to check Dumaria village. When they called me later that day, they said there was no one called Pankaj Saini in that village. We had to find this man. He could be a vital cog in our investigation. He could be one of Samant's associates and might have helped Samant hide in Pakur. Or else Samant had procured a SIM card using Pankaj's identity. I had to make every move with great deliberation now.

I managed to get the address and phone number of the SIM card vendor from the Airtel office. I asked my telephone operator to dial the number of the shop so that I could sound more officious.

Many times during my initial days in the IPS, when I dialled someone's number myself, people thought I was playing a prank. They would think that an SP, being such a senior officer, would never dial anyone's number personally. They expected me to call people only through my PA or telephone operator. Some of the other things they expected me to do were wait for my driver to open the door of the car or to keep finding excuses to scold someone. Thankfully, I had this person called Tanu to keep me firmly on terra firma. Once, during my probationary days, she heard me shouting at a hapless constable, '*Pankhe se latka doonga* (I'll hang you from the fan). I'll teach you a lesson. Blah, blah.'

'Is this the way you talk to a subordinate?' she asked.

'Tanu, this is the way a police officer is supposed to talk. Don't you see, some of my "*kadak*" (tough) colleagues speak like this? Otherwise how are we supposed to keep our juniors disciplined? They should fear us. Only then will people think that I am a strict officer,' I replied.

'They should not fear you, they should respect you—for your work, your ethics,' Tanu quickly retorted. 'And what is the need to shout at your juniors? Your power lies in your rank. You just need to sign a piece of paper and take disciplinary action against any errant personnel.'

'Yeah, yeah, you are right.' I had no option but to agree.

'Wait, I'm not finished. Remember, they don't work under you; they work with you.'

'Phew, that was one heavy-duty speech!' I muttered to myself, but I knew she was right, again. I thanked God for her.

~

'Jai Mata Telecom?' asked my telephone operator.

'*Ji, haan,*' replied the proprietor lazily.

'*SP Sahib, Shekhpura, baat karenge.*'

I heard a chair scrape back; the shopkeeper was probably sitting up straight now.

'Hello, I am the SP of Shekhpura. During our investigation, we learnt that an Airtel SIM card was issued by you on 3 July in the name of one Pankaj Saini. You issued the SIM card without verifying the actual details.'

'Sir, so many people come each day. I must have made a mistake,' he said, sounding very worried.

'Then get ready to pay for your mistake. Do you know that issuing a SIM card without verification is an offence punishable under Sections 419, 465 and 471 of the IPC?'

The proprietor must have been sweating at the other end.

'Listen, if you don't want to go to jail, help us trace this Pankaj fellow.'

'Sir, I have just checked the records. Luckily, in the customer form, he has written his other mobile number.'

'Then call him to your shop. Tell him that his documents have to be verified again,' I said with authority.

'But, sir, why would he come when he got the SIM card on forged documents in the first place?'

'Yeah, yeah,' I said, trying to cover for my silly idea. 'Then tell him that his mobile number 9318**6740 has won a bumper prize—a free mobile phone and free talk time for three months from Airtel. He will definitely come to claim his prize.'

'Are you sure he will come, sir?'

'Absolutely.'

~

'Is that Pankaj Saini?' asked the SIM card vendor.

'*Bol raha hoon* (This is him speaking).'

'*Badhai ho* (Congratulations)! You've won a free Nokia mobile set.'

'Me? What for?' asked a surprised Pankaj.

'You have won a lucky draw organized by Airtel. Please come to Jai Mata Telecom and collect your phone and gift voucher tomorrow before 12 noon. This scheme will lapse after noon.'

Pankaj pondered silently.

Finally, after a few seconds, he asked, 'Does the mobile set have a camera?'

The vendor called me to tell me about the meeting he had fixed up with Pankaj. I smiled triumphantly. I knew the lure of a free mobile phone with a camera would be too much for anyone. Mobile phones with a camera was quite a big thing during those days.

Ranjan, Raju and Krishna waited at Jai Mata Telecom. Around noon, a tall, lean, young man appeared. Excitement was written all over his face.

'Namaste. I'm Pankaj Saini, the winner of the lucky draw.'

'Yeah, sure. Did you buy a SIM card from us on 3 July?' the shopkeeper asked Pankaj.

Ranjan was all ears.

'No, why should I buy another SIM card? I haven't come to your shop in the last one month,' said an indignant Pankaj.

'Oh, then I'm sorry. We can't give you this prize.'

'You idiot, then why did you waste my time? I missed my favourite TV serial just to come here.'

Pankaj abused him for a good four or five minutes and turned around.

Ranjan called me immediately and explained the situation.

'Ranjan, either this Pankaj guy really doesn't know about the new SIM card that Samant is using or he is feigning ignorance. If he is Samant's associate, he might be smart enough not to fall into our trap,' I said.

'Then what am I supposed to do, sir? He's about to board a bus.'

'Follow him. If we're lucky, you might be led straight to the lion's den!'

The Bolero followed the bus through the dusty lanes of Pakur for around half an hour. A weary and angry Pankaj got down and started walking towards a cluster of houses. Ranjan and company followed at a distance.

Pankaj entered a house and closed the door. Ranjan surveyed the area. Everything seemed calm.

Raju went to the *paan-wallah* near the bus stand and casually inquired about Pankaj.

'Arre, bhaiyya, does any Pankaj Saini live here? I am from the Airtel mobile company. I have to give him a surprise gift,' said Raju.

'Pankaj? Oh, he runs a cable business. He's not doing well; he's under heavy debt. Your gift will not be enough to solve his problems,' replied the paan-wallah.

'Does he live alone? Do any outsiders come to meet him?'

'He lives alone. No one comes to see him. Why are you asking questions? Are you a policeman?'

Raju laughed, 'Do I look like a policeman?'

'*Lagte toh gunde ho* (You look like a scoundrel).'

Raju's smile turned into a frown. He swore at the paan-wallah and came back to Ranjan and Krishna. All three of them concluded that Samant was not staying in Pankaj's house. Either Pankaj did not have any connection with Samant or he was smart enough not to have Samant stay with him.

Right from the beginning of our mission, I was very clear that I would not arrest or interrogate any person unless I was absolutely sure that the person would lead us to Samant. I did not want to alert Samant in any way. There was no point questioning Pankaj Saini then.

~

'*Kahe phone kiya, Sanjaywa* (Why did you call, Sanjay)?'

'Bhai, I need to speak to you. It's important,' said Sanjay.

'Wait, let me go to the terrace. This bloody phone doesn't work properly inside the house during the day. Surprisingly, it's quite all right in the night.'

'*Okay, bhaiyya, hold karte hain* (Okay, bhaiyya, I'll hold).'

Samant reached the terrace and said, '*Haan, ab bolo. Network abhi theek hai* (You can talk now. The network is strong).'

'Shanti bhabhi is desperate to meet you. She wants to know your address.'

My heart skipped a beat. Was it going to be that easy, after all this time?

I waited for Samant to speak. I prayed to all the gods to make him say the address.

37

'Ringa Ringa Rojej'

'*Marwayegi woh paagal aurat* (That crazy woman will get me killed)! Has she gone mad? I am having such a tough time surviving and now she wants to create more trouble for me. Lie to her and tell her that I'll come see her soon. I can't come till this SP is transferred. Till then, I have to remain in hiding,' shouted Samant into the phone.

'Samant Bhai, what if the SP does not get transferred?'

'*Abe saale, Sanjaywa, shubh shubh bol* (Hey Sanjay, don't jinx it).'

I could clearly sense the frustration in Samant's voice. The undisputed don, the kingmaker, was sounding like a pale shadow of himself.

I knew that Samant was cornered. He could do nothing, at least not till he was away hiding in some hole in Pakur. Wars cannot be won by generals in exile. They have to lead the army from the front.

I was disappointed that Samant had not revealed his address. The good news was that Samant's mobile location was static. He had not moved. I was confident it was only a matter of days now.

I had managed to get the maps of the Bengal and Jharkhand borders. They were not very detailed, but good enough for me to mark out Samant's possible location. Using the grid reference, I calculated that the circled area was not more than 10 square kilometres. It could still be a difficult task finding someone in that area. But I looked at the positive side—I was within striking distance.

From the other room, I heard 'Ringa ringa rojej, pakit fool of pojej, husha, bussa'. Tanu listened in horror as Avi recited the nursery rhyme 'Ring a Ring o' Roses'. Tanu had started sending Avi to the only nursery school in Shekhpura.

'Oh my God, what kind of an accent have you picked up?' cried Tanu.

'Why are you being so serious? He's sounding so cute,' I said.

'Come on! Would you like him to learn the wrong pronunciations of words?'

'Then what will you do?'

'I'll home-school him, and I am not expecting any help from you.'

'Tanu, this is unfair. Why do you assume that I won't help you with anything? It's just that I am so busy.'

'Please, please. Busy? Who used to watch the stock market on CNBC the entire day? And who's watched *Rambo* and the James Bond films countless times?'

'Oh, those action movies give me an adrenaline rush. It is crucial for my kind of work.'

'My dear Bihari James Bond, you won't get any beautiful woman to support you in your mission. Except a woman with stretch marks on her belly and stitches from a C-section.'

I smirked. 'Tanu, you know it was just friendly banter that day. I am sorry about that. Now don't make me feel guilty each time.'

'Dear hubby, I forgot! You have that Beauty Kumari too.'

She laughed uncontrollably, rolling on the bed in her mirth.

Avi's Bihari accent did not surprise me at all. It was natural for him to pick up certain words and pronunciations from the local dialect. It was the same for the children of my batchmates who were posted to other parts of India.

It is the beauty of India's rich culture and diversity that languages and dialects change from one state to another. In fact, many words sound entirely different as one travels just a few hundred kilometres in the same state!

My own batchmates who were from south India, and did not know a word of Hindi, had quickly learnt the language and spoke it with great fluency. Their vocabulary had become better than that of people who had been speaking the language all their lives. They had even learnt the choicest of Hindi slangs, which sounded quite funny with their distinct twang.

~

Samant was in a particularly romantic and rather horny mood that night. He asked Sanjay to have him talk to Shanti Devi.

'*Kya haal hai, meri jaan* (How are you, my love)? I am missing you very badly. I wish I could take you in my arms and love you all night.'

'What? I can't hear you. There is so much disturbance. What kind of noise is coming from behind you?' asked Shanti Devi.

'Oh, this is the honking of those bloody trucks. Their sound doesn't let me sleep the whole night,' said Samant in an irritated tone.

I could clearly hear the blaring of horns and the typical sound trucks make. Samant was definitely living very close to a highway.

Thoughts churned in my head as Shanti and Samant continued their amorous talk.

Once the call ended, I dialled Ranjan's number. 'You told me about the location where the towers of Airtel and BSNL overlapped, right?'

'Yes, sir. Samant must be somewhere close to that area. But how do we find him? There must be hundreds of houses in that radius.'

'Ranjan, after having listened to his calls for the past few days, I am sure he is living somewhere close to the highway or a busy road. There can be only a few roads or highways in the area that we've identified. Let me know by tomorrow afternoon about all the possible highways or roads where heavy vehicles ply. Also tell me if there are any residential areas along those highways or roads.'

I surmised that there would not be many such residential areas. People prefer to live away from highways because nobody wants to hear the cacophony of trucks and buses, and also because it is unsafe to reside there.

I was quite sure that our target zone would be reduced further.

'Sir, there is only one highway in our zone. It goes from Pakur to Asansol,' said Ranjan the next day.

'Go on,' I listened intently.

'And even better, there are just a few hundred houses along the NH on one side. There are only shops and commercial establishments on the opposite side.'

'Excellent, Ranjan. Just stay put. We should have some good news very soon.'

I knew the stars were aligning in my favour. The chance failure of the Airtel network that morning, Shanti Devi's illicit affair with Samant, the honking on the NH—those were all beautiful clues leading me closer to my quarry.

I knew I was very close to finding Samant's exact hideout. I just needed to find his locality. I had a radical idea. But somehow, I was certain it would succeed.

I picked up my private phone and made the most outrageous call of my life. I dialled Samant's Airtel number.

'*Halloo, Samant Bhai bol rahe ho* (Hello, is this Samant Bhai)?' I spoke in a thick Bihari accent. Surprisingly, I was absolutely calm.

But I think Samant's heart must have skipped a beat. I could sense the tension even hundreds of miles away.

'*Hello, hello, kaun bol raha hai* (Hello, who's calling)?'

I remained quiet.

'Hello, hello,' Samant was desperate now.

'Haan, Samant Bhai, I want to tell you something about Horlicks's arrest,' I spoke with utmost confidence.

'What do you know? *Tum ho kaun, saala* (Who are you)?'

'I can't hear you properly. It seems there is some network problem. I'll call you again.'

I disconnected the phone, quite pleased with the Bihari accent I had pulled off. My plan was audacious, but I was confident that the call would have a profound effect on Samant. Exactly the effect I wanted.

~

Samant was sweating profusely now. 'Who would call me? Nobody knows this number except Sanjay. And who would know the details of Horlicks's arrest?'

His mind was a kaleidoscope of questions, all unanswered. He immediately called Sanjay.

'Sanjay, you asshole, you bastard! Whom have you given my number to? You traitor!'

'Bhaiyya, mind your language. I have grown up with you. You know I can lay down my life for you. And you are suspecting me? Of what? At least tell me what has happened,' Sanjay spoke with absolute conviction. Though he was not a member of Samant's gang, Sanjay was extremely loyal to Samant. He was one of the select few who could argue with Samant.

Samant explained the call in detail to Sanjay, who replied, 'Samant Bhaiyya, I have not given your number to anyone. Why would I share it with anyone? I'll guard your safety with my life.'

'*Mujhe maaf kar de, Sanjaywa* (Please forgive me, Sanjay). But who could have this new number?'

'Let him call you again. He might be a well-wisher. Who knows, he might help us with the identity of our traitor.'

'*Hmm, woh toh theek hai*. But how did he get this number? Can we find out who called me?'

'*Bhai, hum koi police thodi hai* (Bhai, only the police has the power to find out all these things).'

Samant kept pacing in the confines of the small house. How times had changed! He used to roam around with his cronies with absolute authority. His swanky SUVs would own the dusty, pothole-filled roads of Nawada and the adjoining areas. Samant wanted his life back.

~

I enjoyed the conversation between Samant and Sanjay. Samant tried my number, from which I had made the fake call, a few times, but I deliberately did not answer his call. I derived immense sadistic pleasure in breaking Samant down bit by bit.

After the call ended, I looked over at Aish sitting on the floor. She had started crawling all over the house. It was a delight watching her grow in front of me. I had been much busier during Avi's infancy. I had much bigger districts to handle at the time. Naturally, I could not spend much time at home. In fact, I had not been present by Tanu's side during the birth of either of my children.

Since Shekhpura offered me practically no other work apart from chasing the brigand Samant, I could spend a lot of time at home. In any case, eavesdropping on Samant's conversations was more secure and convenient from the privacy of my home. Tanu was quite happy with my presence, even though I was still a very lazy father. I just enjoyed taking pictures of Avi and Aish on my new digital camera. Aish loved to model for me. Her gurgles and squeaks made me happy. I thanked Samant for making me realize the importance of family, and also that things like postings finally do not matter much.

That same day, I received a call from M.A. Hussain. 'Amit, how's it going?' he asked.

'Sir, I am confident of getting Samant soon. My only request is that you please reinstate SI Ranjan when I arrest Samant.'

'Sure, Amit, you've got it,' he replied in his authoritative voice. This time, there was no hesitation in his voice.

~

I called up Ranjan and said, 'Ranjan, get a good sleep in the afternoon. Tonight is going to be a long one.'

'Yes, sir,' replied Ranjan. It was the first time I was actually letting him sleep.

Next, I called the Airtel office.

'Could I speak to the GM? I am the SP of Shekhpura.'

'Yes, sir, what can I do for you?'

'We have been listening to the calls of a very dangerous criminal for the past fortnight. You've been of immense help to us.'

'It's our pleasure, sir. We feel humbled,' replied the GM.

'Thank you. But I need some urgent help from you. I am already observing the number 965498**43 myself. Can one of my colleagues also listen to the calls of that number on his mobile? At the same time?'

The GM pondered for a moment.

'Yes, sir, it's possible.'

'Then please do it as soon as possible.'

The GM of Airtel could sense the earnestness in my voice.

'All I know is that if you help me, we'll be able to arrest one of the biggest criminals in Bihar,' I added. There was a pregnant silence at the other end. 'GM Sahib, you'll always be proud that you helped us nab Samant Pratap.'

'Sir, Samant Pratap, that dreaded ganglord? You have been working on his case?' exclaimed the GM.

'Yes. Now do you understand how important your help will be to us?'

I had done my best to strike an emotional chord with the GM.

'Okay, sir.'

'I will text the number of the officer to you,' I said, barely able to conceal my joy.

I called Ranjan back, 'Ranjan, I have put Samant's number on parallel listening on your number too.'

'Really, sir?'

Ranjan sounded a little taken aback. 'Ranjan, drive along the national highway tonight, close to the houses on the road.'

'Okay, sir,' Ranjan said, not knowing where this was going.

'When you are about to reach the residential area, start honking in a particular sequence. I'll call Samant on his phone at the same time.' Ranjan could not believe his ears. Had I gone out of my mind? No sane person would even think of this idea.

'I called Samant yesterday,' I added.

Ranjan was absolutely shocked. I couldn't be serious.

I told him about my conversation with Samant the day before. 'When I call him, you'll be able to listen to that conversation on your phone. Keep honking your horn in a particular sequence. The moment you are close to his location, you will be able to listen to the honking on the phone as well, after a short lag. Do you understand?'

Ranjan was totally flummoxed. He thought this was straight out of some Hollywood thriller. I didn't explain the physics to him, but I knew that at the point that Ranjan could hear the honking on the phone at nearly the same volume as in his car, he would be closest to Samant's location.

38

'Jagah Mil Gayi'

After an hour, Ranjan reached the houses on the highway.

'Sir, I am ready.'

Raju and Krishna were also huddled up in the Bolero.

'Okay, Ranjan, I am going to call Samant in another five minutes. I'll try to keep him engrossed in my conversation for as long as possible. You keep honking. The moment you hear it on your mobile, slow down. Memorize the exact location and drive away.'

I explained everything to Ranjan once again.

I took a deep breath and dialled Samant's number. Samant's ringtone sounded in my ears. Simultaneously, Ranjan's mobile started ringing. His screen showed Samant's number. Ranjan pressed the green button to initiate the parallel listening.

Ranjan and I were hundreds of miles apart, yet we could almost feel each other's breathing.

I waited for Samant to answer my call.

'Pick up, pick up the phone, for God's sake.'

No institute, not even the glorious National Police Academy, can train any policeman for these situations. Thousands of policeman use all the elements of Chanakya's treatise—*saam, daam, dand, bhed*—to solve crimes all over the country. They have to think like criminals; in fact, be one step ahead of criminals.

That is the reason agencies like the National Investigation Agency (NIA), Intelligence Bureau (IB) and Research and Analysis Wing (R&AW) are so successful in defending our nation.

I was going to rely on my confidence, instinct and, of course, luck.

I was rewarded with the sound of the familiar harsh voice on the other side.

'*Halloo, kaun bol rahe ho* (Hello, who is this)?' shouted a baffled Samant.

'*Arre, Samant Bhai, hum bol rahe hain* (Arre, Samant Bhai, it's me). Listen, there is a mole in your group.'

I spoke with remarkable poise. Ranjan later said that hearing his urbane SP Sahib talk to a criminal in the local dialect had made him grin with glee. He had been so impressed by my accent that he had forgotten to honk for a few seconds.

'I can tell you the identity of the traitor.'

'*Arre, toh bolo na* (Arre, then tell me). Why are you beating around the bush?' Samant was clearly irritated now.

'Samant Bhaiyya, the police are desperately looking for you. A lot of your men have been bought over by the police, particularly Laddua and Gajapati.'

'Laddua, Gajapati? I trusted them so much.'

Samant was shocked to hear the names of his most trusted lieutenants.

'Ranjan, why the hell are you not honking the horn?' I thought.

I knew I could not continue the conversation for very long. My accent would betray me at some point.

Suddenly, I heard the blaring of a horn in a sequence so perfect, it was almost musical.

'Bhai, I can't hear you. There is some very loud sound behind you,' I said deliberately.

'Yes, some fool is blaring his horn. Idiot!' shouted Samant at the top of his voice.

Ranjan kept honking, still waiting to find the location where Samant was hiding. At one point, Ranjan knew that he was at the right spot. The honking of the Bolero's horn and the sound he heard on the phone was almost equally loud. Ranjan heard the honking on the phone an infinitesimal moment after the actual honking. It was the time the radio waves took to transport the digitized sound. All our spoken words are heard a little later by the receiver on their phone. Similarly, all the action we see live on our TV screens actually takes place a little earlier in reality.

Ranjan looked out and memorized the block of houses on the road. He was so close to his target. Ranjan said he could actually feel that the walls were talking to him, beckoning him. He dismissed the thought and drove away.

He immediately texted me on my other phone. '*Sir, jagah mil gayi* (Sir, I've found the place).'

I saw the message and smiled.

'*Achcha, Samant Bhai, jaise hi khabar milti hai bataata hoon* (Samant Bhai, I'll tell you as soon as I have news),' I said, disconnecting the call abruptly.

Samant was absolutely confounded. Who the hell was calling him? And how did the caller have his number? On the other hand, my excitement could hardly be contained. I called Ranjan.

'Ranjan, describe the area to me.'

'Sir, there are some government housing blocks along the road. There are four apartments in each block—two on the ground floor and two on the first floor. The houses are small, the standard size for subordinate staff.'

'Continue,' I said, all ears.

'Sir, I have memorized the exact location. That stretch must not have more than three blocks, each block about 10–15 feet apart.'

I visualized the area. It was typical of a government residential locality in any mofussil town.

'Sir, how do we find Samant? Should I check each and every house?' asked Ranjan.

'And alert Samant? Ranjan, we can't even think of taking any chances. We'll find a way. Remember Horlicks's arrest? Be patient.'

I was so close to Samant, yet so far. I did not want to strike before an opportune moment in my overzealousness. It can be very frustrating when the criminals escape because of one wrong step. In Samant's case, I simply could not afford to make any mistake. It was a matter of life and death, literally. But somehow, I knew I would get some divine help again.

~

Ranjan, Raju and Krishna stayed in a small, dilapidated hotel in Maheshpur, Pakur. I deliberately asked them to lie low. Samant knew Raju and Krishna. After all, they had been brothers in arms earlier. Their loitering around could be disastrous for our mission.

I bided my time. I had a feeling Shanti Devi would be my angel again. She had been the single biggest reason for Horlicks's arrest. She would help me again with Samant.

'*Kitne din se baat nahin kiya hai* (You have not called me for so many days),' Shanti complained when she called Samant the next morning.

'Jaan, I was busy with work,' replied Samant sweetly.

'*Kaam? Kaun sa kaam* (Work? What work)? What work are you doing in hiding?'

'*Chup kar, bewakoof aurat* (Shut up, you silly woman).'

Samant disconnected the call in frustration. He knew that Shanti was right. He felt that even his days in Nawada Jail were better. He was freer inside the jail than he was right now. He was always surrounded by his followers, his cronies. He was treated like a lord even by the jail staff. Here, he was absolutely alone, constantly worried. He felt utterly powerless.

I listened to the conversation with great attention. I knew I would pick up some clue soon. It was not any titbit in the conversation, but a background sound that caught my attention. There was a clear sound of woodwork going on somewhere close to Samant, maybe in his house or the neighbouring house.

The next day, Shanti Devi called again, '*Kya, gussa ho humse* (Why, are you angry with me)? You know how much I love you. *Please maaf kar do* (Please forgive me).'

'*Haan, haan, theek hai!* But you really spoiled my mood. Don't forget, I am Samant Pratap, the king of Nawada, Shekhpura,' roared Samant.

'*Ay hai, mere raja*, your queen is waiting for you.'

This meaningless, silly romantic talk went on for some time. I had to put an end to it.

~

'Ranjan, find the carpenter's shop closest to Samant's location. Immediately,' I said to Ranjan.

'Carpenter's shop? What for, sir?'

'Ranjan, a carpenter is working either near or inside Samant's house. I heard the sound of a hammer and saw yesterday. And I heard exactly the same sound today, in the morning.'

Ranjan understood. The newspaper vendor had been instrumental in Horlicks's arrest. Now the carpenter would lead us to Samant.

'In such a small locality, there can be only one or two carpenters. Ask the carpenter where exactly he is working.

If you don't get the exact address, at least identify the exact block.'

In less than an hour, I got a call from Ranjan.

'Sir, I know the house and the block. Should I raid it? I have Raju, Krishna and Shiv Narayan with me.'

'Don't try anything right now. The houses are small and very close to each other. You never know which house Samant is hiding in. He might be on the first floor and the carpenter might be working on the ground floor. The sound of the hammer can easily travel from the ground floor to the first floor. We will nab him when we are absolutely sure of Samant's location.'

'Sir, I got it. You are absolutely right.'

'Try to find out the details of the residents of the house as clandestinely as possible.'

'Sure, sir.'

'And don't take Raju and Krishna with you. He'll identify them instantly.'

'Yes, sir. This is the first thing I'll do tomorrow morning.'

39

'Aa Gaya Hoon Chhatt Par'

I did not sleep that night. It was more out of excitement, less because of tension. In my mind, I was already celebrating my triumph.

At 6.15 a.m., I got Ranjan's call. He sounded absolutely dejected.

'*Sir, anarth ho gaya* (Sir, disaster has struck). Everything is finished,' said a crestfallen Ranjan.

'Why . . . what happened?' Ranjan gave the phone to Krishna. He was too scared to talk to me.

'Sir, Raju and I had gone to have our morning tea at a local dhaba. As we walked towards our Bolero, we saw Samant washing his face at a *chapakal* across the road.'

'What the **!& is a chapakal?'

'Sir, a handpump.'

'So?'

'Sir, it seems Samant saw Raju.'

I was speechless, bewildered at the turn of events.

'Sir, Samant was splashing water on his face. As he looked up, his eyes met Raju's. I feel as if Samant's eyes followed us all the way till we walked out of his sight,' said Krishna.

It was an absolute anticlimax, a very sad ending to our fairy tale operation.

'Sir, I am still not sure if Samant recognized Raju. He has grown a long beard, and his head was covered by a gamchcha, a small hand towel,' Krishna continued.

'Why the hell did you not catch him?' I asked sternly.

'We did not know how to react. We did not expect Samant to appear in front of us all of a sudden,' Krishna continued.

I regained my composure quickly. My mind was working at a frenetic pace. 'All of you reach that block of houses and take your positions. Call me the moment you are ready.'

I had no time to lose.

I dialled the number of the Pakur DSP. Incidentally, he had worked with me before Bihar and Jharkhand were divided.

'Hello, Rajiv. This is Amit Lodha. Remember me?'

'Jai Hind, sir. Of course. How are you, sir?'

'Rajiv, I have sent a police team from Shekhpura to nab a small-time goon, a petty extortionist. Please ask the SHO of Maheshpur to remain on standby. Just in case.'

'Sure, sir, I'll tell the SHO right away.'

It was a routine matter. Rajiv called the SHO and became busy with his work.

After about ten minutes, Ranjan called.

'Sir, we are ready,' said Ranjan confidently.

'Ranjan, ask Raju and Krishna to block the exits of the building block. Shiv Narayan and you, cock your weapons. I have asked the local police to be ready in case of any trouble,' I spoke with absolute self-assurance.

'Ranjan, keep your phones on silent mode and maintain absolute discretion. I am going to call Samant.'

Ranjan agreed and cut the call, saying, 'Yes, sir.' He was too charged up to talk much.

I dialled Samant's number. This time, he picked up the phone immediately, as if he had been waiting for my call.

'*Abe, kuchch khabar hai toh batao. Gusal mein hoon* (If you have some credible information, tell me. I am in the bathroom). Otherwise go screw yourself,' Samant swore at me.

'Arre, bhai, the police are very close to catching you.'

'What? Are you trying to scare me?' Samant asked, rubbing a Lifebuoy soap on his body.

'Hello, hello, I can't hear you, Samant Bhaiyya. It seems there is some network problem.'

'I can hear you. Speak!' snarled Samant.

'Hello, bhaiyya. Why don't you go outside? Or even better, go to the terrace. I'll be able to hear you properly. I have to tell you something very important about the plans of the police.'

'*Jaata hoon* (I'll go).'

Instinctively, Samant opened the door of his house and climbed up the common staircase of the block.

In the meantime, I called Ranjan from my other mobile phone.

'Ranjan, be ready for my instructions,' I said in a hushed tone.

'Sir, I can listen to your entire conversation,' Ranjan whispered, unable to hide his excitement.

The fact that Ranjan was also observing Samant's number had slipped my mind.

'Even better,' I thought to myself.

'*Haan, aa gaya hoon chhatt par* (Yes, I am on the terrace). Can you hear me now?'

'Much better, Samant Bhai.'

'Now!' I commanded Ranjan.

Ranjan was already clambering up the stairs.

'Sir, yes, sir,' he said, panting hard. Shiv Narayan, his loyal bodyguard, was close on his heels.

Ranjan reached the terrace and flung open the door. There was no one. Ranjan's heart skipped a beat.

'Sir, the other side,' shouted Shiv Narayan.

Ranjan kicked open the other door leading to the terrace of the adjoining house on the first floor.

Right in front of his eyes was Samant Pratap.

Both of them froze.

Samant Pratap, the dreaded outlaw, the man behind the gruesome murders of scores of people, the man who'd been cocking a snook at the police for the last five years, the man whose writ ran large in four districts of Bihar, was absolutely shell-shocked.

'I told you the police would catch you,' I spoke with absolute authority. This time, I spoke in my own voice and accent.

Samant kept holding the phone to his ear, soap dripping from his body. His mind was almost in a trance, refusing to believe what was happening to him.

40

'Sir, Pakad Liya'

Then, all of a sudden, like a cat, Samant darted towards the edge of the terrace.

'*Paagal ho gaya hai* (Have you gone mad)? What the hell are you doing? You can't escape,' shouted Ranjan.

Samant growled. He jumped over the parapet and started slithering down the pipe. Without thinking twice, Ranjan also followed him.

Both hung precariously from the pipe. Somehow, they managed to get down to the first floor.

'Raju Bhai! Krishna! *Pakdo isse* (Get him). Don't let him go,' Shiv Narayan ran down again, calling out to Raju and Krishna for help.

Suddenly, Ranjan's hands slipped. Raju and Krishna looked up in horror.

Luckily, Ranjan's feet struck Samant, who also lost his grip and tumbled down. Both of them fell to the ground, Ranjan over Samant, the latter grimacing in pain. He bore the brunt of the fall. Still, surprisingly, he rolled over and sprang to his feet. Falling from the first floor had probably not caused much damage.

Samant's lungi came undone, confusing Raju and Krishna for an instant, just the way a lizard's tail diverts the attention of a predator.

'*Grenade toh nahin hai* (Is there a grenade in his lungi)?' Shiv Narayan asked. Of course, there was nothing in his lungi. It was an urban legend that Samant kept a grenade or two in his lungi. So formidable was Samant's reputation that people actually believed it.

Things were happening too fast. Raju and Krishna tried to catch him, but Samant wriggled out of their grip, just like a slippery eel. The soap on his body probably helped him.

But before he could run away, Samant was knocked to the ground with a resounding thud. Ranjan looked at Shiv Narayan with deep admiration. Shiv had been a tremendous support. This was the second time he had knocked down a dreaded criminal, the first being Horlicks.

Samant looked at him with venom in his eyes.

Ranjan punched Samant hard on the cheekbone. That was the wrong place to hit. He hurt his hand, but it did not stop him from punching Samant again, this time on his jaw.

Raju and Krishna tied his hands with a lanyard and hurriedly pushed him into the Bolero. Ranjan and Shiv Narayan jumped in too.

As soon as this was done, Ranjan called me. '*Sir, sir, pakad liya, sir* (Sir, sir, we've got him),' he said jubilantly.

I had been waiting for this for the last two and a half months. I went absolutely quiet. I didn't know how to react. There was no emotion, just a vacuum. Now I realize how a mountaineer feels on climbing Mount Everest. He or she has no more summits to conquer. They feel totally drained—physically, mentally and emotionally.

Tanu entered the living room and instantly gestured to ask what happened. It seems my wife has a sixth sense about what is going on in her husband's mind.

I just gave her a thumbs up. Tanu started jumping around with sheer delight. She was so happy for me. I hugged her.

Ajit was standing in a corner, allowing us our private celebration, but I could see his eyes welling up with tears. He was such a loyal person, very much a part of my family. I went to him and patted his back.

I called Kumar Sir to break the news.

'Congratulations, Amit, well done,' he said, reticent as always. But I knew how much of a support he had been to me. Apart from Tanu, of course, he was the one who had always believed in me. Most importantly, he did not interfere in my work at all. There was no nagging and no irrelevant questions, and he had not issued a single order. That is a rarity because quite a few bureaucrats love to write letters, giving hundreds of instructions, and believe that they have done their job.

Next, I called M.A. Hussain Sir.

'Sir, we are about to catch Samant Pratap, maybe in the next half an hour. I sincerely request you to revoke the suspension of Ranjan. He is leading the team that will arrest Samant.'

For the first time, Hussain laughed heartily.

'Okay, Amit. I'll send the orders right away.'

Hussain was experienced enough to know that in all probability, we had already arrested Samant. He knew I was bluffing, but he did not mind. The order rolled out of my fax machine in ten minutes: 'The suspension order of SI Ranjan Kumar is hereby revoked—by the order of IG, Bhagalpur'.

The IG had kept his word. I was so happy for Ranjan. He deserved that and much more. He had almost single-handedly arrested two of Bihar's most dangerous criminals, Horlicks and Samant. Not only had Ranjan shown remarkable presence of mind, he had displayed bravery of the highest order. Samant was known to come after the families of the policemen who crossed his path, yet Ranjan and Shiv Narayan had not flinched from this mission even once.

After half an hour, an angry Ranjan called me, '*Sir, sir, yeh saala gaali de raha hai. Bahut gussa aa raha hai. Kya karoon* (Sir, sir, this piece of scum is swearing at me. I'm very angry. What should I do)?'

Ranjan was absolutely flustered. Samant was constantly swearing at Ranjan and company. He was back to his old ways. I pondered for a moment.

Suddenly, my official phone rang. It was Kumar Sir.

'Amit, I hope you are not thinking of harming Samant in any way.'

How the hell had Sir known what was going on in our minds? How could he have a premonition?

'Uh, sir, it was just a fleeting thought,' I muttered.

'Don't get any ideas. Samant belongs to a powerful community and still has considerable clout. And gone are the days when cops could go scot-free,' Kumar Sir said sternly.

'Yes, sir, I understand.'

'Ranjan, there is a clear no from the DIG,' I explained to Ranjan.

'But, sir, he has been using the choicest expletives for my family, my mother, my sister.'

'Then gag his mouth.'

~

Ajit had already gone to purchase sweets.

'Sir, I am going to distribute mithai to all the policemen and staff working at the *kothi*,' Ajit beamed.

I was quite amused by Ajit's excitement, and him calling my small two-and-a-half-room house a 'kothi'. Such hubris!

On the inside, I was still a little worried. Samant was an extremely dangerous man. If he could escape from Nawada Jail, he could very well slip from Ranjan's custody.

I kept pacing in my small garden.

Every minute felt like an hour. It was strange. I had been so patient for the past so many days, and now, I could not wait any longer.

Around 6 p.m., Ranjan's Bolero entered my compound. A beaming Ranjan got down with a lovely smile on his face. I hugged him.

Ranjan had already dropped Raju and Krishna off a few kilometres from my residence. Shiv Narayan remained seated in the back with his fully loaded carbine pointing at Samant's head.

Ranjan opened the door. A gaunt, weary man slowly crawled out. Finally, I saw Samant Pratap, the villain of my story. He was very thin and short, nothing like the persona he had cultivated over the years.

Ranjan removed the gag from Samant's mouth.

'SPaiyya kahaan hai (Where is the SP)?' snarled Samant as he surveyed the group. He was down but not yet out.

By this time, my entire house guard and staff had assembled. They could scarcely believe that the dreaded fugitive was standing right in front of them.

'Hum hain yahaan ke SP (I am the SP of Shekhpura),' I said in a commanding voice.

Samant, clad in his lungi and ganji, looked at me incredulously. From the look on his face, I could tell he found me way too young to be the leader of a district's police. My casual attire of shorts and T-shirt made me look even more boyish. Samant did not like the fact that he had been outfoxed by someone so young and inexperienced—at least, according to his expectations. That is the beauty of the IPS. The service trains an officer to lead the police force from the very beginning of his career. An IPS officer becomes the equivalent of a CEO at the average age of twenty-seven or twenty-eight.

'*Kal yahaan par hum garda chhuda denge* (I'll knock all of you to smithereens tomorrow). You'll know who the king of Shekhpura is,' Samant growled. It was clear that he was trying to put on a brave front.

Ajit moved forward, seething with rage.

'*Saale, aukat mein rah* (Stay in your limits),' he raised his hand to slap Samant.

'Ajit, wait.'

Ajit stopped at my command.

'Go and call my cook, Bhim Singh.'

Everybody looked at each other. Why on earth was I calling my cook? Surely I was not going to offer Samant some Bihari delicacies like litti chokha?

Bhim Singh, the rotund cook, came running out.

'Ji, huzoor.'

I pointed towards Samant.

'Push this guy hard, as hard as possible.'

Bhim Singh was quite taken aback at my order. He was, after all, a simple cook, even though outrageously bad at his job. He wondered why he was being asked to assault a scrawny, lungi-clad man when the compound was teeming with policemen.

But I knew Bhim Singh was delighted. He had always secretly desired to be like his uniformed colleagues. The rolling pin was not for him. He wished to use his hands to hold a rifle. Today, he finally had a chance to act like a tough guy. 'Must be some petty criminal,' he thought.

He pushed Samant softly. Samant growled, flashing his gutkha-stained brown teeth.

'*Abe, itna bada hai* (You are so big and look at you). You are behaving like a sissy. Shove him so hard that he falls,' I commanded Bhim.

Bhim did not like being slighted in front of everyone. This time, he put all his weight behind it and shoved Samant hard.

Samant fell to the ground and lay motionless. I got a little worried. I checked his pulse and gestured to Ajit to get some water.

Bhim looked around triumphantly.

Samant was already dehydrated and fatigued. The last thing I wanted was for him to pass out in my residential compound.

41

'Put On Your Uniform'

Ajit sprinkled some water on Samant's face. He got up, abusing all of us. And then, just like that, he started sobbing uncontrollably. Finally, it dawned on him that he had been arrested. The shove from Bhim Singh had totally shattered his fragile ego.

The DSP took Samant to the town police station. I called the DG and briefed him about Samant's arrest. He was pleased and immediately broke the news to the CM.

I asked Ranjan to wait. I went inside to pick up the IG's order. I waved the paper at Ranjan and gave it to him to read. Tears trickled down his checks.

'Put on your uniform. You look very good in it.'

Ranjan wiped his tears and saluted me. He went to a corner and called his wife.

~

There was hot kadhi–chawal, my favourite, for dinner. I called Bhim Singh to the table.

'Do you know whom you pushed today?'

'Ji, huzoor. It was Samant Pratap. I didn't know earlier. I wish I had recognized him.'

'You know, Samant was asking about you. He said that he would teach you a lesson for life.'

Bhim Singh put the utensils down and started shaking. 'Sir, what did I do wrong? Why have you put my family and me in so much danger?' Bhim started sobbing.

Tanu consoled him, '*Arre, mazaak kar rahe hain* (Arre, he's just joking).'

Once he had been pacified and had left the room, Tanu looked at me sternly and admonished me. 'What was the need to scare him? And why did you ask him to shove him?'

I remained silent. Samant's myth had to be shattered. People had to be freed from the shadow of his fear.

I went to the bedroom and looked at the dozen mobile phones that had been my constant companions for the last few months. I switched them off and put them in my drawer.

~

The next morning, I reached my office to hold a press conference.

'I had promised that I would arrest Samant before Independence Day. Well, today is 13 August.'

Ajit ushered in Samant, the erstwhile don of Shekhpura and Nawada. There was pin-drop silence for a moment. Then all hell broke loose.

The flashlights kept going off, and the press went berserk. It was the biggest news in the state that day. I just kept smiling and answering questions. I did not disclose Ranjan's role. Not only would that lead to a lot of uncomfortable questions, it could potentially put Ranjan in jeopardy.

All of a sudden, Samant shouted, 'These powermongers have used me and cheated me. They will pay a heavy price.'

Before he could make any more disclosures, Ajit took Samant away from there. I felt relieved. I knew Samant was telling the truth, but I did not want the press to be diverted by his tactics right now. He was a criminal and deserved no sympathy. I came out of the office and was greeted by a thunderous applause from the crowd. All my officers and jawans had a jubilant smile on their faces.

'Sir, that lady there is Shanti Devi,' whispered Havaldar Shiv Narayan in my ear.

I walked towards Shanti Devi, my path through the throng being cleared by my bodyguards.

'I can't thank you enough. You have done the Shekhpura police a great service.' I left her with an absolutely confused look on her face. I had kept my promise of thanking Shanti Devi.

I was about to go home when I got a call from Rajesh Charan.

'Sir, sir. Come quickly to the Shekhpura Chowk. Look at what has happened to Samant Pratap.'

I rushed to the chowk and was appalled by the sight of Samant. He had been garlanded with shoes and slippers. Someone had shaved off half his moustache and also half his head.

It was absolutely shocking. Samant was being paraded on the streets of Shekhpura. People were spilling out on the roads, pushing each other to get a glimpse of Samant, the terror of Shekhpura.

The circus went on for some time before everyone could be rounded up. I rebuked the escort party and put an end to the spectacle. Samant looked at me with bloodshot eyes. I could see absolute hatred in them. I did not explain anything to Samant, though I knew that he was holding me responsible for this public humiliation. Though Samant was more of a beast, his human rights still had to be respected.

Samant was sent to the prison amid extremely high security. I put a special guard outside the Shekhpura Jail lest Samant try some Nawada jailbreak-type escape. The guard comprised thirty to thirty-five jawans of the BMP and SAP.

~

'Sir, the petty criminal you talked about that day, was he Samant Pratap?'

It was DSP Rajiv from Pakur.

'Yes,' I replied gingerly.

'Sir, you could have told me,' said an upset Rajiv. 'My SP was not very happy with me. I had to listen to a lot, sir.'

'I am sorry, Rajiv. The situation was such that we did not have time to tell you anything,' I lied.

Of course, I could not tell Rajiv the real identity of Samant. I had learnt from my bad experience during Horlicks's arrest in Deoghar.

My phone kept buzzing for the next two days. I got congratulatory messages from all over Bihar. I was more relieved than happy. Finally, it was over. Eventually, I switched off even my personal phones. I did not want to hear the ringtone of any phone, at least for a few days.

~

Tanu was very, very happy for me. It was finally time to relax a bit. I switched on the TV and looked for the 'Krazy Kiya Re' song.

'Chun, there is no need to search the TV channels. Your heroine is right in front of you.'

I looked up. Tanu was wearing a short dress and looking absolutely stunning.

'Wow,' I whistled.

She was back to her fit avatar. In fact, I had put on some weight. I had hardly exercised in the last two months.

'I'll just get some chocolates from the fridge.' I got up to go to the kitchen.

When I went back to my room, I got a huge shock. Bhim Singh was standing in our bedroom. His mouth was wide open, wide enough to stuff a handful of rasgullas into it.

'Bhim Singh, what are you doing here?' I was livid.

'Huzoor, an important message has come from DM Sahib. I just came to give it to you.'

'*Darwaaza toh knock karna tha na* (Couldn't you knock)? You imbecile.'

'Huzoor, the door was open.'

'Now get out!' I pointed to the door.

Bhim Singh scurried away, glancing back one more time before leaving.

Tanu looked at me and started laughing.

'Couldn't you have locked the door?' I asked.

'Arre, how could I have known that someone would enter the bedroom?'

She hugged me. I shrugged her away, still angry.

'Arre, hero, Shekhpura ke James Bond. Why are you so angry? Don't you also ogle at heroines?'

'Tanu, this is not a movie and you are the SP's wife.'

'Don't be so old-fashioned.'

Tanu started laughing again. I could not control my laughter any more.

'Saala Bhim Singh!'

~

The scourge of Shekhpura was behind bars, but I still had some unfinished business. I summoned Rajesh Charan to my office.

'Jai Hind, sir.'

'Rajesh, you slimy creature. You are a shame to the department. It's because of you that honest policemen get a bad name,' I said, seething with uncontrollable rage.

'Sir, sir . . . what have I done?' Rajesh asked, shaking like a leaf.

'Don't you know what you have done?'

I threw the printout with the call details of Rajesh's phone in front of him.

'I would shame you publicly if I had my way. You are suspended with immediate effect. I'll ensure that you are dismissed.'

Rajesh went pale immediately. '*Sir, maaf kar do. Galti ho gayi* (Sir, please forgive me. I made a mistake).' He started crying.

'Just get out before I lose my cool. Out, right now!'

Ajit motioned for Rajesh to leave.

'And take off that uniform. You don't deserve it.'

Just then, Ranjan entered my office, looking smart in his police uniform. He was beaming from ear to ear. I felt proud of him.

'Ranjan, you have done an extraordinary service to society. But we need to ensure that Samant and Horlicks are convicted. Get me a list of cases pending against them.'

'Sir, that is easier said than done. There are dozens of cases against Samant and Horlicks. But who will become a witness? Who will depose against them in court?'

I realized that we had to strategize to get this trial on track. So Kumar Sir, I, the SP of Nalanda and the SP of Nawada got together for an official meeting. The four of us discussed which case to try Samant for. After much debate, we decided that the escape from Nawada Jail would be our best bet because the police staff themselves were both witnesses and victims and would be able to testify more easily than laypersons who did not have the same level of security and the means to defend themselves. Finally, we had a plan to put these dreaded criminals behind bars for good.

42

'Saregama'

I had been quite fit during my training days. I loved sports, squash being my favourite. In the past few months, partly because of my stiffness due to arthritis and mostly due to my obsessive pursuit of Samant, I had not exercised at all. The small love handles on my sides were a blow to my vanity. I needed to get back in shape. Unfortunately, there was no gym or sports facility in town.

'Do we have any badminton or tennis courts in Shekhpura?' I asked the DSP.

'Sir, you know the state of affairs here. Even the bigger towns like Gaya and Muzaffarpur have no sports infrastructure. Clubs in Patna allow marriages to take place on the lawns of their tennis courts these days. Who bothers about sports in our country?'

He was right, but I still prodded him to find a place with any kind of sports activity.

That evening, the DSP took me to a small club and proudly showed me a TT table.

'*Sir, tennis toh nahin mila* (Sir, I couldn't find any tennis court). But you can play table tennis here.'

The TT table had only two legs—the other two were missing. Somebody had put bricks in place of the missing legs to balance it.

I was quite disappointed. I had never been interested in playing TT, that too, on a table with crutches!

~

Later that day, I got a call. 'Boss, I have heard you are planning to start playing sports. Why don't we play badminton?'

It was Shrikanth, the affable DM of Shekhpura. He had worked with me as a subdivisional officer (SDO) during my Nalanda days.

'Where do you intend to play? There's no court in the entire town,' I asked.

'Arre, sir, we will play in the FCI godown. I'll ask someone to arrange for a net and put the markings. See you tomorrow evening.'

I was delighted. Tanu, Shrikanth and I started playing in the evenings. Soon, the chief judicial magistrate (CJM) and a few other officers joined us. We had our own court now. So what if it had uneven cement floors, yellow bulbs that flickered and rats devouring the sacks of grains lying all around?

It was our own Siri Fort Stadium!

~

Life continued at a languorous pace. I watched all the movies that I had missed not only in the past few months, but in the past few years.

I also focused on honing my inner Kishore Kumar and sought the services of a music teacher.

He came home with his harmonium. '*Sir, gaaiye.* Please sing sa, re, ga, ma,' urged the teacher earnestly.

After listening to me a few times, the music teacher realized that I simply did not have the talent for music. Unable to bear the cacophony, the teacher vented his frustration on the harmonium.

'Oh! Sir, I think the harmonium has been damaged. Please give me a few days to get it repaired.'

I still believe he deliberately damaged the harmonium. That was the only way he could save himself from the third-degree torture.

~

After a week, the government transferred Samant to Gaya Jail. Horlicks was sent to Bhagalpur. It was the right decision—Shekhpura Jail was not secure enough to keep both of those highly dangerous criminals, that too, together.

Meanwhile, I could finally concentrate on my family. Aishwarya was crawling all over the house, and I would chase her on my knees. Avi was doing well in his studies, and this made Tanu quite happy.

'Chun, I think we should try to make Aish walk now.'

'*Tanu, ho jaayega.* She will walk. What is the hurry?'

'You have a tendency to avoid everything. You did the same when Avi was growing up. Even during the potty training of both the kids, you did not help me at all.'

'Yaar, you are always complaining. Come on, this is not my job. I am busy arresting criminals,' I replied. Anyway, I was not good at these things.

'Mister, you might be a "sahib" everywhere else, but not in this house. Don't expect only me to do all the kids' chores just because I am a woman.'

As always, I knew she was right. So we made Aish walk around the edges of the table in our living room. I walked behind her to support her in case she lost her balance. It turned out to be great fun.

My idyllic life was interrupted by a phone call from the ADG (Intelligence).

'Amit, I have some disturbing news for you'. The ADG's tone was quite sombre.

I wondered what it was. Everything that could go wrong for me had gone wrong three months ago. Now my life was finally back on track after a long time.

'Amit, Samant is targeting you. Tell me, do you go to play badminton every day?'

'Yes, sir, I do.'

'Then please stop. We have confirmed intel from our sources in Gaya Jail. Samant has instructed his men to attack you at the badminton court. You'll be an easy target there.'

'Sir, thank you. I'll take care.'

I put the phone down and pondered.

The ADG was absolutely right. My fixed routine and the totally unguarded premises of the FCI godown were ideal for someone to ambush me. I would be a sitting duck in the badminton court.

I decided to stop playing. For a few days, I managed to stay home, but I did not like this house arrest. It was just too much for me. Not only was it extremely depressing, it was a challenge to me. As a district SP, I could not live like a coward. What would people think if they came to know?

I requested Kumar Sir to send me a bulletproof Gypsy from the Munger police lines. I also got an AK-47 from the Patna Police HQ. I already had my 9 mm Glock pistol, but an AK-47 would be better in a gun battle at close quarters. I increased the security around my house by deploying Special Task Force–trained commandos and some SAP jawans. Still, my house was quite unsafe. It was in an isolated corner of Shekhpura, with almost no habitation close by. Power outages were quite common. I started storing extra diesel for the generator. I even installed an inverter to have the lights on in case of an emergency.

A few days later, I noticed that a Bolero would frequently cross our house late at night. It was as if someone was doing a reconnaissance of our house. The children would play in the small garden—it was their only entertainment in Shekhpura. I thought that it would be quite easy for anyone to just lob a country-made bomb into our compound and harm the kids. All these thoughts constantly ran through my mind. It was difficult sleeping at night with a cocked AK-47 next to me.

~

The DM was quite shocked—there was an AK-47 lying next to my badminton racquets.

'Boss, what is this?'

'Arre, it's nothing, yaar.'

'Then why are you carrying a gun with you inside the court? What if it goes off?'

'Shrikant, don't worry. An AK-47 or any gun will not fire when the safety catch is down.'

'AK-47! It is an AK-47!' the CJM joined the DM and subdivisional magistrate as they all looked at the gun.

'Sir, you are scaring us. Everything all right, no?'

'Yes. Come on, let us play.'

Nobody enjoyed the game. There was no focus or energy. It seemed that all the civil and judicial officers were distracted by the sight of the AK-47 lying next to the badminton kit.

The next day, I kept waiting at the FCI godown—none of the players turned up. I picked up my phone to call the DM.

'*Huzoor, koi faayda nahin hai* (Sir, it's no use calling anyone),' said my driver.

I put the phone aside and looked at him.

'Huzoor, DM Sahib got quite worried yesterday. When he came out, he saw a posse of guards all around the court, absolutely ready in their crouching positions. And he got really unnerved when he saw the bulletproof Gypsy outside the godown,' said my driver with a hearty laugh.

But the DM and other officers did not find it funny. As so my dream of becoming a badminton champ came to a premature end. Instead, I started doing some martial arts training in my house to keep myself fit.

~

Back in the office, I received a letter from a human rights organization.

To,
The SP, Shekhpura,
Sub: Violation of the human rights of an accused undertrial

This is to inform you that the Helping Hands Organization hereby takes cognizance of the recent incident pertaining to one Samant Pratap.
You are directed to explain your actions by Friday to the office of the undersigned.

Yours faithfully,
Sd
Member Secretary,
Helping Hands Organization

I was quite angry, naturally. Firstly, Samant Pratap was not 'one Samant Pratap'. He was the most feared criminal of Bihar. I failed to understand why the organization cared so much about his human rights. Secondly, I had done no wrong personally. I was the one who had stopped the humiliation of Samant that day. Instead of bouquets, I was getting brickbats.

The DSP, Yash Sharma, was a mature person, well-versed with the functioning of various agencies and organizations.

'Sir, don't worry. No harm will come to you.'

'Have you read the letter? I have been asked to explain my actions,' I said, unable to hide my anguish.

'Sir, I will prepare a defence on your behalf.'

'Still, what answer do I give them? How do I explain the incident?'

'You tell them it was the public of Shekhpura that garlanded Samant with shoes. And that is a fact. We have witnesses. Moreover, the police party escorting Samant was suspended that very day for dereliction of duty. I knew that this issue would snowball and Samant would try his best to trouble you. Legally and otherwise.'

I smiled and thanked Sharma. The police department has many such loyal and experienced people to bail you out of trouble.

Later, I learnt that the organization had been flooded with complaints against me and the Shekhpura police. Obviously, they were all sent by Samant's men. But this was just one of the sinister plans Samant had plotted against me.

I knew I had to get Samant convicted quickly. I requested the district judge of Nawada to start the trial on a priority basis. We arranged all our witnesses and got the evidence in order.

~

The trial was held in the fast-track court in Nawada. The quick trial of the accused by these fast-track courts is one of the reasons crime in Bihar has gone down significantly since. The SP of Nawada would go to the trial every day with adequate BMP and SAP staff to make sure that everything was conducted properly. Samant would be transported every day in a special anti-landmine vehicle to prevent attacks from his enemies as well as to discourage his own gang members from trying to free him.

The evidence we had put together ensured that we had a watertight case against Samant. We used the fact that he was always absent during roll call in jail in the days after his escape in 2001 as proof that he had got out by force. It was as if an errant student had been marked absent by the class teacher. Apart from that, the post-mortem and injury reports of the jail staff and guards who had been killed and hurt in the escape attempt also contributed to the evidence. It was a landmark verdict, wherein Samant was sentenced to life imprisonment. Our joy knew no bounds. The judgment was a brilliant culmination of the hard work of the entire police department.

43

The Attack on Avi

After a few months, I was transferred to Begusarai, the lovely place I had wanted to be the SP of when I was officiating in place of Rajesh Bhushan, my friend. Life had come a full circle. Tanu was the happiest. The kids were growing up. Aishwarya had started eating greens and dals without much fuss and Avi had started going to the DAV school in the IOC campus. We too had gone back to playing regularly in a proper badminton court. The DM, Hansraj, was a dear batchmate from IIT. Life could not have been better. Or so we thought.

One day, Tanu was sitting with Mona, the DM's wife, at the IOC's annual charity event.

'*Madam, madam, jaldi aaiye.* Come fast!' the havaldar said frantically.

'What happened? Tell me!'

Tanu could sense something catastrophic had happened.

'There has been an attack on us!'

'What? Who all were with you?'

'Sir and Avi Bhaiyya,' the havaldar said and started crying.

Tanu dropped to her knees, unable to control her emotions.

'Both of them are all right, Memsahib. Chandi Mata has saved them.'

Tanu rushed to Begusarai Chowk, which was swarming with policemen. DSP Pankaj and Kotwali SHO Sanjiv came forward to meet her.

'Madam, your son is safe.'

She ignored them. Her eyes were searching for Avi and me. There was a sea of humanity in the area. Thousands of people had gathered for Durga Visarjan, one of the most important festivals in Bihar. Her eyes kept moving to and fro, but then stopped suddenly. She saw Ajit inside a shop, holding Avi tightly in his arms, shielding him from any imminent danger.

Avi was giggling with joy and slurping his favourite mango ice cream.

She started walking towards them and instinctively increased her pace.

Avi looked at her and jumped into her arms. She hugged him as tightly as possible, controlling her tears with great difficulty.

'*Sahib kahaan hain?* How is sir?' she asked, her voice choking with tears.

'*Aa rahe hain sir* (Sir is coming). I just spoke to one of the guards with him,' replied Ajit. 'Madam, bhaiyya was getting bored in the house. So, sahib asked me to take him around the marketplace. We thought Avi Babu would enjoy the mela, he would see the various idols of Durgaji.'

She remained quiet while she checked the wound on Ajit's temple. Luckily, it was not deep.

'We got down from the Gypsy as the market was very crowded. Sir and I could sense that some people were following us. I instructed the guards to keep watch around us. Then bhaiyya asked for ice cream,' Ajit paused to catch his breath. 'Suddenly, sir saw two suspicious-looking characters coming towards us. Their hands were in their pockets. Sir sensed that something was wrong. Instinctively, he shouted at the guys.

They just stopped in their tracks and turned around. Sir started running after them, which was not the right thing to do. He was unarmed as he had no reason to carry a weapon. So many of us were with him. Initially, we did not know what to do—to run after sir or stay with Avi Babu. Obviously, we could not let sir go alone after those criminals. I sent the guards to help sir. The havaldar and I stayed back with bhaiyya,' Ajit continued.

'We waited for sir to come back. All of a sudden, from the corner of my eye, I saw two more people running towards us. Before I could take out my pistol, one of the goons hurled a desi bomb at us.'

Tanu immediately visualized how Ajit must have curled himself around Avi and taken the entire impact of the bomb. He had been extremely lucky. The bomb maker had probably not put the right amount of explosives in the bomb. The bomb did explode on impact, but the shrapnels did not travel with enough velocity to cause any lethal damage.

The havaldar was shaken too, but had taken position and fired some random shots in the air. The goons realized that they had missed their chance and beat a hasty retreat.

Just then, Tanu saw me limping down the street, escorted by three constables.

'I am fine, Tanu,' I said and smiled at her.

The floodgates opened. Tanu could not hold back her tears any more. We embraced each other, with Avi trying to hold on to his dripping ice cream between us. I had never felt happier or more relieved. I might not have taught my children their ABCs, but like any other parent in the world, I loved them more than my life.

I looked at Ajit. Blood was oozing out of his temple, and his shirt was torn to shreds.

'Are you all right? You need to see a doctor immediately.'

'Sir, I am all right.'

'Tell me, what exactly happened?' asked Tanu.

There was no need for her to ask who did it. Samant.

'Sahib had almost caught hold of one of the assailants when he started limping. We thought he had twisted his ankle,' said one of the guards who had followed me.

'We tried to catch the criminals, but they had a head start and vanished in the dark,' said another constable.

Tanu immediately understood. It must have been an attack of ankylosing spondylitis. She looked at me angrily, 'What was the need to show such bravado? What if the assailant had fired at you?' I tried to hold her, but she pulled her hand away.

~

We took Ajit to a doctor in Sadar Hospital. 'Sir, this guy is very lucky. Had the injuries been serious, or had he lost a lot of blood, we would not have been able to do much.'

The doctor was telling the hard truth.

I looked at Tanu's face. Tears had dried on her cheeks.

'Chun, do something please. Promise me that no harm will come to our children. Ever.'

I held her hands. 'Yes, I promise you.'

The next day, I got a series of calls from my seniors and well-wishers. They were all concerned about my safety.

That morning, there had been a report of the Special Branch lying on my table. It mentioned the previous night's attack and advised me to be cautious about my family. I smiled wryly when I read it. So much for the 'warning'. This often happens with the field units of the Special Branch. Field units are often poorly equipped and understaffed. More often than not, the poor unit in-charge, a junior officer, prepares a report after an incident takes place, that too, after taking inputs from the district police. Ironically, this is the exact opposite of the very purpose for which the Special Branch exists—to provide intelligence in advance to the district police.

I put the report aside. I was hopeful that I would not get any more reports on any threat perception. But things were not going to cool down any time soon.

44

An Attack on the MLA

26 August 2012

Krishna was a busy man. He had been attending back-to-back functions and delivering speeches all over the district. He was returning from a 'Brahmbhoj', a luncheon in memory of a villager who had died a few days ago. In the evening, he had to attend a wedding. But he was not complaining. He had come a long way from being known as just Krishna, the owner of an arms shop in Shekhpura. He smiled at this change of fortune.

His car was about to enter Murarpur, his native village. He was expecting a grand reception at the wedding. After all, he was the local MLA. As he was thinking about it all, his driver drove smoothly, making good time. Just then, in the blink of an eye, he felt a powerful blast shake the frame of the car as it turned over twice. The next moment he felt as if his eardrums had ruptured.

A dazed Krishna somehow managed to get out of his vehicle. His driver and bodyguards were badly injured. He looked at his vehicle and the crater under it. The front of his car had been blown to smithereens. He looked around fearfully for any attackers hiding nearby. Luckily, a few villagers came rushing to his aid.

'*MLA Sahib, aap theek toh hain?* Are you all right, Krishna Bhaiyya?' the villagers asked.

The assailants had triggered the device when the car was a few metres away from the bomb. The attackers had misjudged the position of the car due to poor visibility in the fog. Krishna thanked the gods. He knew it was Samant. Nobody else could be so daring. Even after six years in jail, Samant was not finished.

~

Later, as he was recuperating in the All India Institute of Medical Sciences (AIIMS) in Delhi, the Shekhpura police apprised Krishna of the progress in the investigation. The conspiracy to eliminate Krishna had indeed been hatched by Samant Pratap and his accomplices in jail.

Krishna was not surprised. Apart from Naxalites, only Samant Pratap had the capability to plant a landmine. The planning had been meticulous. Even a 'rehearsal' of the explosion had been carried out a few days ago. A battery recovered from the blast site led the police to the perpetrators of the crime. A similar device and battery had been used in the fields of Thalpos village in Nawada. Chhotu Samrat, who was out on bail, was the brains behind the plan.

Krishna had to take a decision. He remembered the murder of ex-MP Kesho Singh. He knew he would not be so lucky each time. Krishna knew that Samant would come after him again.

Once he was back in Patna, he called Raju immediately. He knew it was late in the night, but it did not matter.

Raju was in his veranda in half an hour.

'Raju, let me be very clear. We know that Samant was behind the attack on me. He attacked SP Lodha Sahib also some time ago. Samant has started this war against us, and we will end it.'

'Krishna Bhai, what do you want?' asked Raju.

Krishna stared hard at him.

'What do you think?'

They talked till the wee hours of the morning. Both of them discussed each and every minute detail of their plan. They were sure that this was going to be the endgame. Samant had brought it upon himself.

45

'Woh Hi Laddu Hain'

13 June 2013

'*Kaisan ho, Horlicks* (How are you, Horlicks)?'

Samant was delighted to meet Horlicks after so many days. He embraced Horlicks and showered kisses all over his face.

'*Kya baat hai* (Is something wrong)?' asked Samant, a little concerned by Horlicks's lukewarm response.

'*Nahin, bhaiyya, sab theek hai* (No, bhaiyya, everything is fine). Just missing my children.'

'Haan, but don't worry. *Sab theek ho jaayega* (Everything will be all right). Don't you remember the Nawada jailbreak?'

Samant started laughing loudly. He looked at Horlicks, who was not showing any emotion.

Samant and Horlicks were meeting after a while. They had been kept apart during the trial, but had been sent back to Nawada Jail for their entire sentence. It was poetic justice indeed.

For Horlicks, it had all started in this jail. He had had such a happy family life at one point, but Samant had changed everything. He had been a simple man whose only desire was a better future for his children. That dream had to be fulfilled. Even if he was behind bars for the rest of his life.

~

'*Kya soch raha hai* (What are you thinking about)?' asked Samant, tapping Horlicks on the shoulder.

'*Kuchch nahin*, just thinking of what I have done with my life,' replied Horlicks glumly.

'Arre, you should be happy. What were you? Just an ordinary man. Now you are my right-hand man. The entire state of Bihar fears you.'

'Haan, bhai, you are right. People know me as the killer of innocent children.'

'Abe, it seems you have got depressed. This *sazaa*, this life imprisonment, this is all meaningless. We will be free birds again.'

Horlicks smiled faintly. Samant grinned.

'Come on, cheer up.'

'Ji, Samant Bhaiyya. You are absolutely right. How can I forget? You are the king, the emperor.'

'*Yeh hui na baat* (That's more like it),' Samant patted him.

'Yes, yes. Let us celebrate,' exclaimed Horlicks.

Horlicks opened his tiffin and took out a few laddus.

'Khao, bhaiyya, these are your favourite.'

'*Oh ho, mazaa aa gaya* (Wow, this is amazing)! How did you get them?'

'*Bhaiyya, aapne hi toh kaha tha* (Bhaiyya, you're the one who told me), everything can be made available in the jail. You just have to pay the price!'

'Of course, of course!'

'Enough of the talking now. Let us eat.'

'*Yaar, Horlicks, tune mood achcha kar diya* (Horlicks, you've really cheered me up).'

'Then you should take two of them.'

Horlicks offered the laddus to Samant.

'They are delicious. Thank you, bhai,' Samant said, eating them happily.

'Then have one more. *Ek mere haath se* (Let me put one in your mouth).'

'*Kitna khilaayega* (How many will you make me eat)?'

Samant's mouth was full of laddus. He looked rather funny.

'Bhai, this is my love for you.'

'Yes, I know how much you love me, Horlicks.'

Both of them laughed heartily. The other inmates also smiled, but from a distance. They dared not get close to Samant. Not even now.

After a few minutes, Samant stopped laughing. He felt dizzy and was having trouble moving his limbs.

All the inmates got up and looked at Samant. Something was seriously wrong.

Samant dragged himself towards Horlicks.

'*Kya milaya tha laddu mein* (What did you put in the laddus)? You snake! You . . . bastard!'

He lunged forward, somehow managing to grab Horlicks collar, but lost his grip and slowly fell to the ground. He lay motionless for a minute. Then, all of a sudden, he coughed violently. The blood in his sputum soaked his shirt crimson red.

Horlicks hovered over Samant and looked into his eyes.

'*Woh hi milaya tha joh jailbreak ke time mein milaya tha* (The same poison used during the jailbreak). It's just that the dose was stronger this time.'

Samant stared at Horlicks, and then went limp.

Epilogue

Krishna is an honourable MLA from Shekhpura now. Raju is the head of Aphani village.

Ranjan has been promoted to the rank of an inspector. His wife is doing much better now. Of course, being able to live with her husband is a major factor in her recovery.

Kumar Sir is the ADG of the Bihar Police.

Ajit Singh, my bodyguard, has been promoted to the rank of an ASI of police. He cannot be my bodyguard any longer, but his loyalty remains unflinching.

I just let go of Manish. Kumar Sir told me to forgive and forget him.

Shanti Devi is still baffled. She lost both the men in her life and she does not know how. She got married soon after. Maybe she will be third time lucky!

Netaji surrendered before the court in the jailbreak incident.

Aishwarya is growing into a beautiful girl. Her mother, Tanu, is worried that I will pamper her badly.

Horlicks is serving his time in Nawada Jail.

~

Right after the unsuccessful attack on Krishna, Raju and Krishna went to the Bhagalpur Jail to make a deal with Horlicks—a deal he could not refuse.

'*Horlicks Bhaiyya, ek waqt aap hum kitne achche dost the* (Horlicks Bhaiyya, we were bosom friends once),' said Raju and Krishna with earnestness.

Of course, all of them had worked together in Samant's gang. They had bonded over guns and booze during those days. Raju, in particular, had doted on Horlicks's son, Chhotu.

'*Aap ko toh ab jail rehna hai* (You have to spend your entire life behind bars now). Don't you want to fulfil your dreams for your children?' said Krishna.

'Horlicks, I still think Chhotu can become a policeman. Imagine, your Chhotu!' added Raju.

'Really? How?' Horlicks had asked with hope in his eyes.

Raju explained the deal to Horlicks. He agreed instantly.

'And I think you already know that Samant had an affair with Shanti Bhabhi,' added Krishna. Horlicks turned his head away. He did not want them to see his tears.

~

I went to meet Avi, my son, in his hostel in Netarhat School, the most prestigious school in all of Bihar and Jharkhand. The school has a tradition of producing IAS and IPS officers.

'Avi, where is your friend Chhotu? Call him.'

'Papa, please! Don't call him Chhotu. We are teenagers now,' retorted Avi.

'Okay, sorry. I know he is your best friend and all grown up, but I've known him from his "Chhotu" days.'

A smart, immaculately dressed young boy walked over and wished me. 'Morning, uncle, how are you?'

'I am fine, beta. How are you doing?'

'Papa, do you know, Shivam stood first in the essay competition!'

'Excellent, Shivam! What was the topic for the essay?'

'Uncle, it was "What do you want to be when you grow up"?'

'Oh, and what did you write?'

'I want to become an IPS officer.'

I just ruffled Shivam's hair and looked heavenwards. I am sure the gods will definitely answer Horlicks Samrat's prayers.

Acknowledgements

When I narrated the idea of a film to my friend, acclaimed director Neeraj Pandey, he instantly suggested I write a book too. I procrastinated as I thought that it was quite an onerous task to pen down my thoughts. But probably I was destined to become an author.

It was Emraan Hashmi who introduced me to India's best-known crime writer Hussain Zaidi, who, in turn, connected me to Milee Ashwarya, my publisher at Penguin Random House India. Contrary to his screen image, Emraan is suave and very well read. It was our bonding over books and sons that led me to wielding the pen along with the gun.

I have to put on record my appreciation for all the policemen, the unsung heroes, who put duty over everything else and who stood by me during my 'bad' times too. Shri Sunil Kumar, IPS, has always been a wonderful mentor. Inspector Ranjan Kumar and Havaldar Shiv Narayan are the epitome of courage and valour. My bodyguard for years and now an ASI, Ajit Kumar has been like my shadow. These are the kind of policemen who instil a tremendous sense of pride in all of us. I am fortunate to have the DG of Border Security Force (BSF), Shri K.K. Sharma, IPS, be so supportive of all my endeavours.

There is one person I have learnt a lot from and look up to and that is the National Film Award winner Akshay Kumar. Special thanks also to the lovely and ever witty Mrs Funnybones, Twinkle Khanna, for writing the foreword.

Of course, I can't thank God enough for making me marry my amazing wife, Tanu, the light of my life. I thank my children, Aditya and Aishwarya, for patiently listening to my songs every day and tolerating my idiosyncrasies. Aditya has become my friend, confidant and the toughest rival on the tennis court. I was confident of my writing skills only after his critical appraisal.

This book could not have been completed without the assistance of Ravinder Mahur. I also thank Avantika Poddar Dalmia, Verun S. Mehta, my father-in-law, Arun Dugar, and my parents, Dr Narendra Lodha and Asha Lodha, for going through the manuscript umpteen times and making invaluable suggestions. My brother, Namit, has always been a solid support, right from my childhood. I am also very lucky to have wonderful friends like Sameer Gehlaut and others from IIT Delhi, St Xavier's, Jaipur, and the civil services.

Thank you so much, Hussain, for your constant support, and Milee, Roshini and Aditi from Penguin for your editorial inputs.

I have to also put on record my deep appreciation for the marketing team of Penguin, particularly Preeti Chaturvedi, who is an indefatigable bundle of energy. I'm so glad the book has become a bestseller so soon, else I'd have kept getting calls at most unearthly hours from her. And also, a big word of thanks to Sameer, Twinkle, Vijesh and Harish for taking so much initiative for the book.